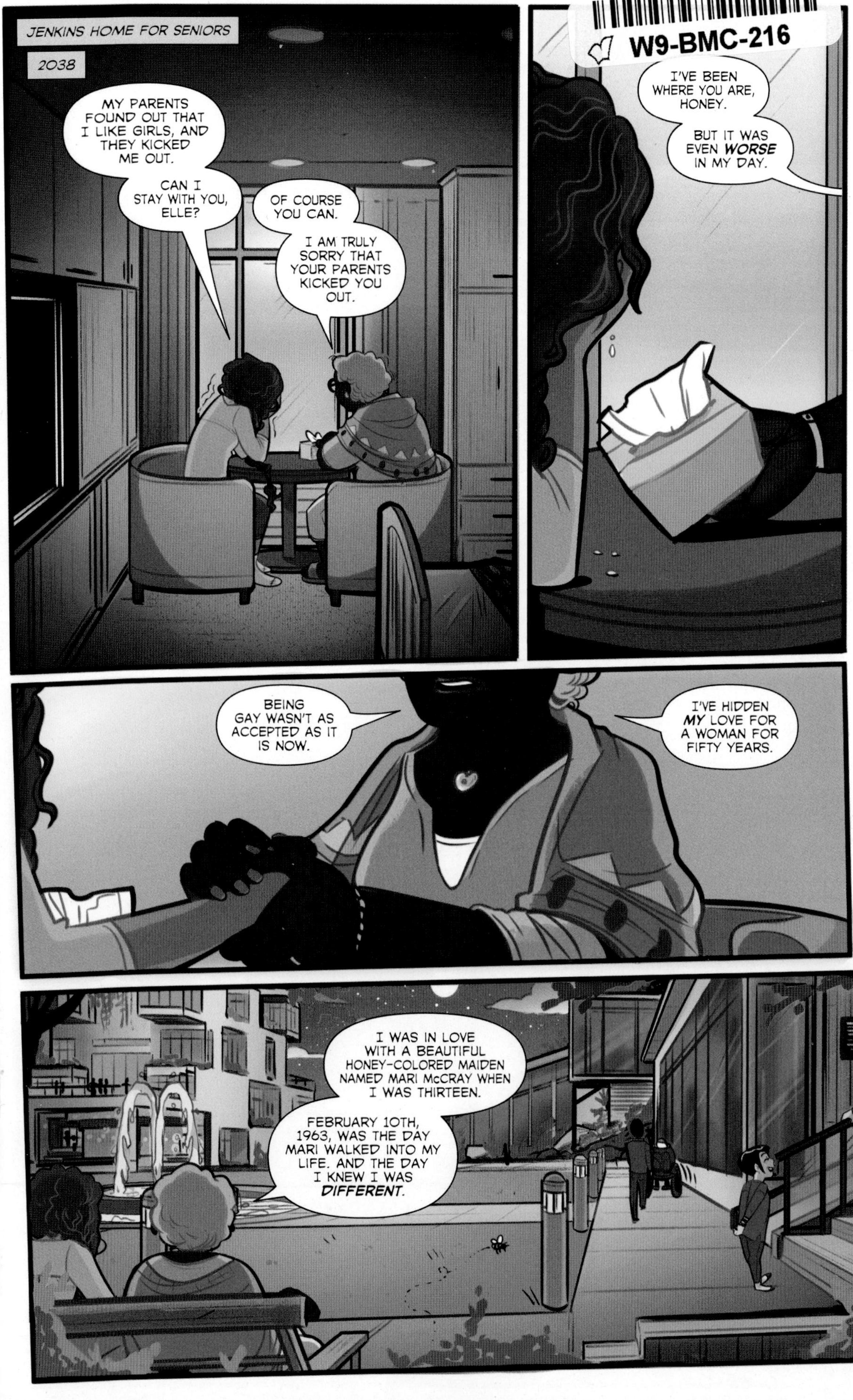
JENKINS HOME FOR SENIORS
2038
MY PARENTS FOUND OUT THAT I LIKE GIRLS, AND THEY KICKED ME OUT.
CAN I STAY WITH YOU, ELLE?
OF COURSE YOU CAN.
I AM TRULY SORRY THAT YOUR PARENTS KICKED YOU OUT.
I'VE BEEN WHERE YOU ARE, HONEY.
BUT IT WAS EVEN WORSE IN MY DAY.
BEING GAY WASN'T AS ACCEPTED AS IT IS NOW.
I'VE HIDDEN MY LOVE FOR A WOMAN FOR FIFTY YEARS.
I WAS IN LOVE WITH A BEAUTIFUL HONEY-COLORED MAIDEN NAMED MARI McCRAY WHEN I WAS THIRTEEN.
FEBRUARY 10TH, 1963, WAS THE DAY MARI WALKED INTO MY LIFE. AND THE DAY I KNEW I WAS DIFFERENT.

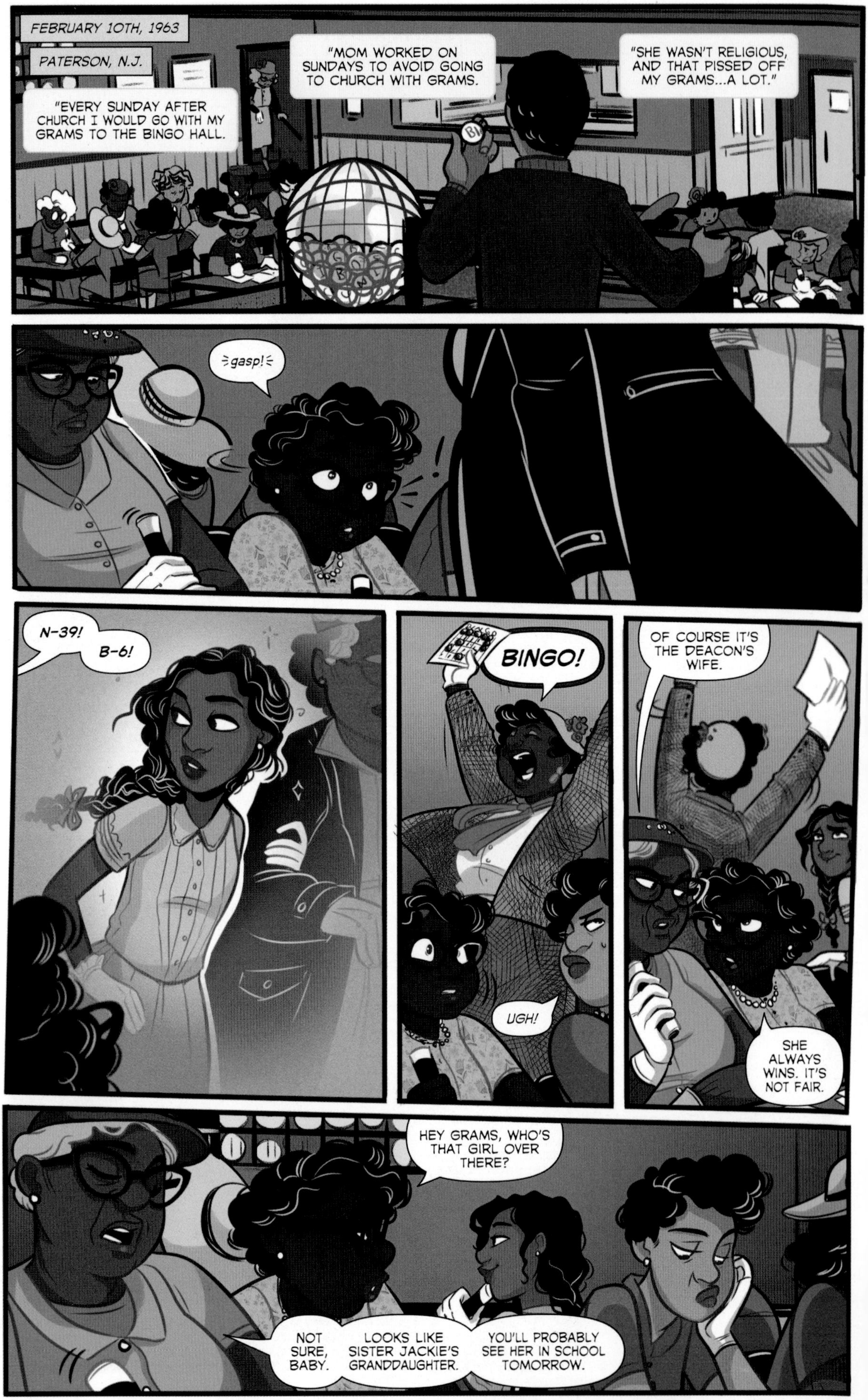
FEBRUARY 10TH, 1963
PATERSON, N.J.
"EVERY SUNDAY AFTER CHURCH I WOULD GO WITH MY GRAMS TO THE BINGO HALL.
"MOM WORKED ON SUNDAYS TO AVOID GOING TO CHURCH WITH GRAMS.
"SHE WASN'T RELIGIOUS, AND THAT PISSED OFF MY GRAMS...A LOT."
gasp!
N-39!
B-6!
BINGO!
UGH!
OF COURSE IT'S THE DEACON'S WIFE.
SHE ALWAYS WINS. IT'S NOT FAIR.
HEY GRAMS, WHO'S THAT GIRL OVER THERE?
NOT SURE, BABY.
LOOKS LIKE SISTER JACKIE'S GRANDDAUGHTER.
YOU'LL PROBABLY SEE HER IN SCHOOL TOMORROW.

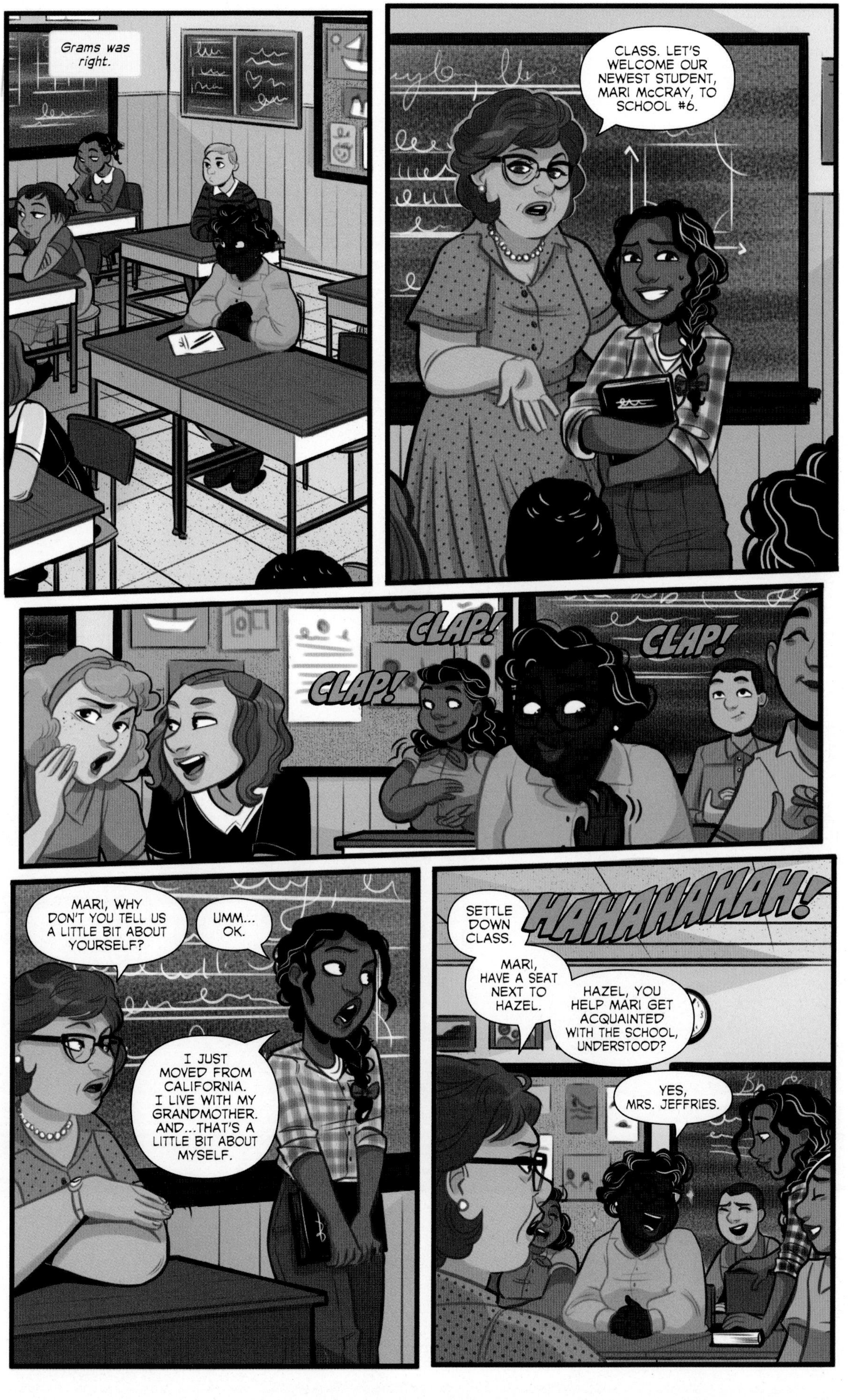

Grams was right.
CLASS. LET'S WELCOME OUR NEWEST STUDENT, MARI McCRAY, TO SCHOOL #6.
CLAP!
CLAP!
CLAP!
MARI, WHY DON'T YOU TELL US A LITTLE BIT ABOUT YOURSELF?
UMM... OK.
I JUST MOVED FROM CALIFORNIA. I LIVE WITH MY GRANDMOTHER. AND...THAT'S A LITTLE BIT ABOUT MYSELF.
HAHAHAHAH!
SETTLE DOWN CLASS.
MARI, HAVE A SEAT NEXT TO HAZEL.
HAZEL, YOU HELP MARI GET ACQUAINTED WITH THE SCHOOL, UNDERSTOOD?
YES, MRS. JEFFRIES.

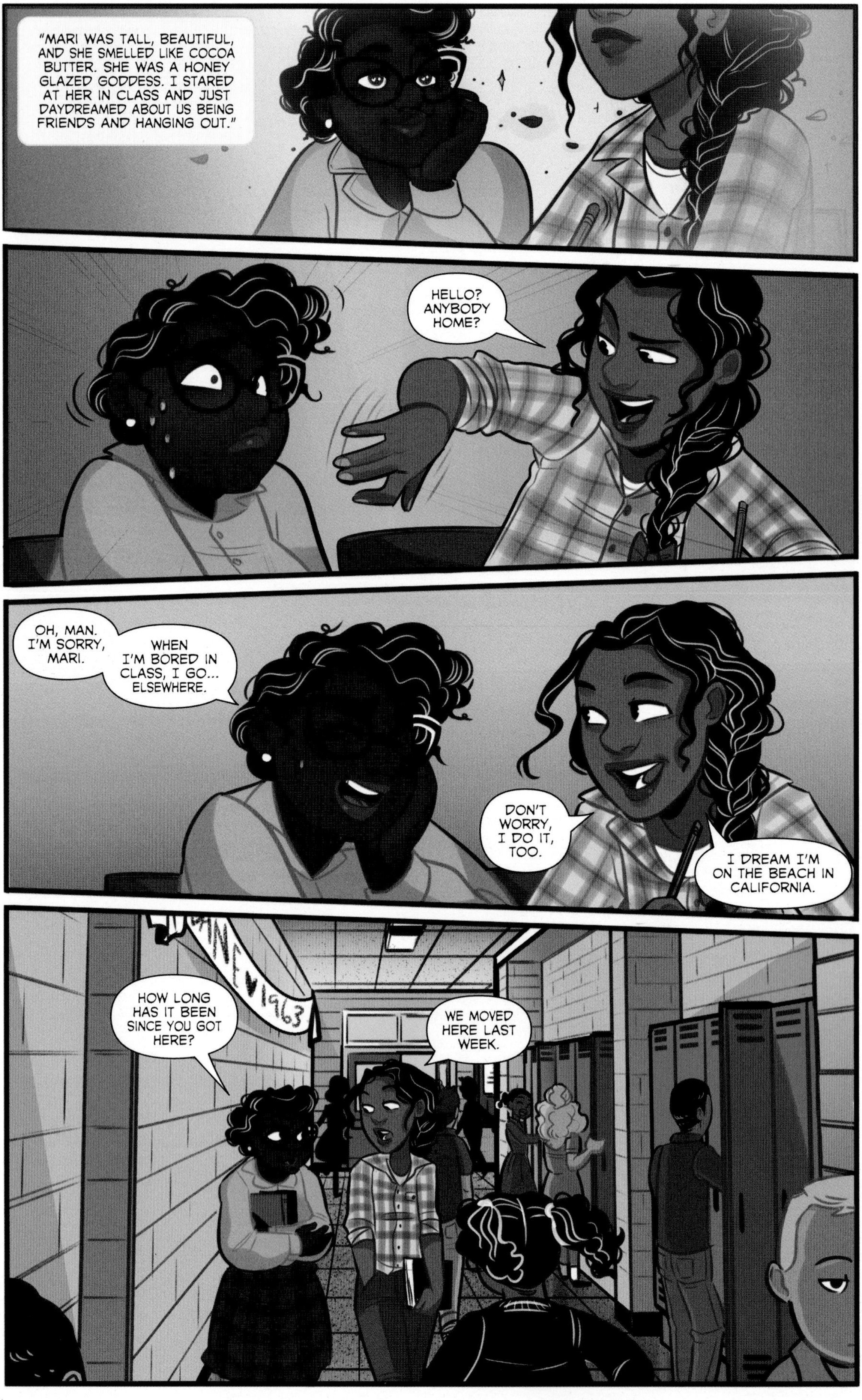
"MARI WAS TALL, BEAUTIFUL, AND SHE SMELLED LIKE COCOA BUTTER. SHE WAS A HONEY GLAZED GODDESS. I STARED AT HER IN CLASS AND JUST DAYDREAMED ABOUT US BEING FRIENDS AND HANGING OUT."
HELLO? ANYBODY HOME?
OH, MAN. I'M SORRY, MARI.
WHEN I'M BORED IN CLASS, I GO... ELSEWHERE.
DON'T WORRY, I DO IT, TOO.
I DREAM I'M ON THE BEACH IN CALIFORNIA.
HOW LONG HAS IT BEEN SINCE YOU GOT HERE?
WE MOVED HERE LAST WEEK.

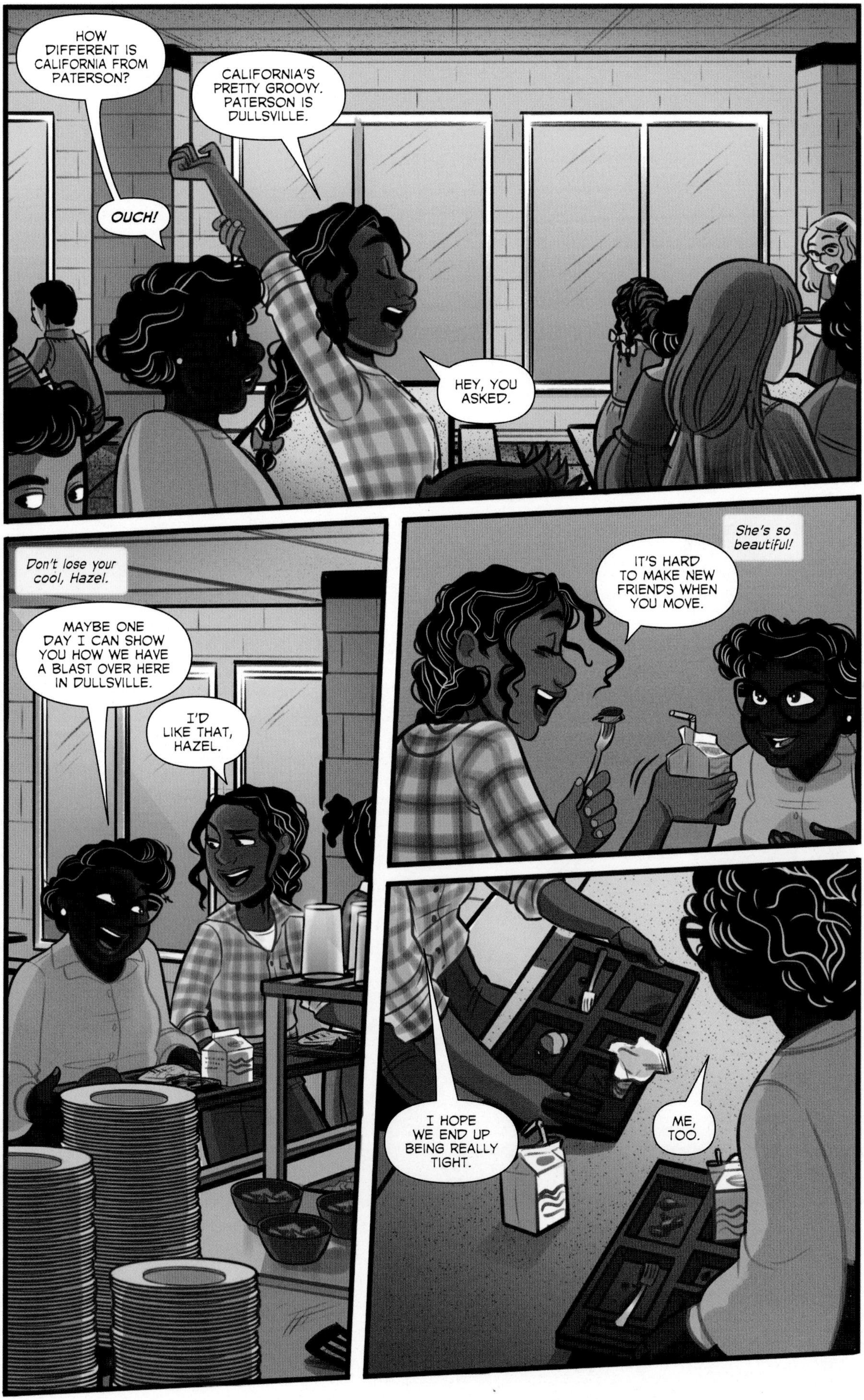
HOW DIFFERENT IS CALIFORNIA FROM PATERSON?
CALIFORNIA'S PRETTY GROOVY. PATERSON IS DULLSVILLE.
OUCH!
HEY, YOU ASKED.
Don't lose your cool, Hazel.
MAYBE ONE DAY I CAN SHOW YOU HOW WE HAVE A BLAST OVER HERE IN DULLSVILLE.
I'D LIKE THAT, HAZEL.
She's so beautiful!
IT'S HARD TO MAKE NEW FRIENDS WHEN YOU MOVE.
I HOPE WE END UP BEING REALLY TIGHT.
ME, TOO.

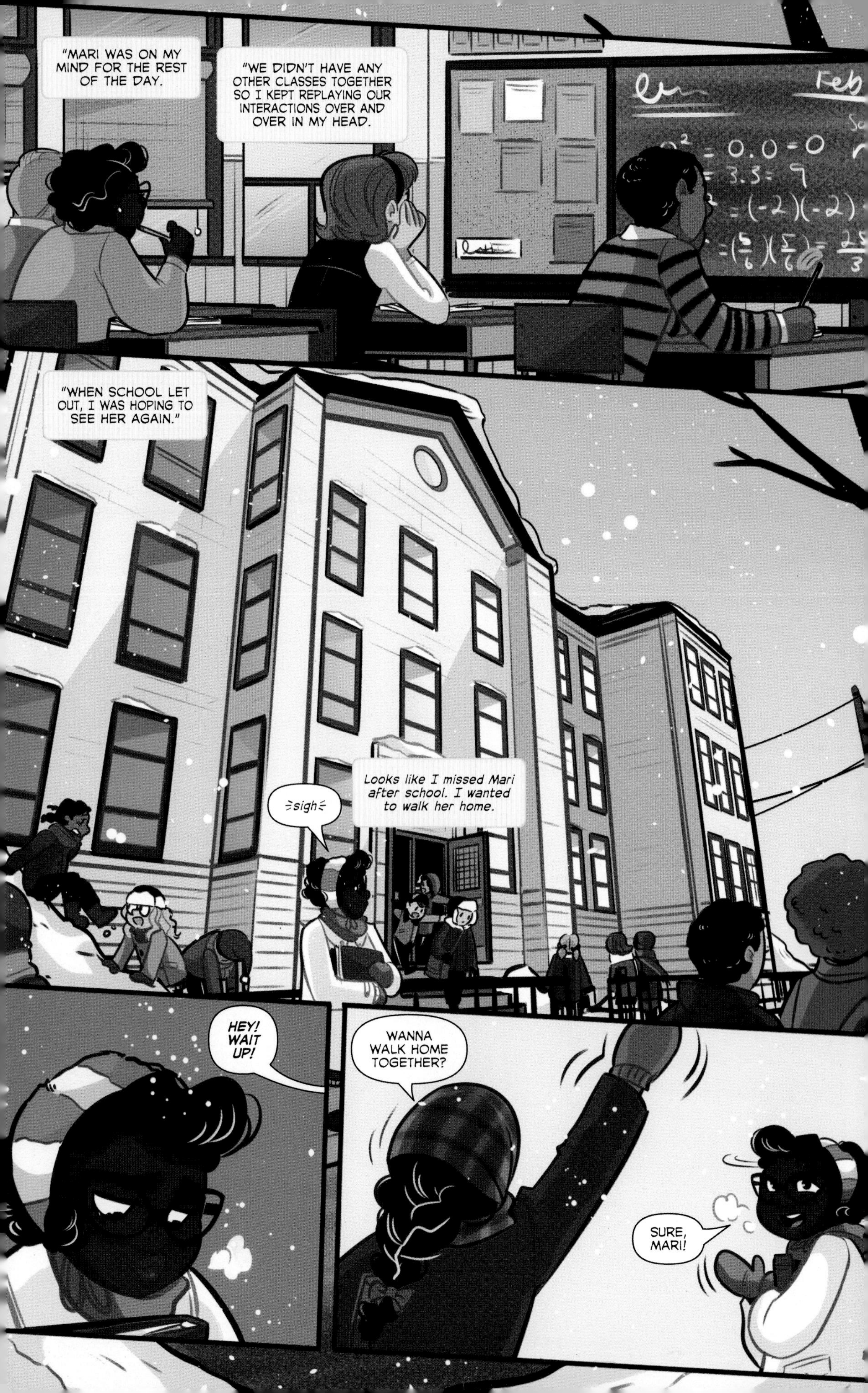
"MARI WAS ON MY MIND FOR THE REST OF THE DAY.
"WE DIDN'T HAVE ANY OTHER CLASSES TOGETHER SO I KEPT REPLAYING OUR INTERACTIONS OVER AND OVER IN MY HEAD.
"WHEN SCHOOL LET OUT, I WAS HOPING TO SEE HER AGAIN."
sigh
Looks like I missed Mari after school. I wanted to walk her home.
HEY! WAIT UP!
WANNA WALK HOME TOGETHER?
SURE, MARI!

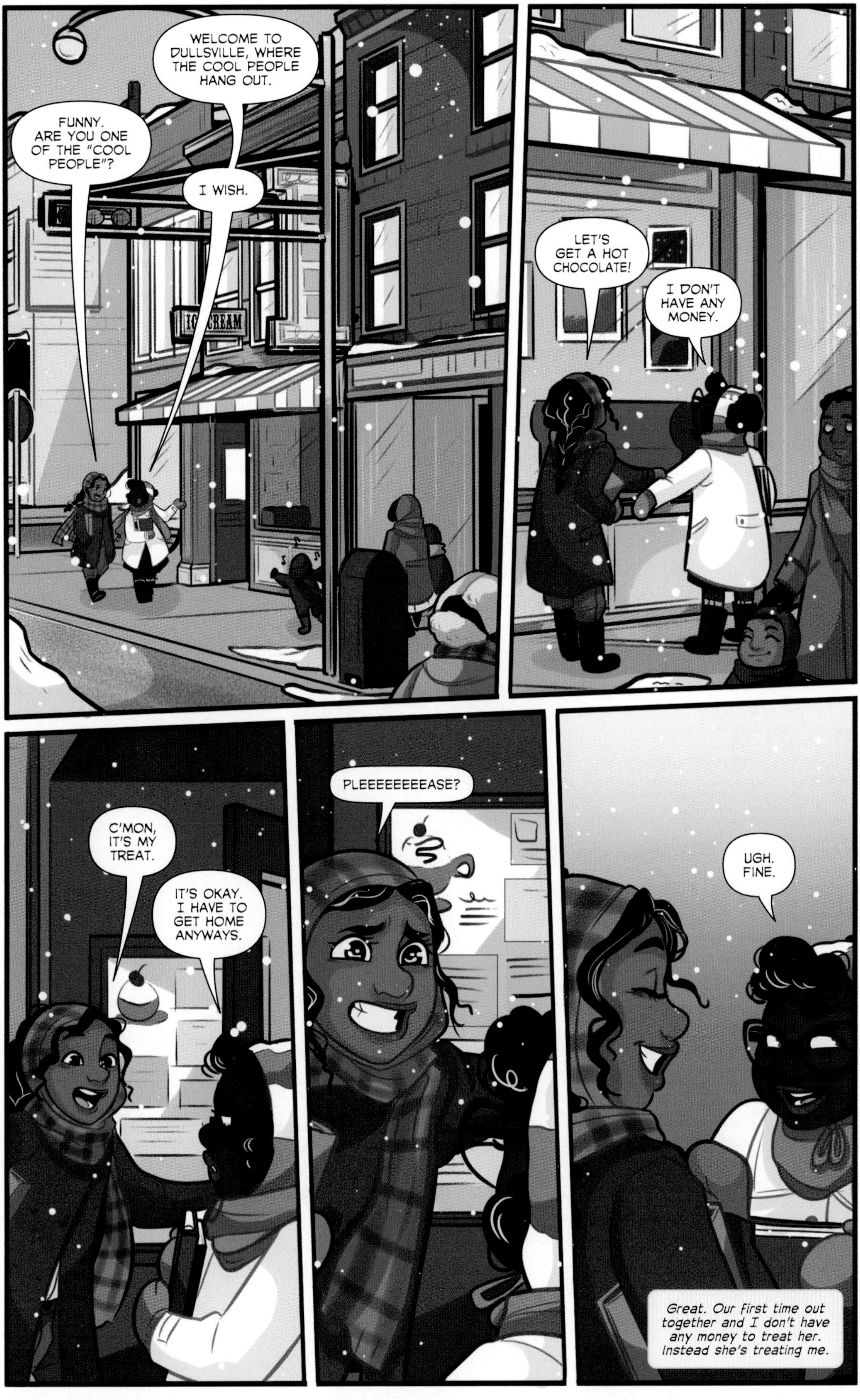
WELCOME TO DULLSVILLE, WHERE THE COOL PEOPLE HANG OUT.
FUNNY. ARE YOU ONE OF THE "COOL PEOPLE"?
I WISH.
ICE CREAM
LET'S GET A HOT CHOCOLATE!
I DON'T HAVE ANY MONEY.
C'MON, IT'S MY TREAT.
IT'S OKAY. I HAVE TO GET HOME ANYWAYS.
PLEEEEEEEEASE?
UGH. FINE.
Great. Our first time out together and I don't have any money to treat her. Instead she's treating me.

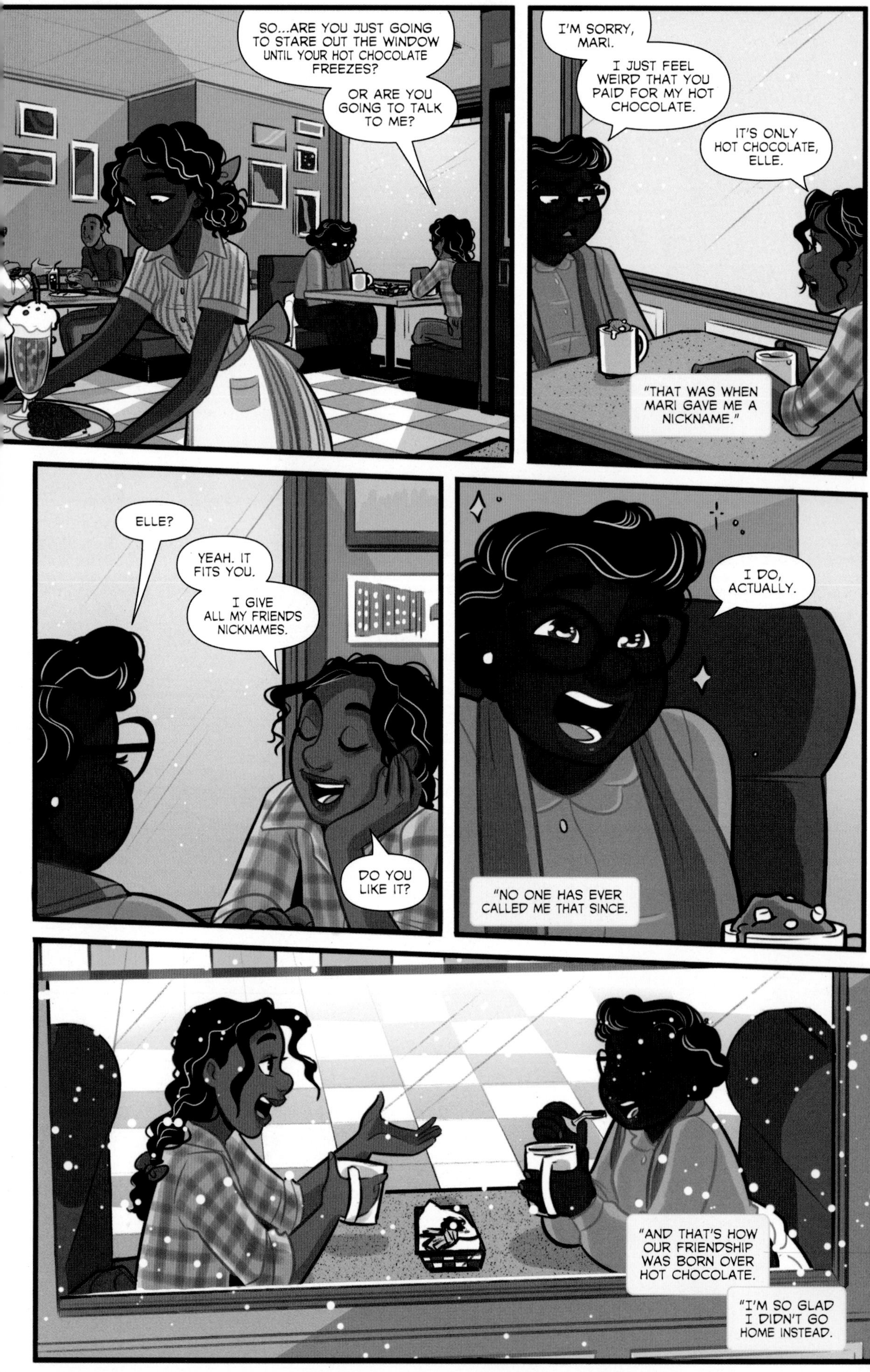

SO...ARE YOU JUST GOING TO STARE OUT THE WINDOW UNTIL YOUR HOT CHOCOLATE FREEZES?
OR ARE YOU GOING TO TALK TO ME?
I'M SORRY, MARI.
I JUST FEEL WEIRD THAT YOU PAID FOR MY HOT CHOCOLATE.
IT'S ONLY HOT CHOCOLATE, ELLE.
"THAT WAS WHEN MARI GAVE ME A NICKNAME."
ELLE?
YEAH. IT FITS YOU.
I GIVE ALL MY FRIENDS NICKNAMES.
DO YOU LIKE IT?
I DO, ACTUALLY.
"NO ONE HAS EVER CALLED ME THAT SINCE.
"AND THAT'S HOW OUR FRIENDSHIP WAS BORN OVER HOT CHOCOLATE.
"I'M SO GLAD I DIDN'T GO HOME INSTEAD.

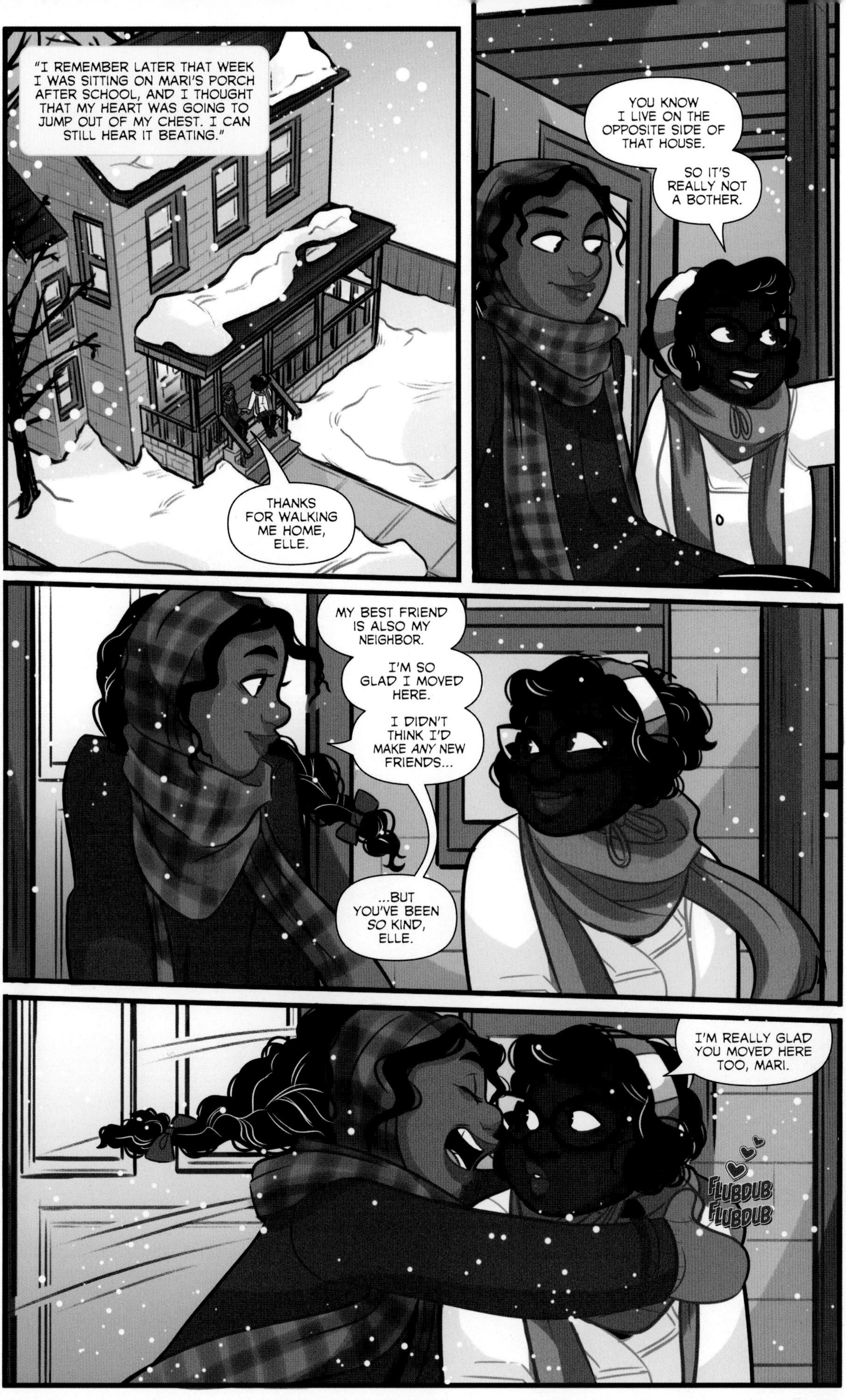
"I REMEMBER LATER THAT WEEK I WAS SITTING ON MARI'S PORCH AFTER SCHOOL, AND I THOUGHT THAT MY HEART WAS GOING TO JUMP OUT OF MY CHEST. I CAN STILL HEAR IT BEATING."
THANKS FOR WALKING ME HOME, ELLE.
YOU KNOW I LIVE ON THE OPPOSITE SIDE OF THAT HOUSE.
SO IT'S REALLY NOT A BOTHER.
MY BEST FRIEND IS ALSO MY NEIGHBOR.
I'M SO GLAD I MOVED HERE.
I DIDN'T THINK I'D MAKE *ANY* NEW FRIENDS...
...BUT YOU'VE BEEN *SO* KIND, ELLE.
I'M REALLY GLAD YOU MOVED HERE TOO, MARI.
FLUBDUB FLUBDUB

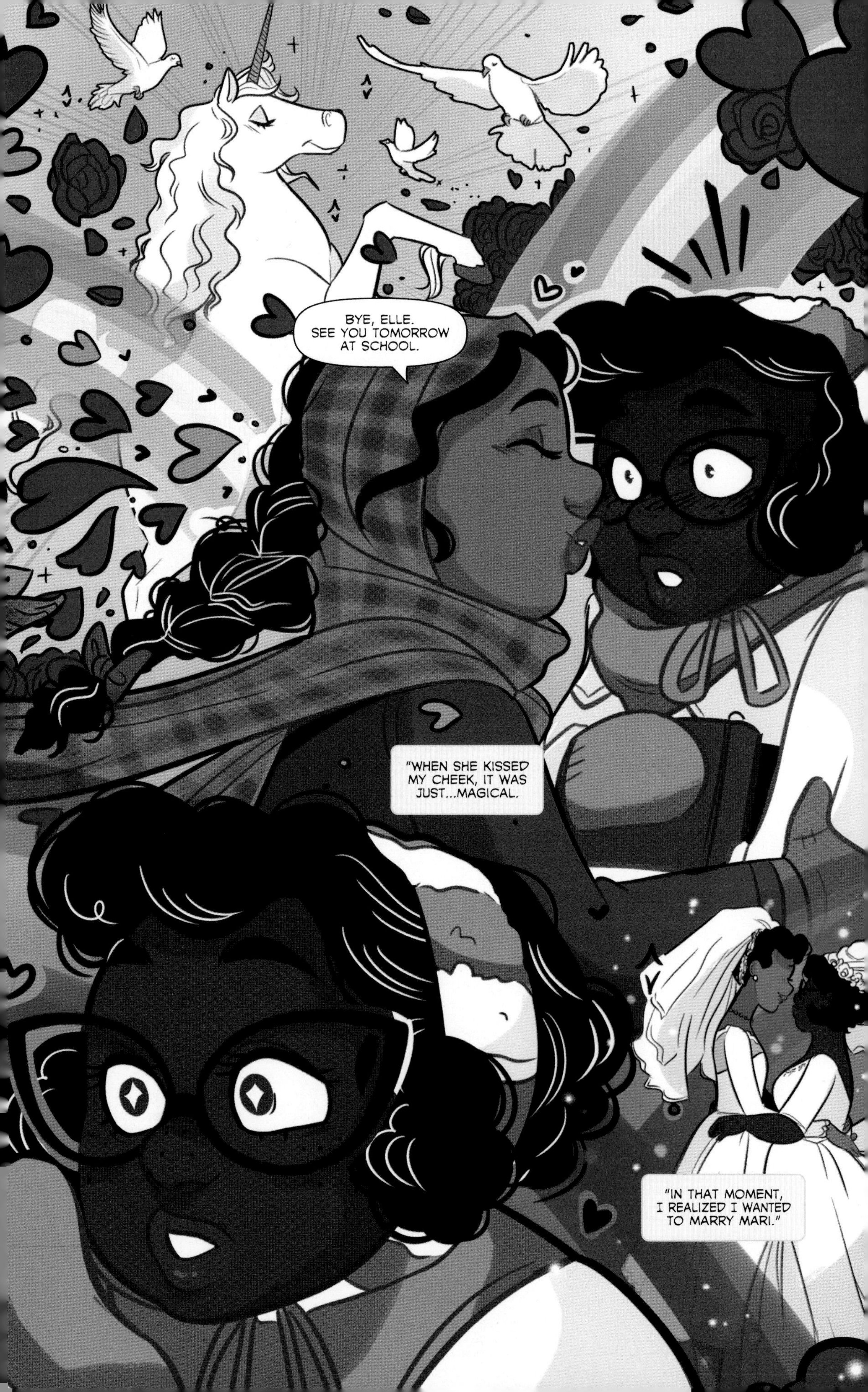
BYE, ELLE. SEE YOU TOMORROW AT SCHOOL.
"WHEN SHE KISSED MY CHEEK, IT WAS JUST...MAGICAL.
"IN THAT MOMENT, I REALIZED I WANTED TO MARRY MARI."

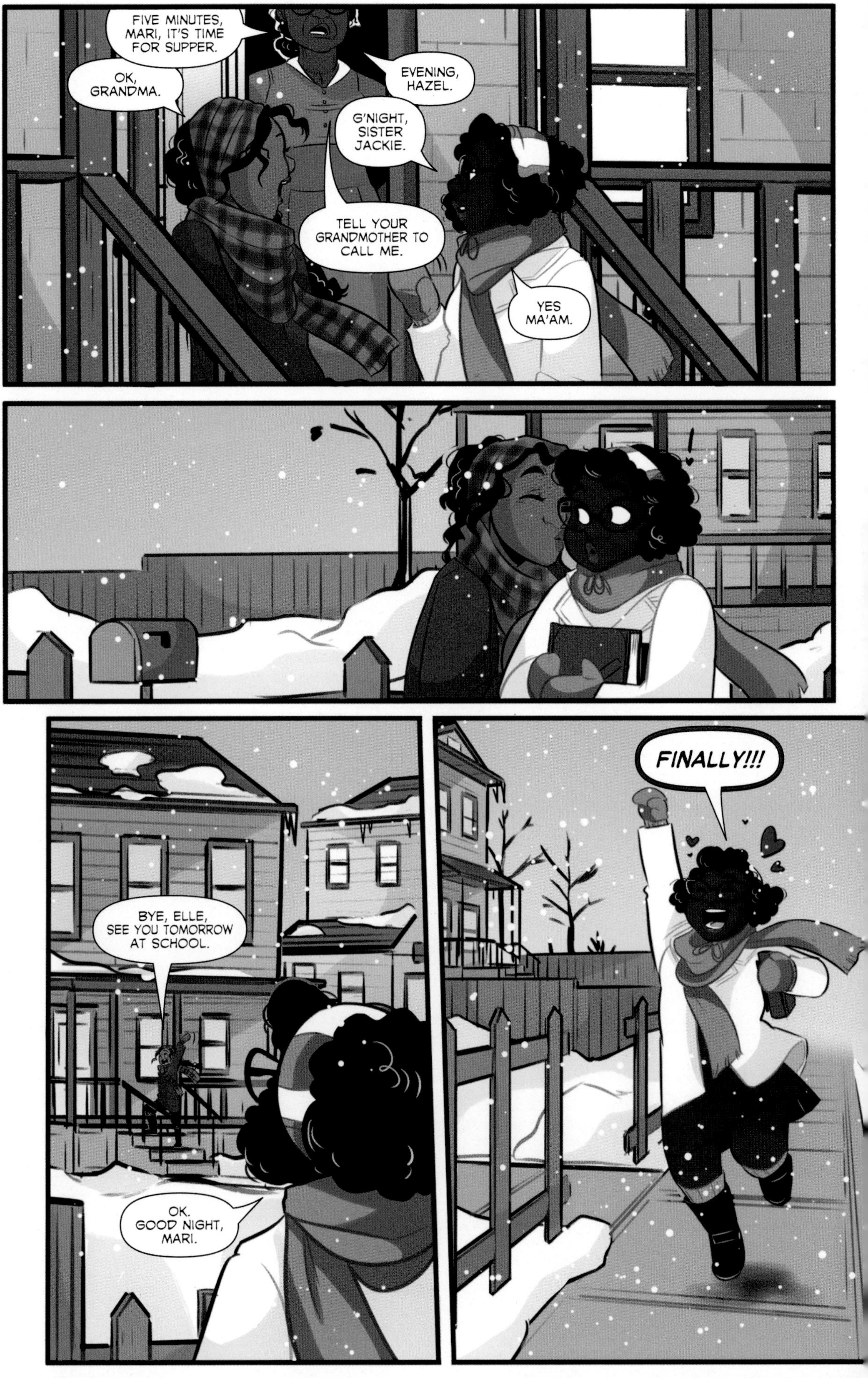
FIVE MINUTES, MARI, IT'S TIME FOR SUPPER.
OK, GRANDMA.
EVENING, HAZEL.
G'NIGHT, SISTER JACKIE.
TELL YOUR GRANDMOTHER TO CALL ME.
YES MA'AM.
!
BYE, ELLE, SEE YOU TOMORROW AT SCHOOL.
OK. GOOD NIGHT, MARI.
FINALLY!!!

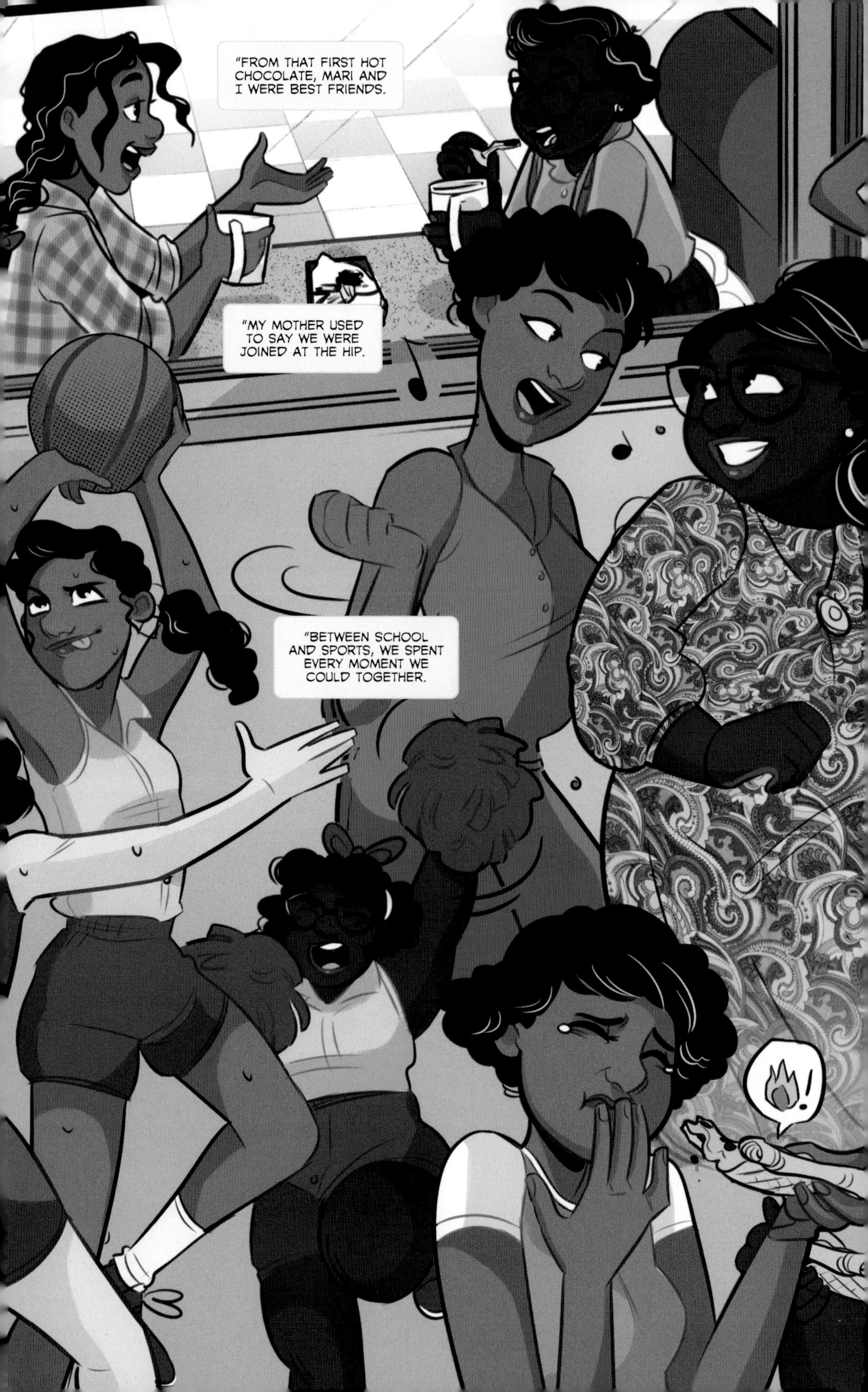
"FROM THAT FIRST HOT CHOCOLATE, MARI AND I WERE BEST FRIENDS.
"MY MOTHER USED TO SAY WE WERE JOINED AT THE HIP.
"BETWEEN SCHOOL AND SPORTS, WE SPENT EVERY MOMENT WE COULD TOGETHER.
!

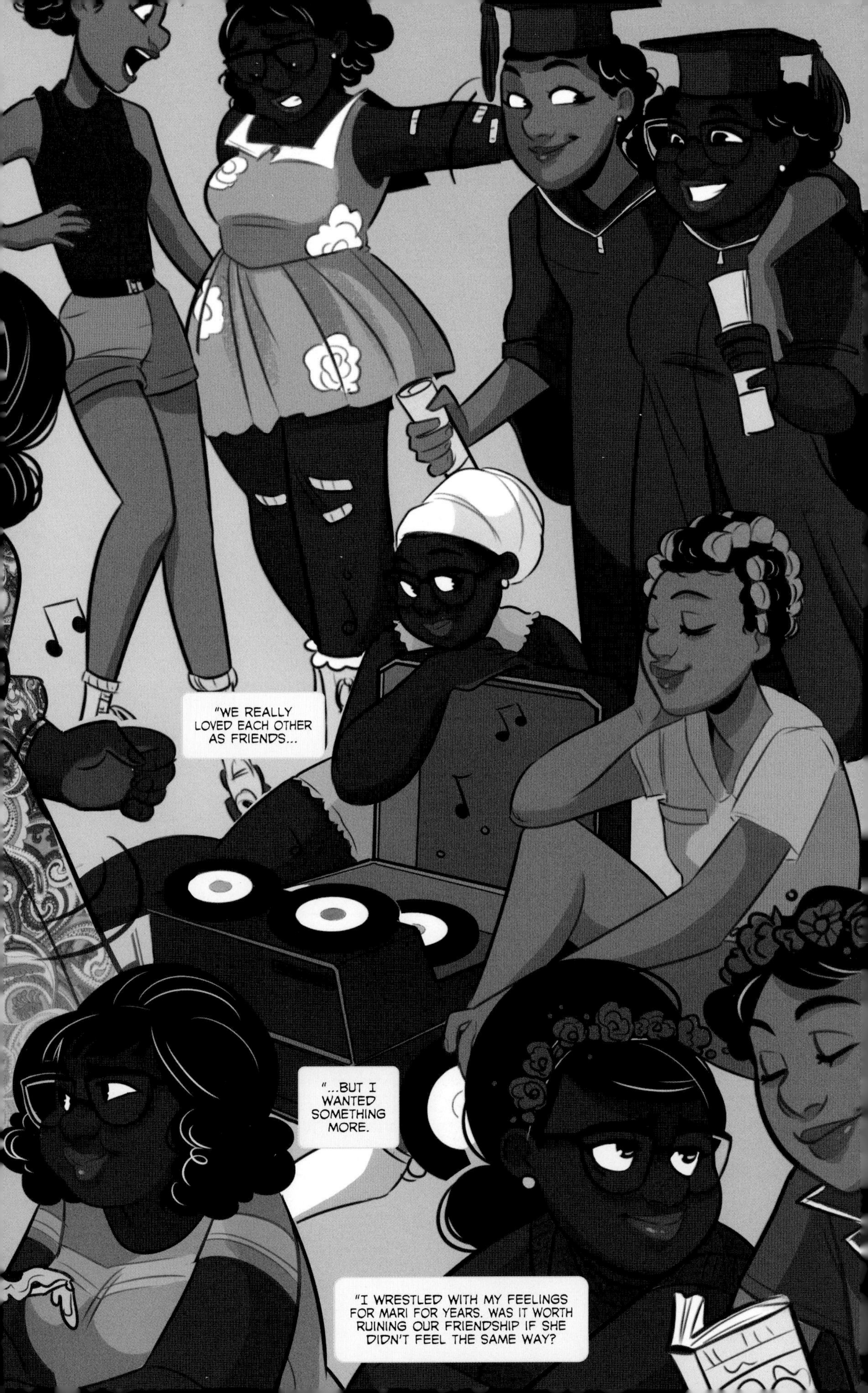
"WE REALLY LOVED EACH OTHER AS FRIENDS...
"...BUT I WANTED SOMETHING MORE.
"I WRESTLED WITH MY FEELINGS FOR MARI FOR YEARS. WAS IT WORTH RUINING OUR FRIENDSHIP IF SHE DIDN'T FEEL THE SAME WAY?

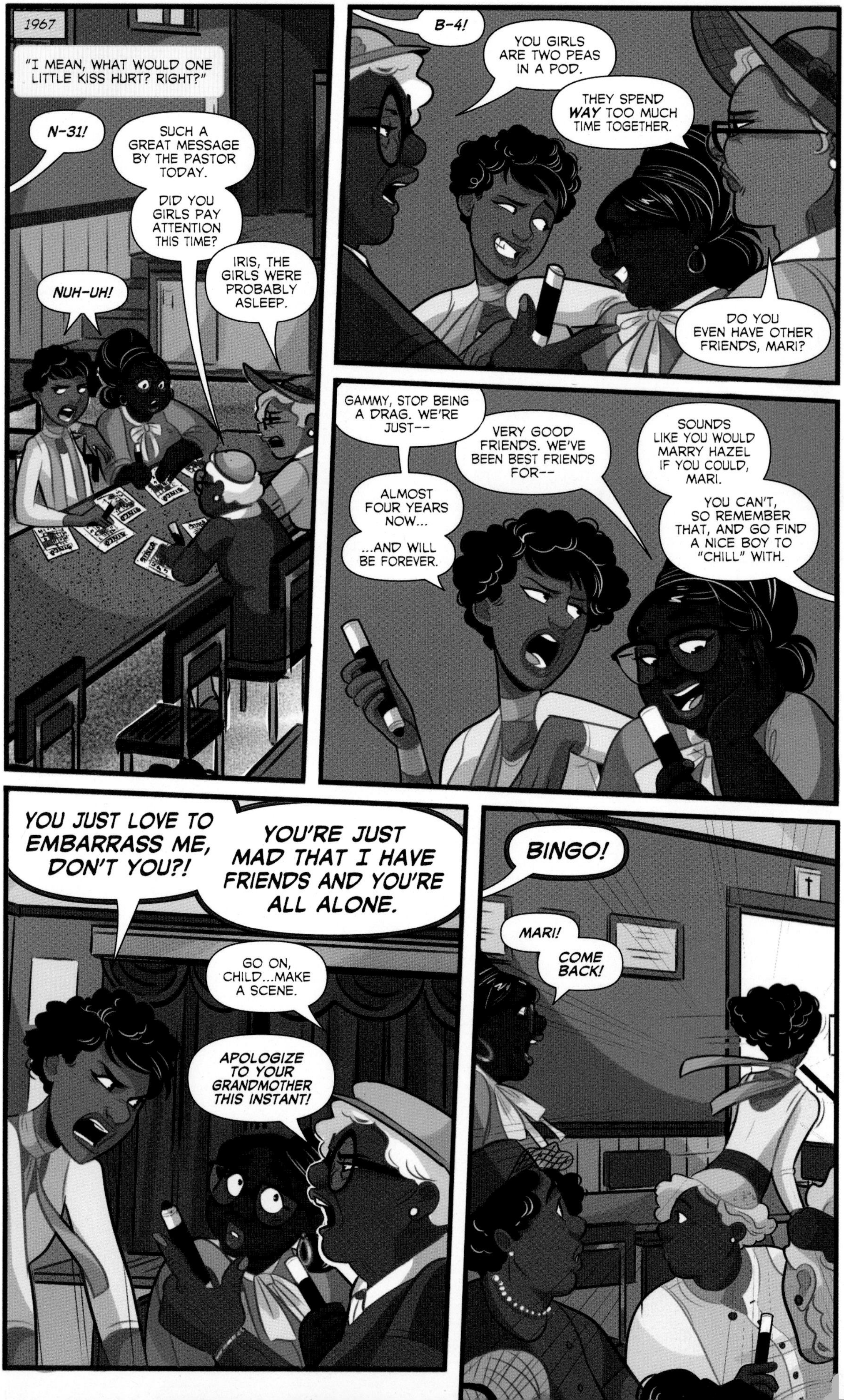
1967
"I MEAN, WHAT WOULD ONE LITTLE KISS HURT? RIGHT?"
N-31!
SUCH A GREAT MESSAGE BY THE PASTOR TODAY.
DID YOU GIRLS PAY ATTENTION THIS TIME?
IRIS, THE GIRLS WERE PROBABLY ASLEEP.
NUH-UH!
B-4!
YOU GIRLS ARE TWO PEAS IN A POD.
THEY SPEND WAY TOO MUCH TIME TOGETHER.
DO YOU EVEN HAVE OTHER FRIENDS, MARI?
GAMMY, STOP BEING A DRAG. WE'RE JUST--
VERY GOOD FRIENDS. WE'VE BEEN BEST FRIENDS FOR--
ALMOST FOUR YEARS NOW...
...AND WILL BE FOREVER.
SOUNDS LIKE YOU WOULD MARRY HAZEL IF YOU COULD, MARI.
YOU CAN'T, SO REMEMBER THAT, AND GO FIND A NICE BOY TO "CHILL" WITH.
YOU JUST LOVE TO EMBARRASS ME, DON'T YOU?!
YOU'RE JUST MAD THAT I HAVE FRIENDS AND YOU'RE ALL ALONE.
GO ON, CHILD...MAKE A SCENE.
APOLOGIZE TO YOUR GRANDMOTHER THIS INSTANT!
BINGO!
MARI!
COME BACK!

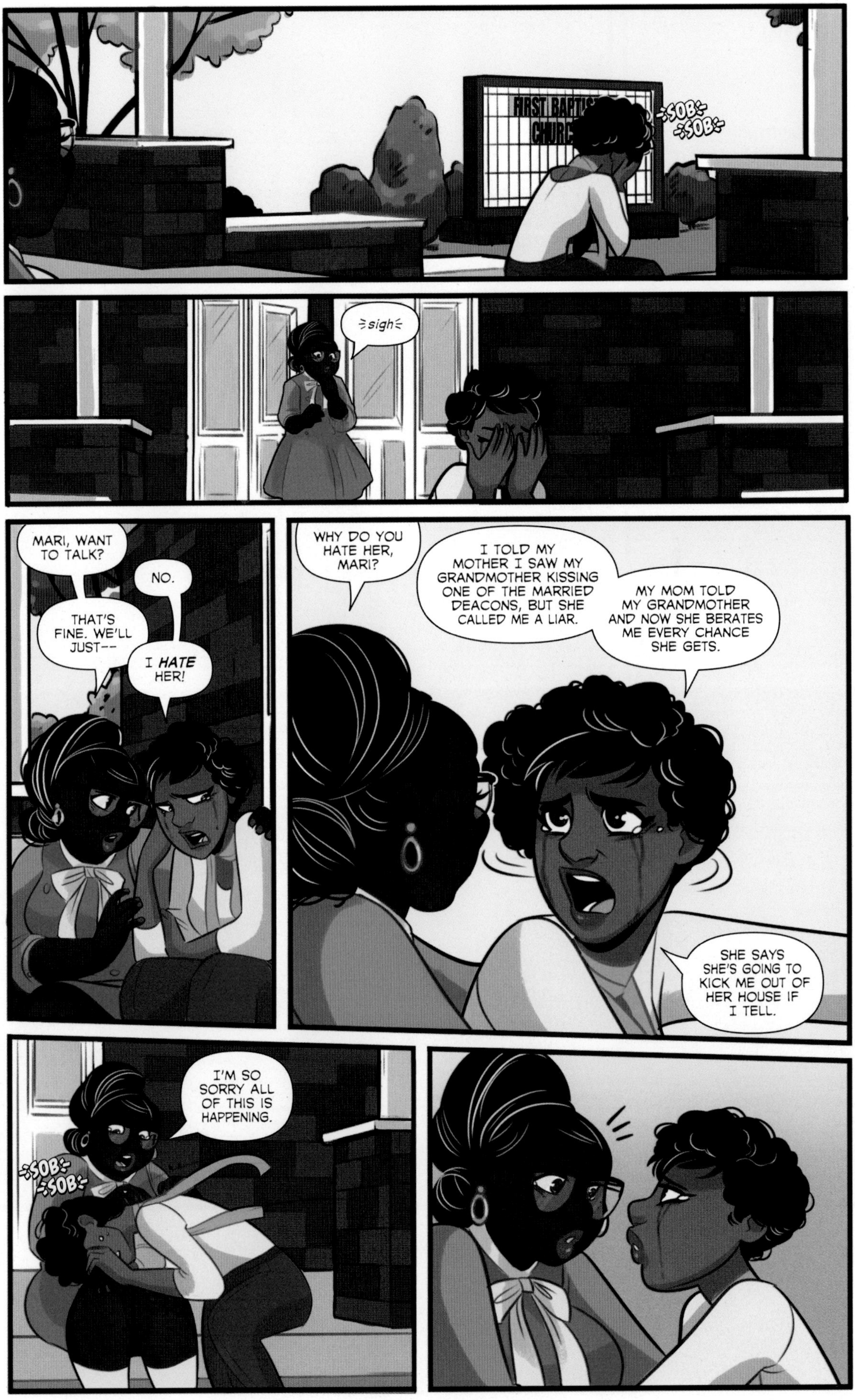
FIRST BAPTIS
CHURC
SOB
SOB
sigh
MARI, WANT TO TALK?
NO.
THAT'S FINE. WE'LL JUST--
I HATE HER!
WHY DO YOU HATE HER, MARI?
I TOLD MY MOTHER I SAW MY GRANDMOTHER KISSING ONE OF THE MARRIED DEACONS, BUT SHE CALLED ME A LIAR.
MY MOM TOLD MY GRANDMOTHER AND NOW SHE BERATES ME EVERY CHANCE SHE GETS.
SHE SAYS SHE'S GOING TO KICK ME OUT OF HER HOUSE IF I TELL.
SOB
SOB
I'M SO SORRY ALL OF THIS IS HAPPENING.

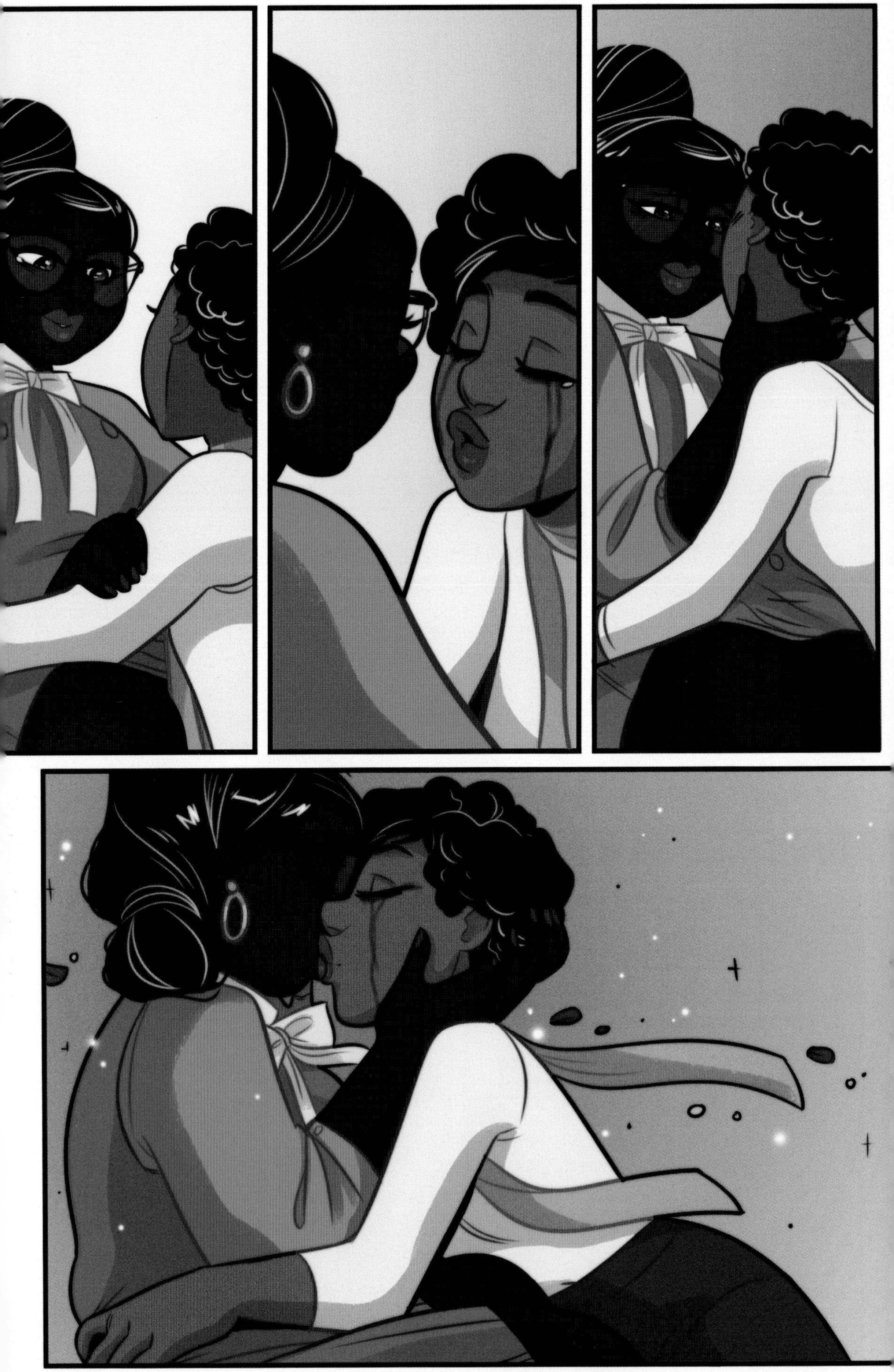

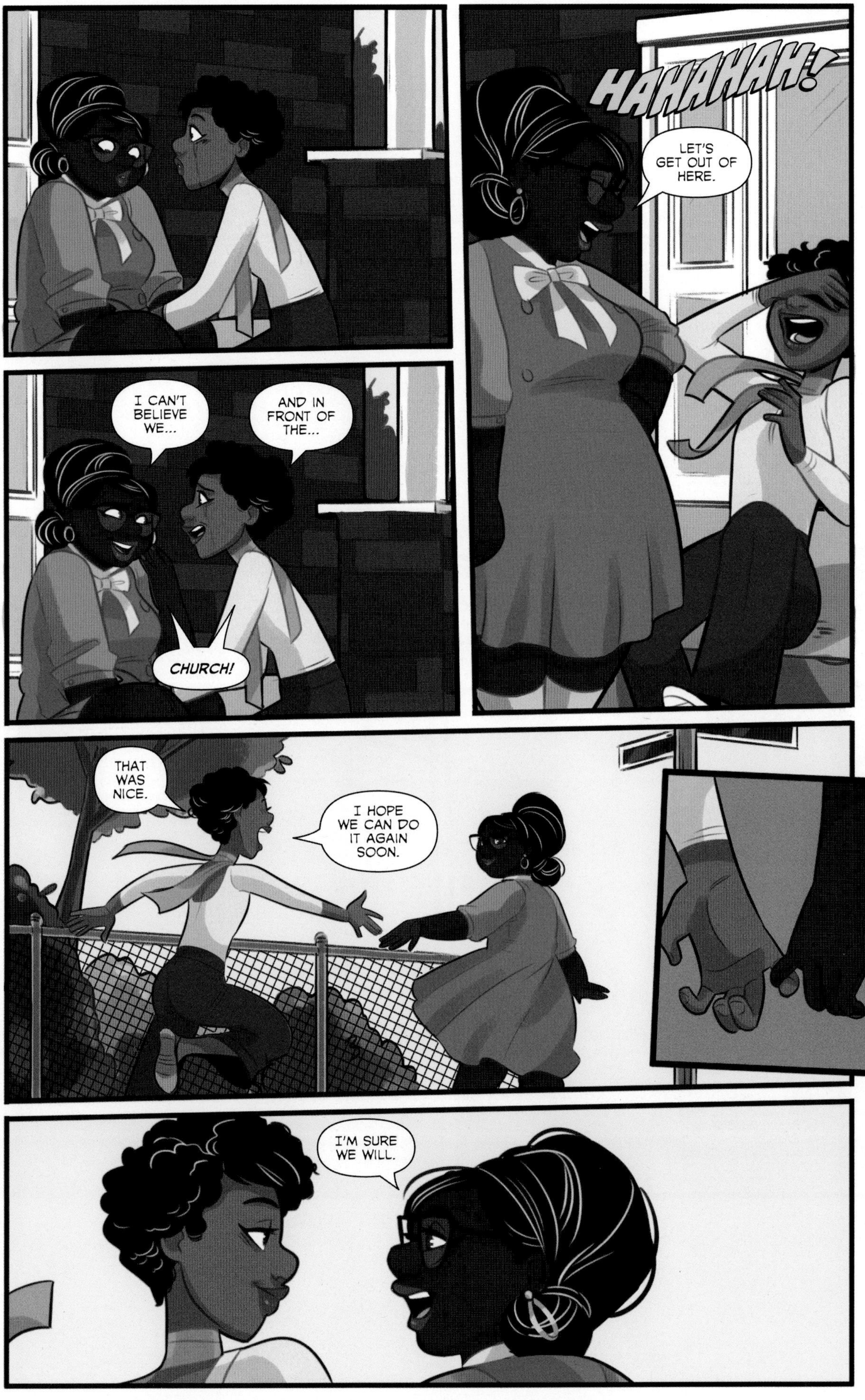
HAHAHAH!
LET'S GET OUT OF HERE.
I CAN'T BELIEVE WE...
AND IN FRONT OF THE...
CHURCH!
THAT WAS NICE.
I HOPE WE CAN DO IT AGAIN SOON.
I'M SURE WE WILL.

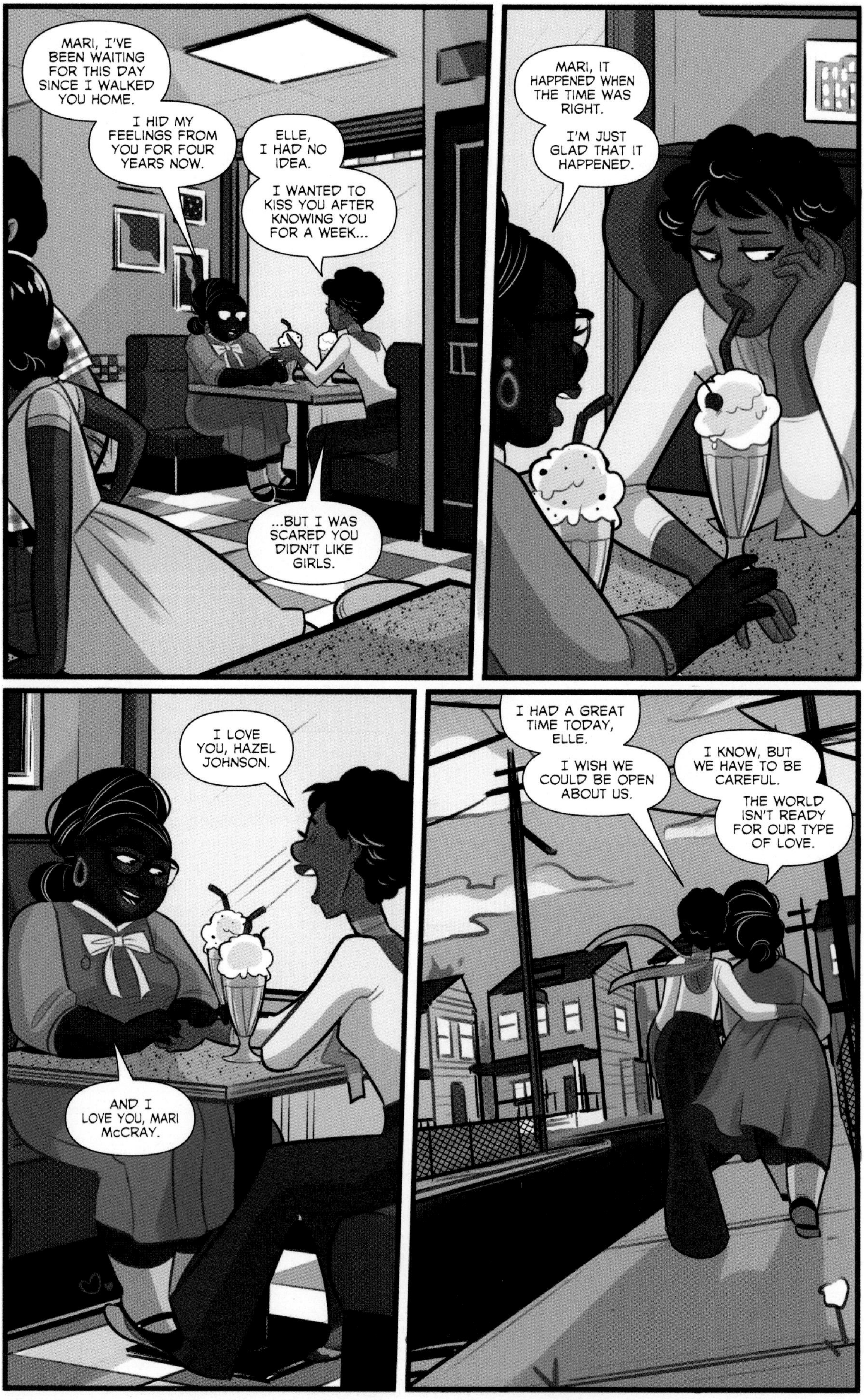
MARI, I'VE BEEN WAITING FOR THIS DAY SINCE I WALKED YOU HOME.
I HID MY FEELINGS FROM YOU FOR FOUR YEARS NOW.
ELLE, I HAD NO IDEA.
I WANTED TO KISS YOU AFTER KNOWING YOU FOR A WEEK...
...BUT I WAS SCARED YOU DIDN'T LIKE GIRLS.
MARI, IT HAPPENED WHEN THE TIME WAS RIGHT.
I'M JUST GLAD THAT IT HAPPENED.
I LOVE YOU, HAZEL JOHNSON.
AND I LOVE YOU, MARI McCRAY.
I HAD A GREAT TIME TODAY, ELLE.
I WISH WE COULD BE OPEN ABOUT US.
I KNOW, BUT WE HAVE TO BE CAREFUL.
THE WORLD ISN'T READY FOR OUR TYPE OF LOVE.

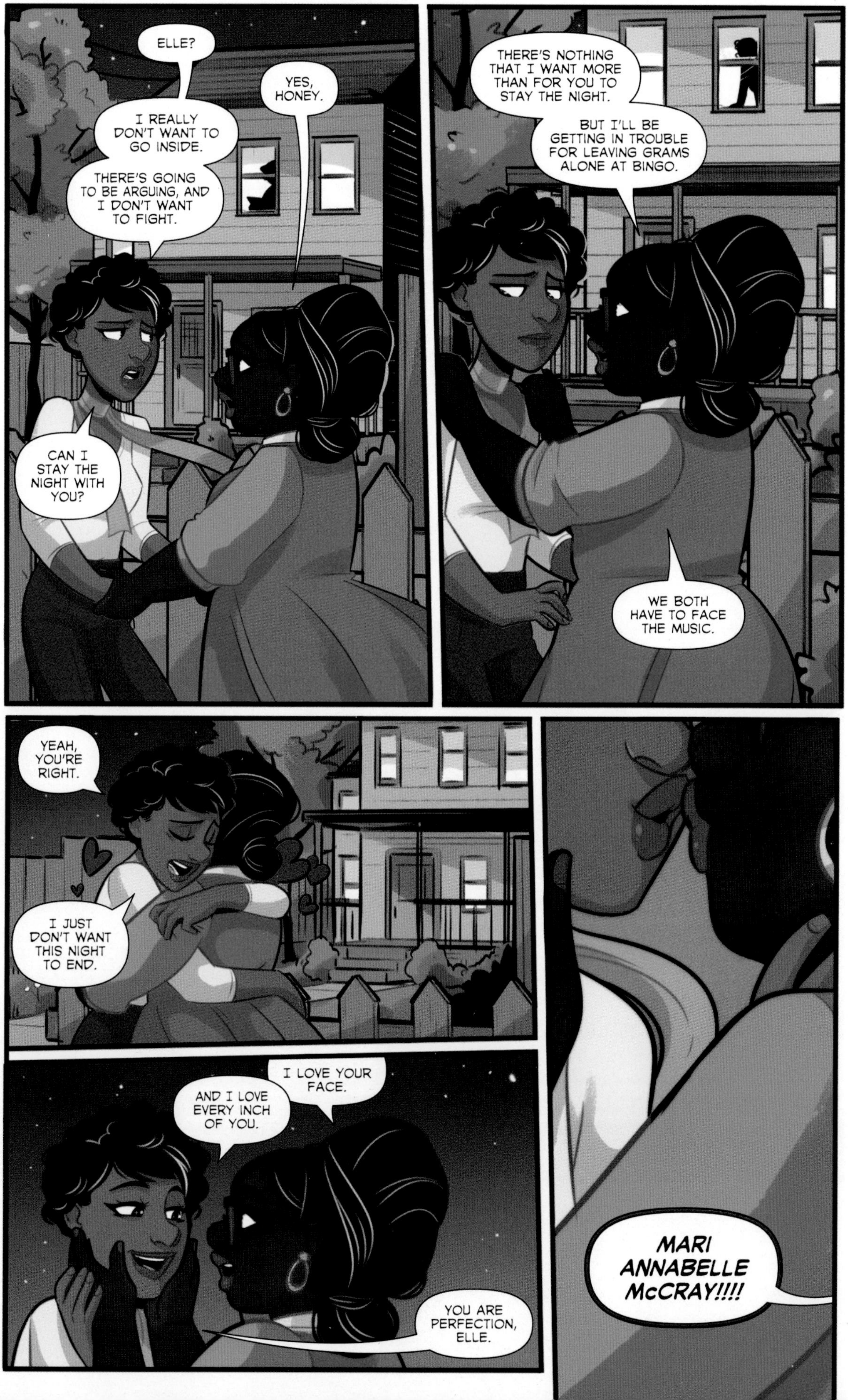

ELLE?
YES, HONEY.
I REALLY DON'T WANT TO GO INSIDE.
THERE'S GOING TO BE ARGUING, AND I DON'T WANT TO FIGHT.
CAN I STAY THE NIGHT WITH YOU?
THERE'S NOTHING THAT I WANT MORE THAN FOR YOU TO STAY THE NIGHT.
BUT I'LL BE GETTING IN TROUBLE FOR LEAVING GRAMS ALONE AT BINGO.
WE BOTH HAVE TO FACE THE MUSIC.
YEAH, YOU'RE RIGHT.
I JUST DON'T WANT THIS NIGHT TO END.
I LOVE YOUR FACE.
AND I LOVE EVERY INCH OF YOU.
YOU ARE PERFECTION, ELLE.
MARI ANNABELLE McCRAY!!!!

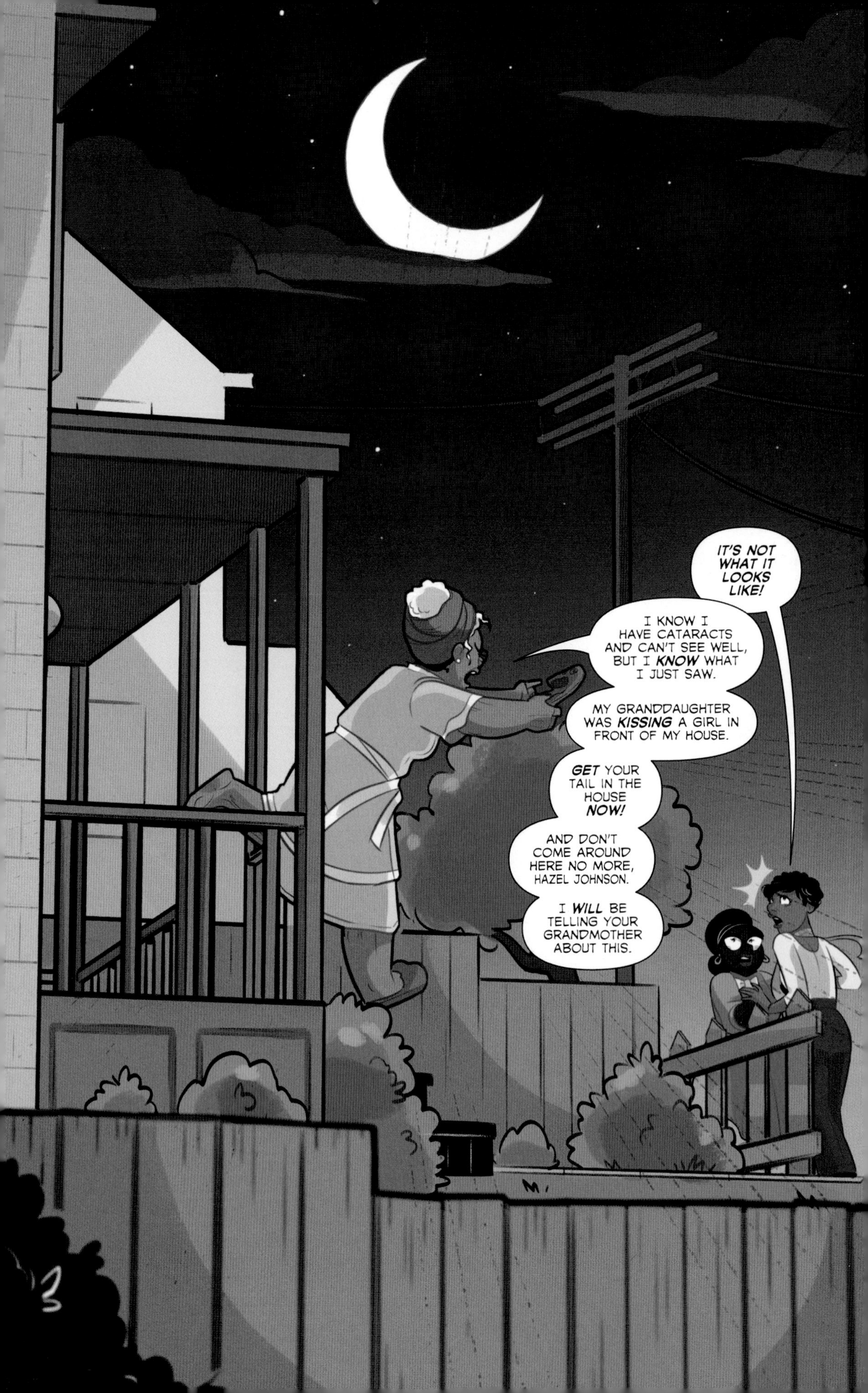
I KNOW I HAVE CATARACTS AND CAN'T SEE WELL, BUT I KNOW WHAT I JUST SAW.
MY GRANDDAUGHTER WAS KISSING A GIRL IN FRONT OF MY HOUSE.
GET YOUR TAIL IN THE HOUSE NOW!
AND DON'T COME AROUND HERE NO MORE, HAZEL JOHNSON.
I WILL BE TELLING YOUR GRANDMOTHER ABOUT THIS.
IT'S NOT WHAT IT LOOKS LIKE!

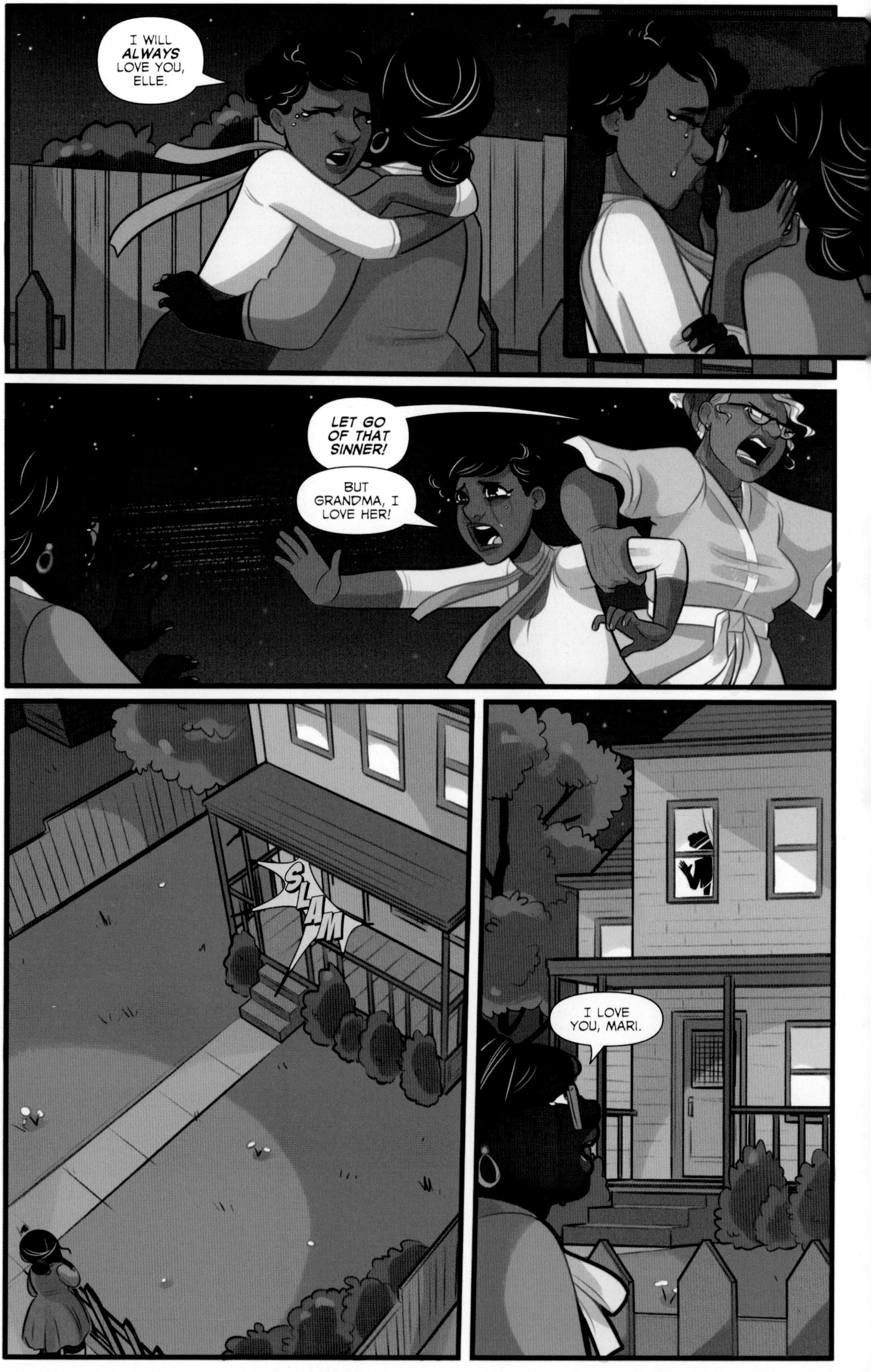
I WILL *ALWAYS* LOVE YOU, ELLE.
LET GO OF THAT SINNER!
BUT GRANDMA, I LOVE HER!
SLAM
I LOVE YOU, MARI.

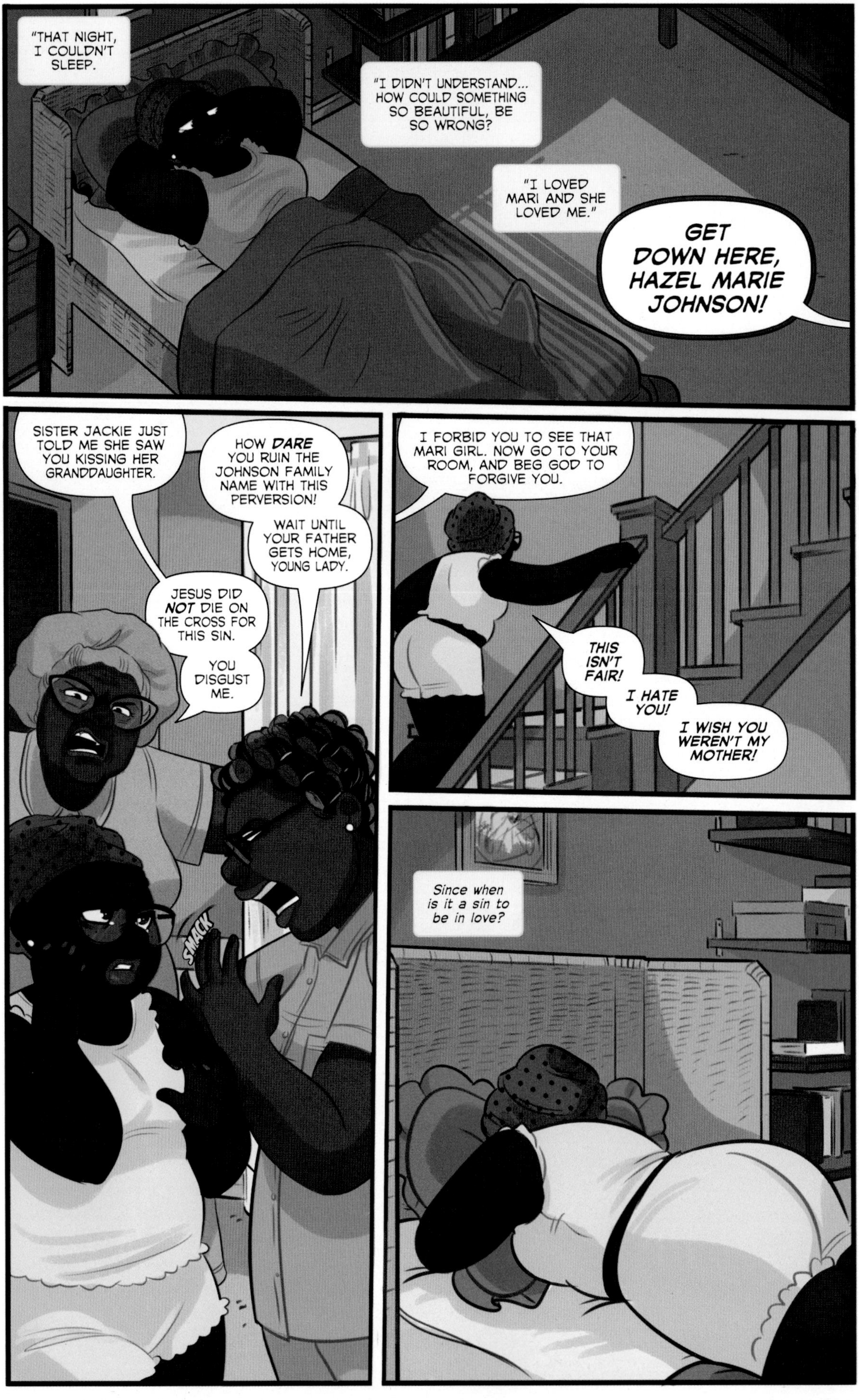
"THAT NIGHT, I COULDN'T SLEEP.
"I DIDN'T UNDERSTAND... HOW COULD SOMETHING SO BEAUTIFUL, BE SO WRONG?
"I LOVED MARI AND SHE LOVED ME."
GET DOWN HERE, HAZEL MARIE JOHNSON!
SISTER JACKIE JUST TOLD ME SHE SAW YOU KISSING HER GRANDDAUGHTER.
HOW DARE YOU RUIN THE JOHNSON FAMILY NAME WITH THIS PERVERSION!
WAIT UNTIL YOUR FATHER GETS HOME, YOUNG LADY.
JESUS DID NOT DIE ON THE CROSS FOR THIS SIN.
YOU DISGUST ME.
SMACK
I FORBID YOU TO SEE THAT MARI GIRL. NOW GO TO YOUR ROOM, AND BEG GOD TO FORGIVE YOU.
THIS ISN'T FAIR!
I HATE YOU!
I WISH YOU WEREN'T MY MOTHER!
Since when is it a sin to be in love?

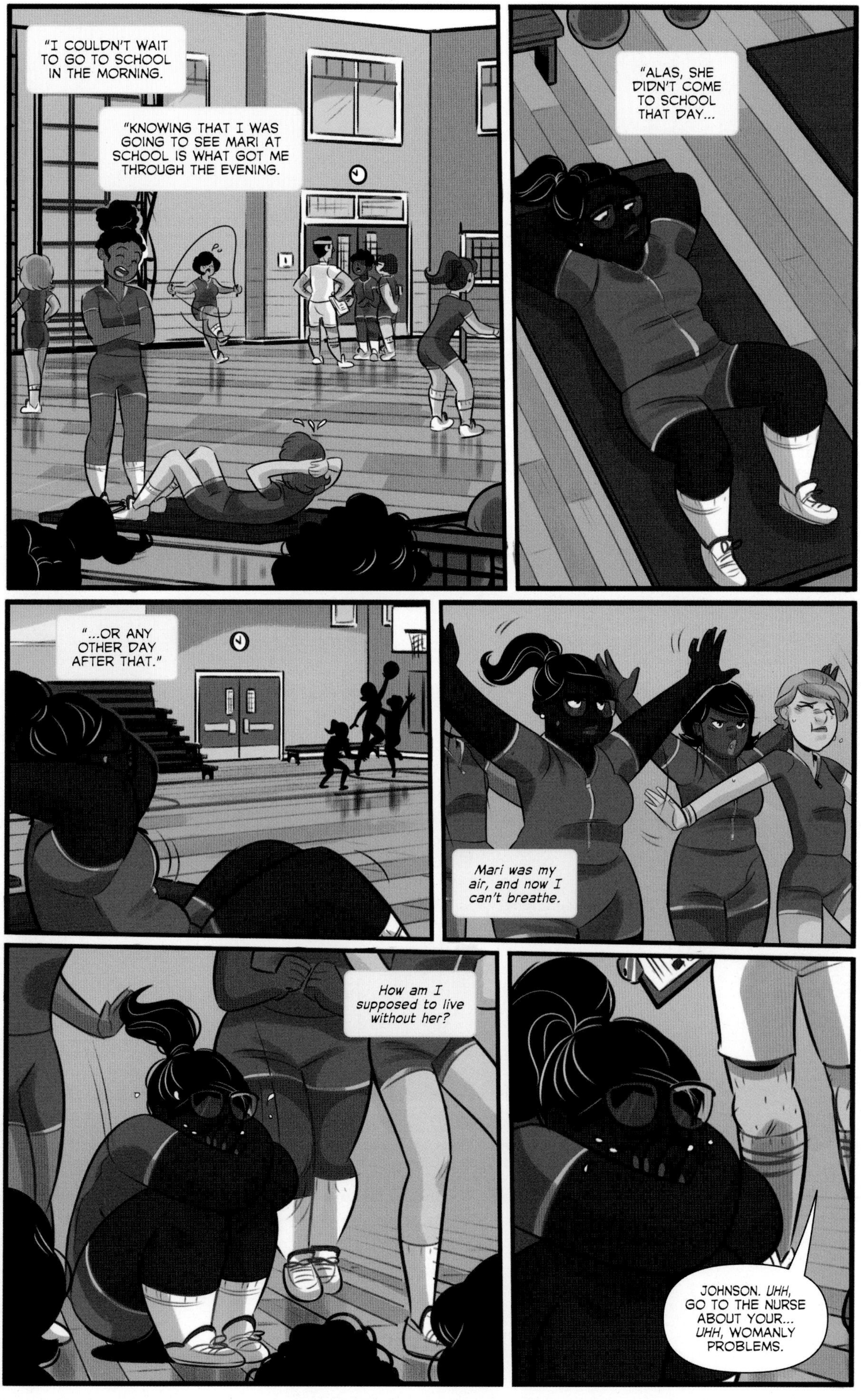
"I COULDN'T WAIT TO GO TO SCHOOL IN THE MORNING.
"KNOWING THAT I WAS GOING TO SEE MARI AT SCHOOL IS WHAT GOT ME THROUGH THE EVENING.
"ALAS, SHE DIDN'T COME TO SCHOOL THAT DAY...
"...OR ANY OTHER DAY AFTER THAT."
Mari was my air, and now I can't breathe.
How am I supposed to live without her?
JOHNSON. *UHH*, GO TO THE NURSE ABOUT YOUR... *UHH*, WOMANLY PROBLEMS.

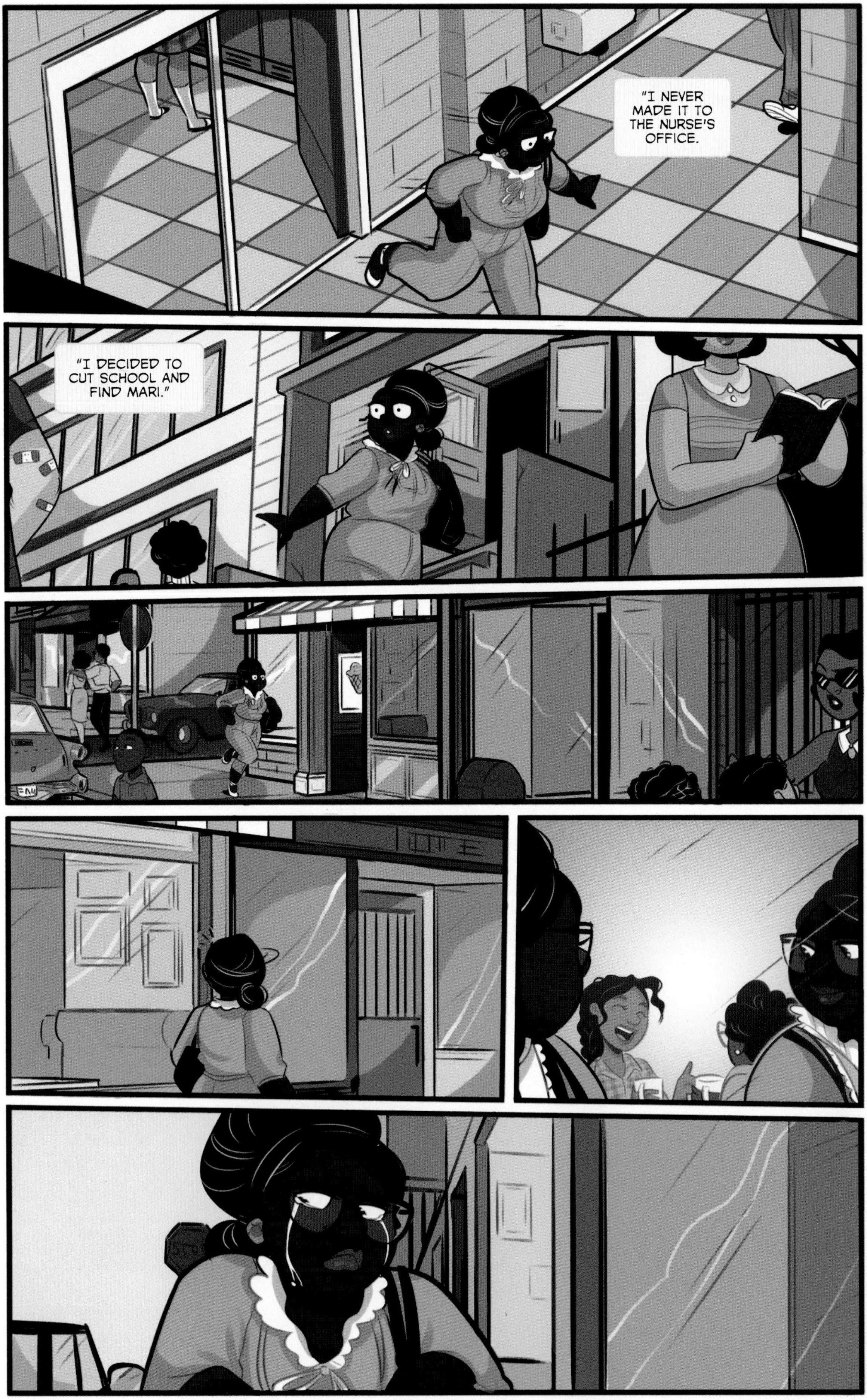
"I NEVER MADE IT TO THE NURSE'S OFFICE.
"I DECIDED TO CUT SCHOOL AND FIND MARI."

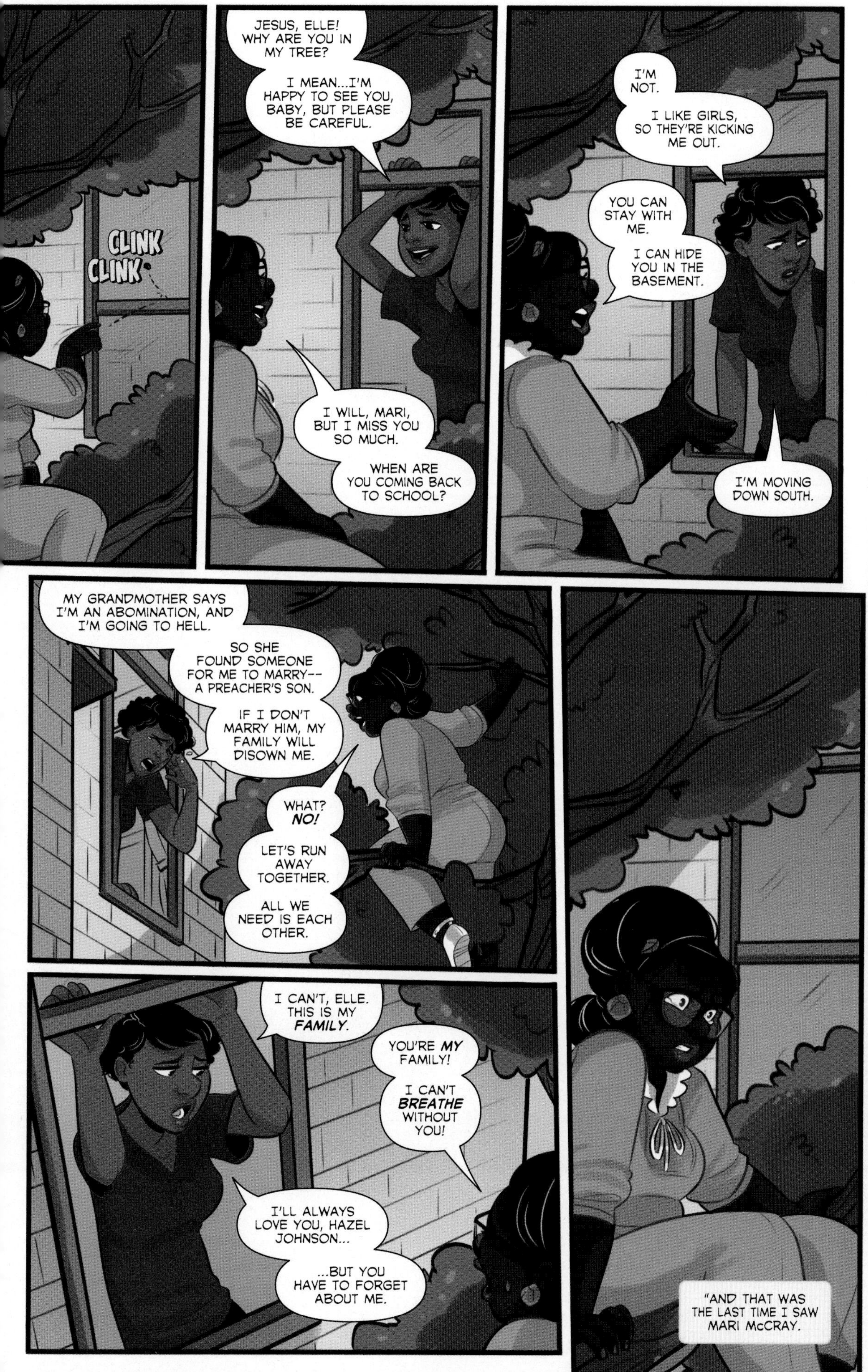
CLINK
CLINK
JESUS, ELLE! WHY ARE YOU IN MY TREE?
I MEAN...I'M HAPPY TO SEE YOU, BABY, BUT PLEASE BE CAREFUL.
I WILL, MARI, BUT I MISS YOU SO MUCH.
WHEN ARE YOU COMING BACK TO SCHOOL?
I'M NOT.
I LIKE GIRLS, SO THEY'RE KICKING ME OUT.
YOU CAN STAY WITH ME.
I CAN HIDE YOU IN THE BASEMENT.
I'M MOVING DOWN SOUTH.
MY GRANDMOTHER SAYS I'M AN ABOMINATION, AND I'M GOING TO HELL.
SO SHE FOUND SOMEONE FOR ME TO MARRY-- A PREACHER'S SON.
IF I DON'T MARRY HIM, MY FAMILY WILL DISOWN ME.
WHAT? NO!
LET'S RUN AWAY TOGETHER.
ALL WE NEED IS EACH OTHER.
I CAN'T, ELLE. THIS IS MY FAMILY.
YOU'RE MY FAMILY!
I CAN'T BREATHE WITHOUT YOU!
I'LL ALWAYS LOVE YOU, HAZEL JOHNSON...
...BUT YOU HAVE TO FORGET ABOUT ME.
"AND THAT WAS THE LAST TIME I SAW MARI McCRAY.

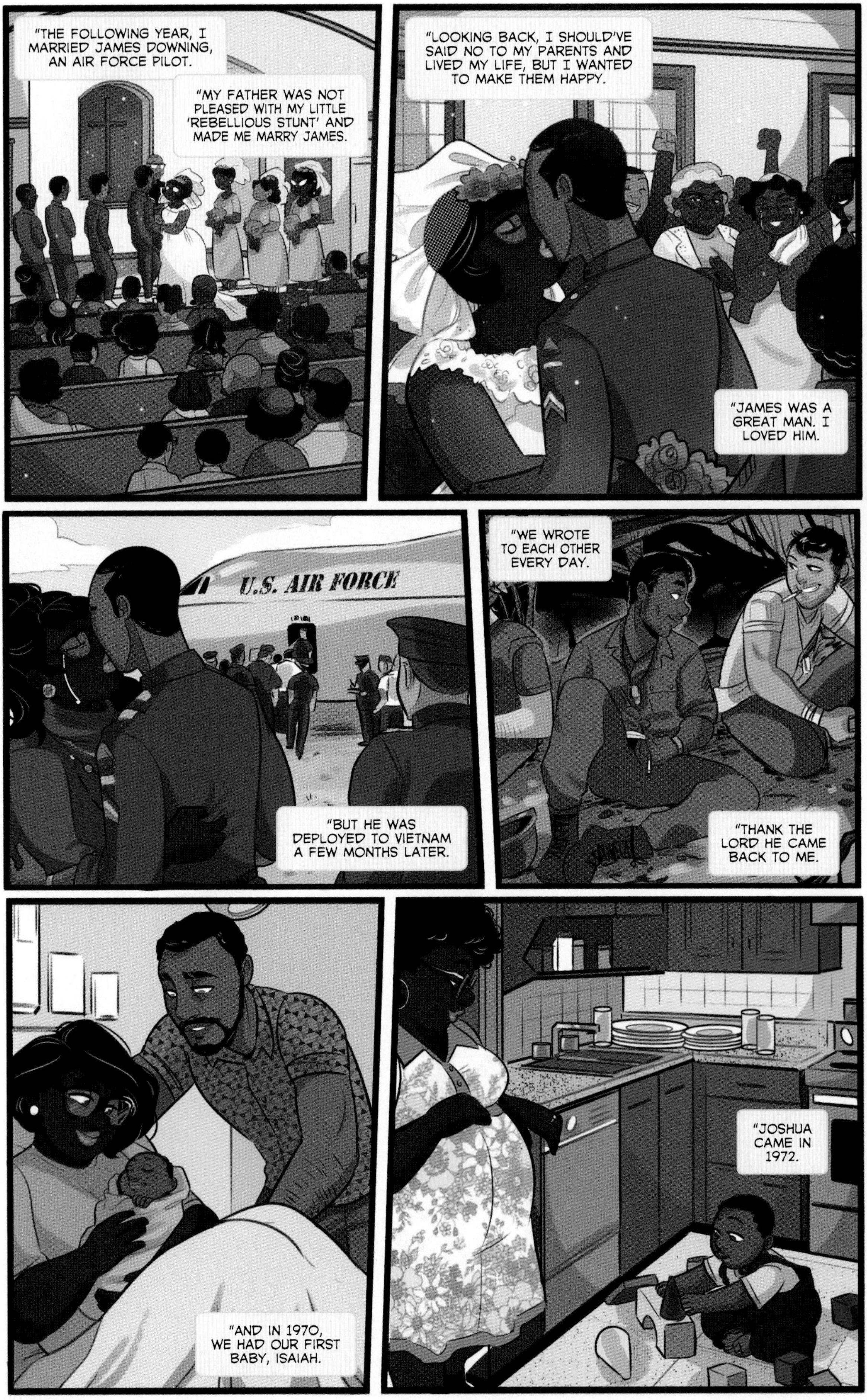
"THE FOLLOWING YEAR, I MARRIED JAMES DOWNING, AN AIR FORCE PILOT.
"MY FATHER WAS NOT PLEASED WITH MY LITTLE 'REBELLIOUS STUNT' AND MADE ME MARRY JAMES.
"LOOKING BACK, I SHOULD'VE SAID NO TO MY PARENTS AND LIVED MY LIFE, BUT I WANTED TO MAKE THEM HAPPY.
"JAMES WAS A GREAT MAN. I LOVED HIM.
U.S. AIR FORCE
"BUT HE WAS DEPLOYED TO VIETNAM A FEW MONTHS LATER.
"WE WROTE TO EACH OTHER EVERY DAY.
"THANK THE LORD HE CAME BACK TO ME.
"AND IN 1970, WE HAD OUR FIRST BABY, ISAIAH.
"JOSHUA CAME IN 1972.

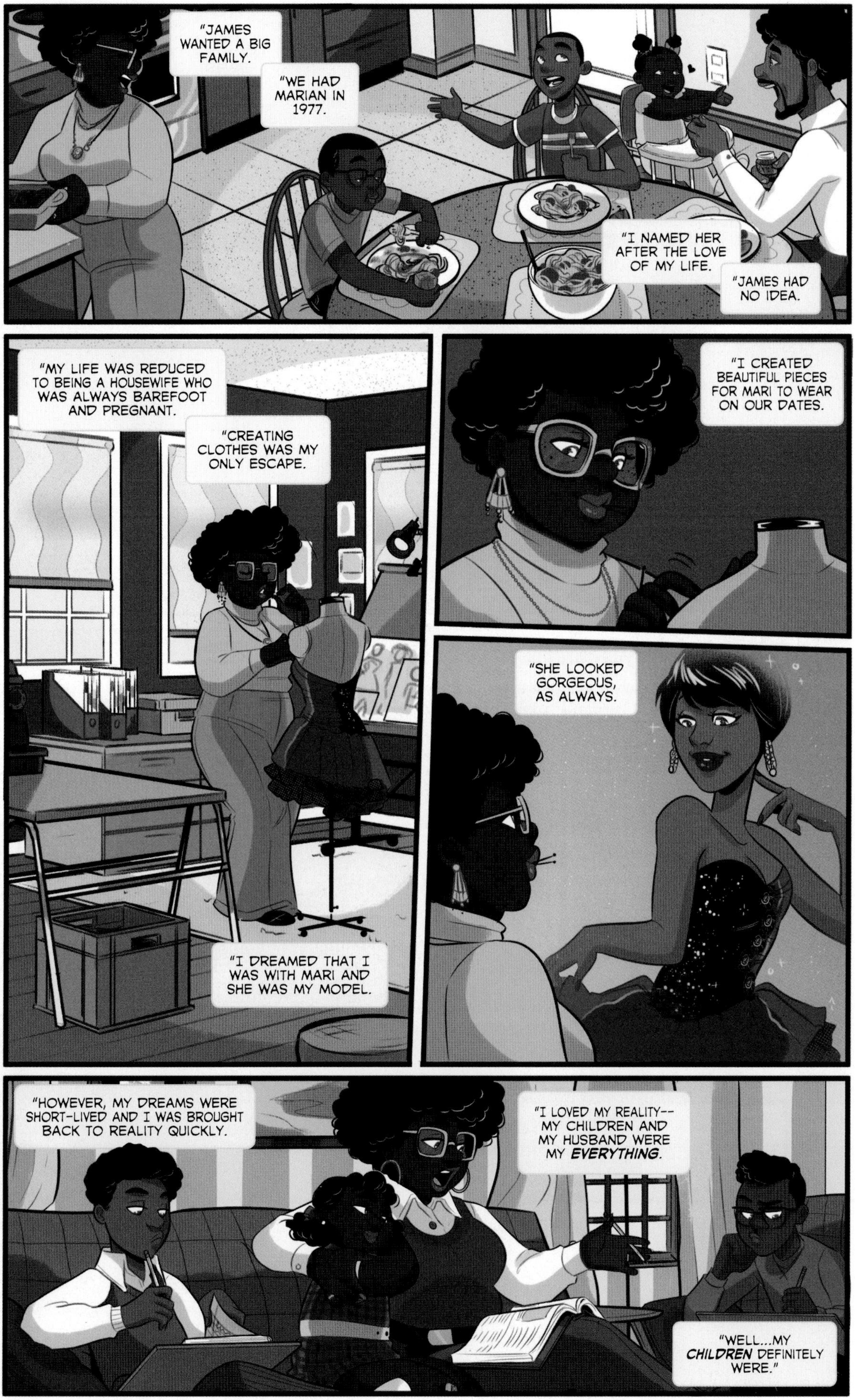
"JAMES WANTED A BIG FAMILY.
"WE HAD MARIAN IN 1977.
"I NAMED HER AFTER THE LOVE OF MY LIFE.
"JAMES HAD NO IDEA.
"MY LIFE WAS REDUCED TO BEING A HOUSEWIFE WHO WAS ALWAYS BAREFOOT AND PREGNANT.
"CREATING CLOTHES WAS MY ONLY ESCAPE.
"I DREAMED THAT I WAS WITH MARI AND SHE WAS MY MODEL.
"I CREATED BEAUTIFUL PIECES FOR MARI TO WEAR ON OUR DATES.
"SHE LOOKED GORGEOUS, AS ALWAYS.
"HOWEVER, MY DREAMS WERE SHORT-LIVED AND I WAS BROUGHT BACK TO REALITY QUICKLY.
"I LOVED MY REALITY-- MY CHILDREN AND MY HUSBAND WERE MY ***EVERYTHING***.
"WELL...MY ***CHILDREN*** DEFINITELY WERE."

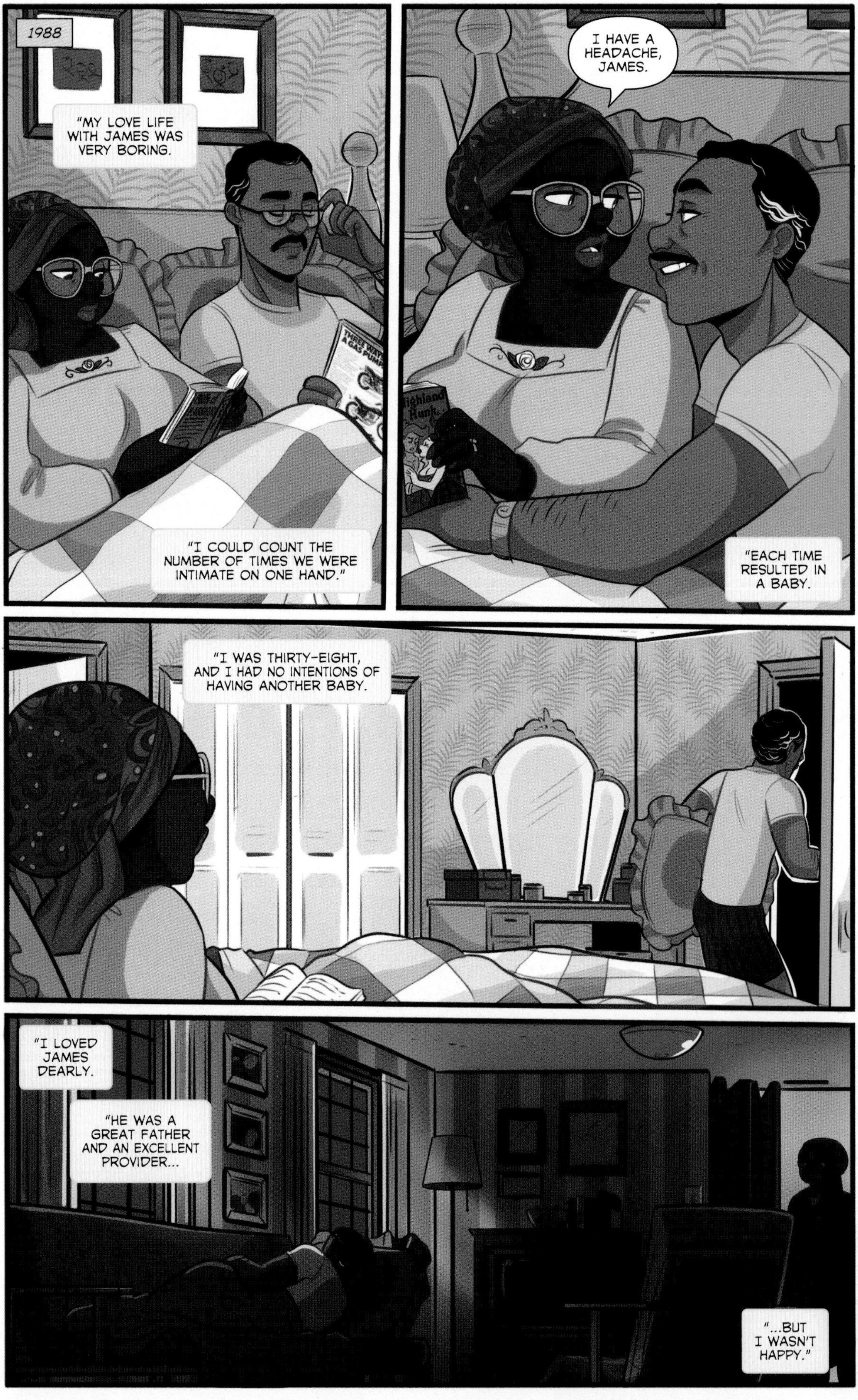
1988
"MY LOVE LIFE WITH JAMES WAS VERY BORING.
"I COULD COUNT THE NUMBER OF TIMES WE WERE INTIMATE ON ONE HAND."
I HAVE A HEADACHE, JAMES.
"EACH TIME RESULTED IN A BABY.
"I WAS THIRTY-EIGHT, AND I HAD NO INTENTIONS OF HAVING ANOTHER BABY.
"I LOVED JAMES DEARLY.
"HE WAS A GREAT FATHER AND AN EXCELLENT PROVIDER...
"...BUT I WASN'T HAPPY."

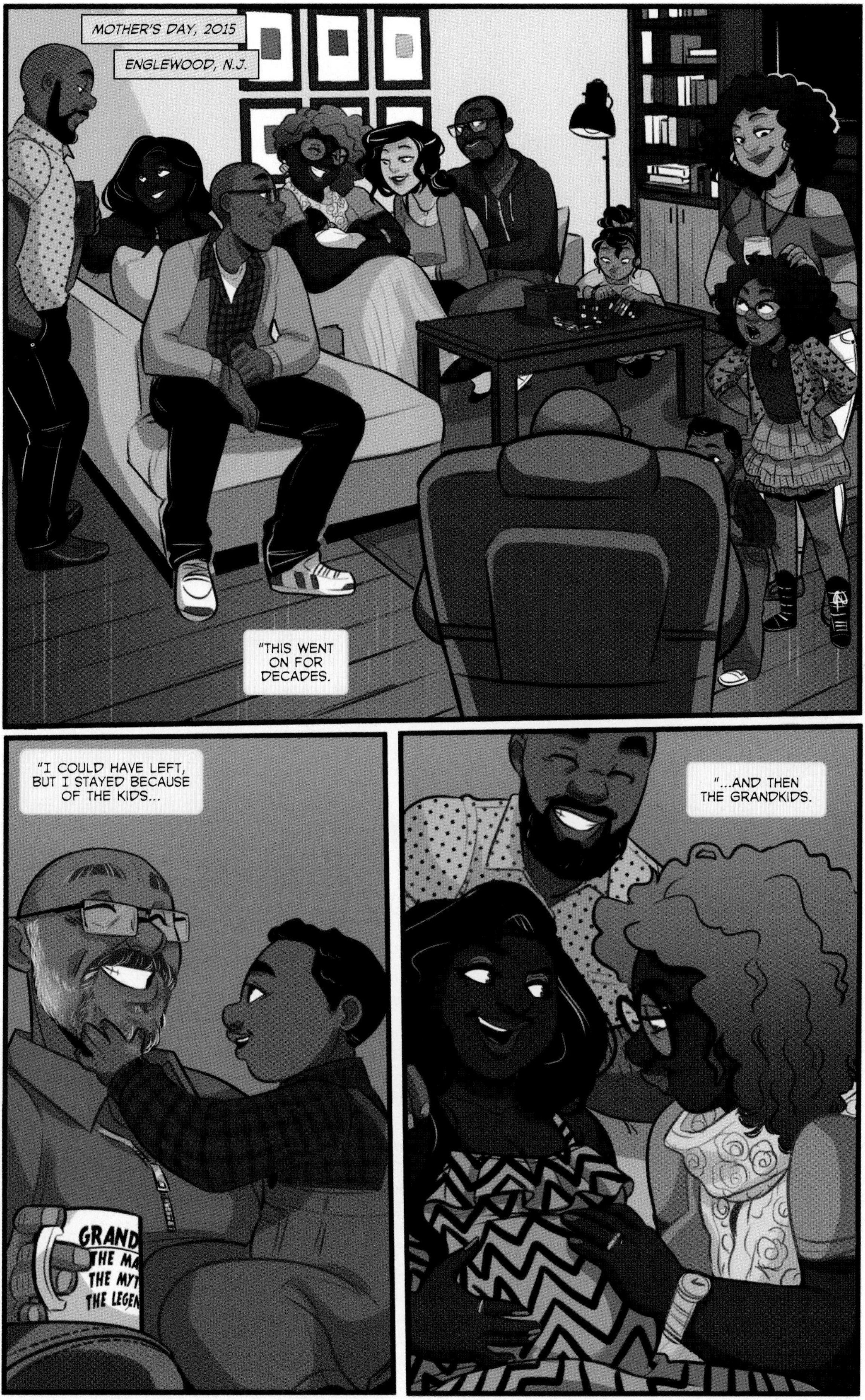
MOTHER'S DAY, 2015
ENGLEWOOD, N.J.
"THIS WENT ON FOR DECADES.
"I COULD HAVE LEFT, BUT I STAYED BECAUSE OF THE KIDS...
"...AND THEN THE GRANDKIDS.

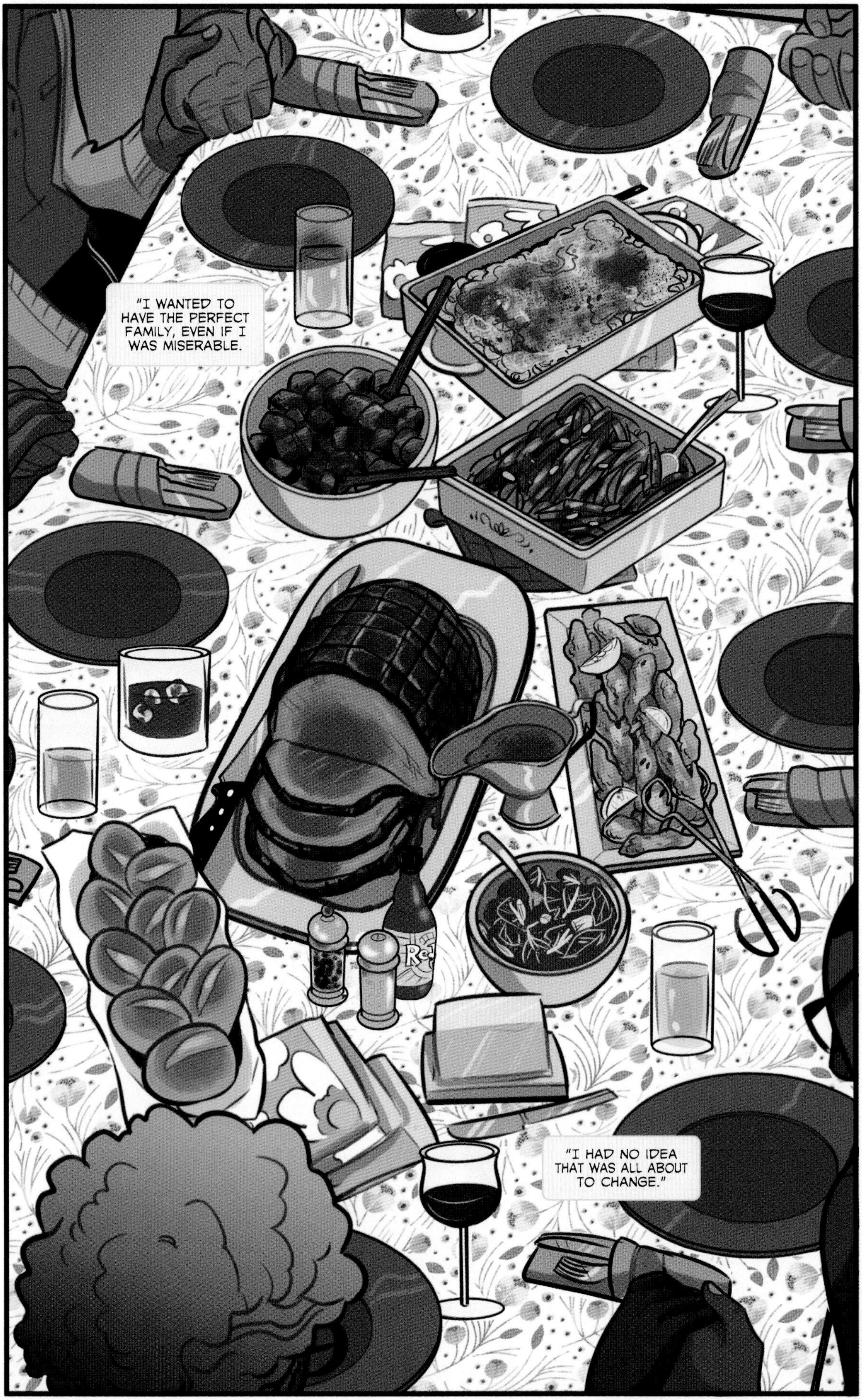
"I WANTED TO HAVE THE PERFECT FAMILY, EVEN IF I WAS MISERABLE.
"I HAD NO IDEA THAT WAS ALL ABOUT TO CHANGE."

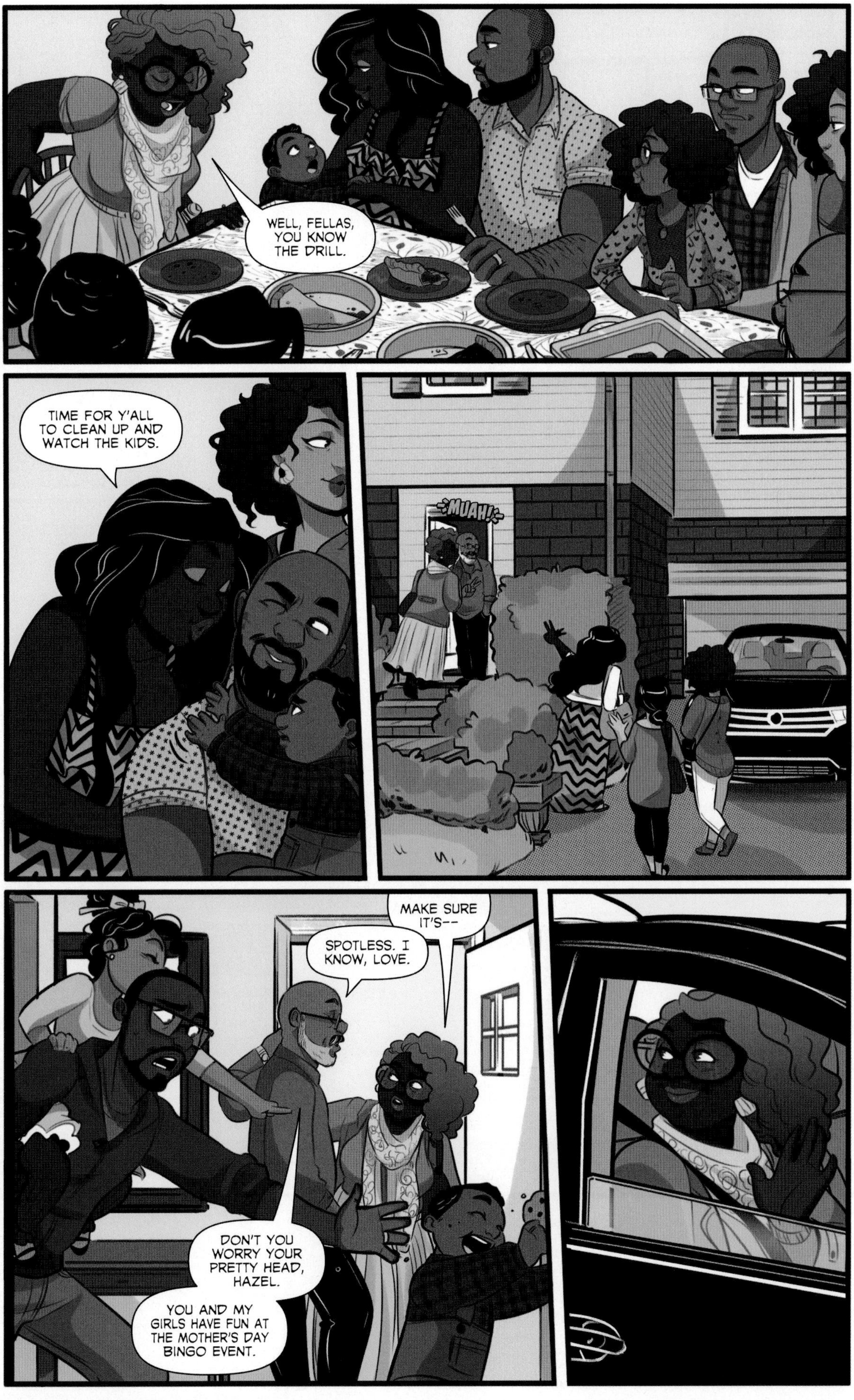

WELL, FELLAS, YOU KNOW THE DRILL.
TIME FOR Y'ALL TO CLEAN UP AND WATCH THE KIDS.
MUAH!
MAKE SURE IT'S--
SPOTLESS. I KNOW, LOVE.
DON'T YOU WORRY YOUR PRETTY HEAD, HAZEL.
YOU AND MY GIRLS HAVE FUN AT THE MOTHER'S DAY BINGO EVENT.

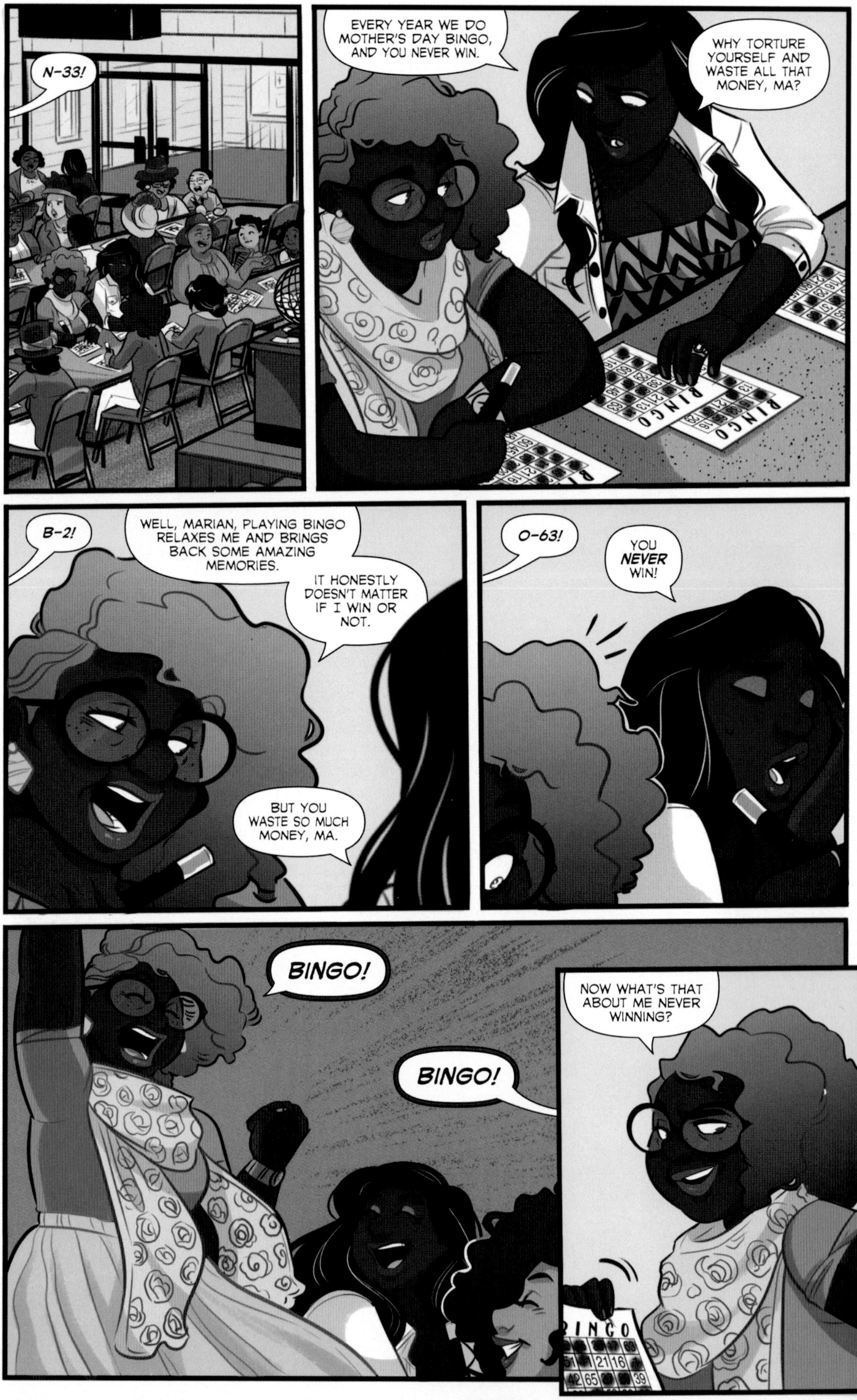
N-33!
EVERY YEAR WE DO MOTHER'S DAY BINGO, AND YOU NEVER WIN.
WHY TORTURE YOURSELF AND WASTE ALL THAT MONEY, MA?
B-2!
WELL, MARIAN, PLAYING BINGO RELAXES ME AND BRINGS BACK SOME AMAZING MEMORIES.
IT HONESTLY DOESN'T MATTER IF I WIN OR NOT.
BUT YOU WASTE SO MUCH MONEY, MA.
O-63!
YOU *NEVER* WIN!
BINGO!
BINGO!
NOW WHAT'S THAT ABOUT ME NEVER WINNING?

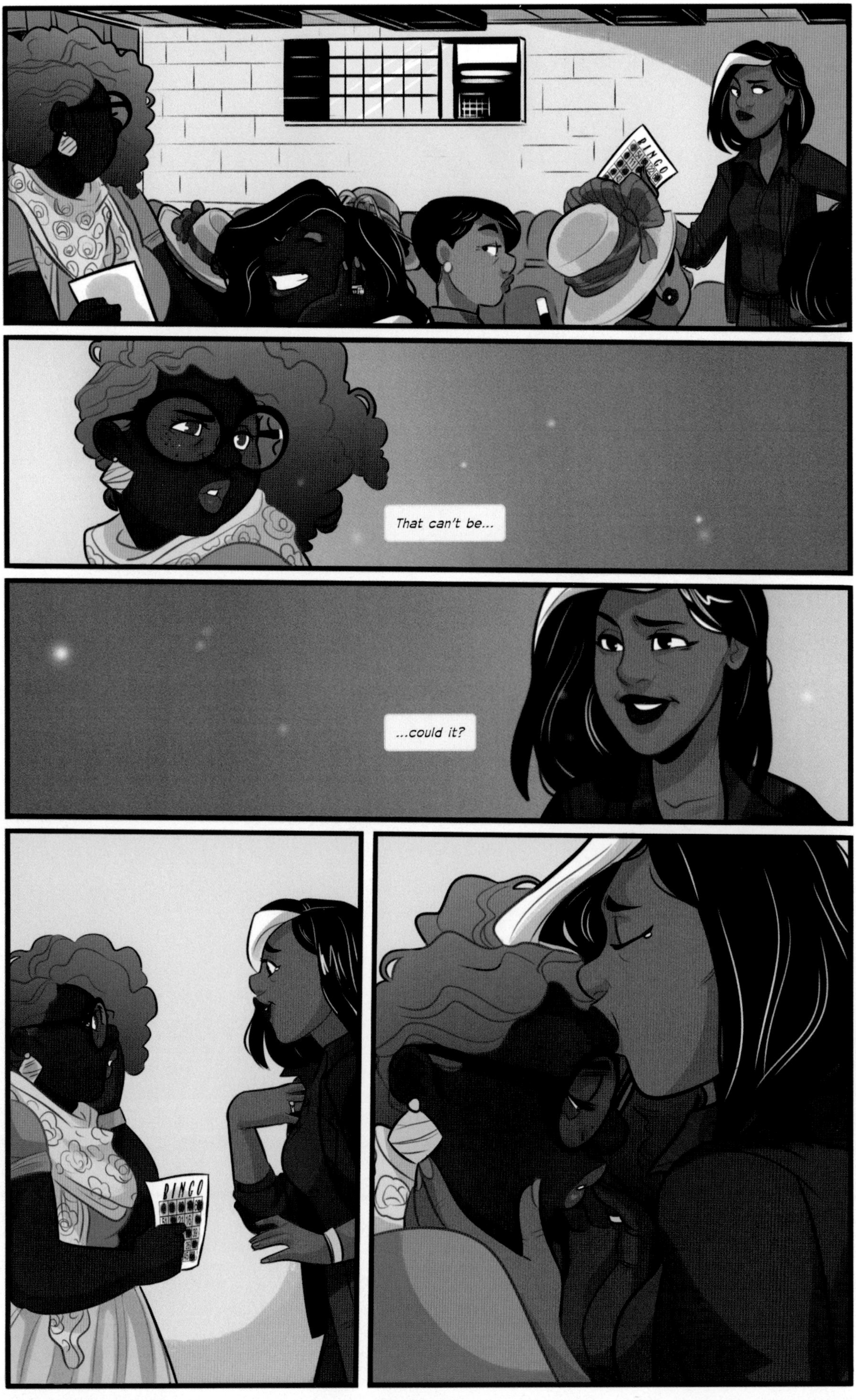
BINGO
That can't be...
...could it?
BINGO

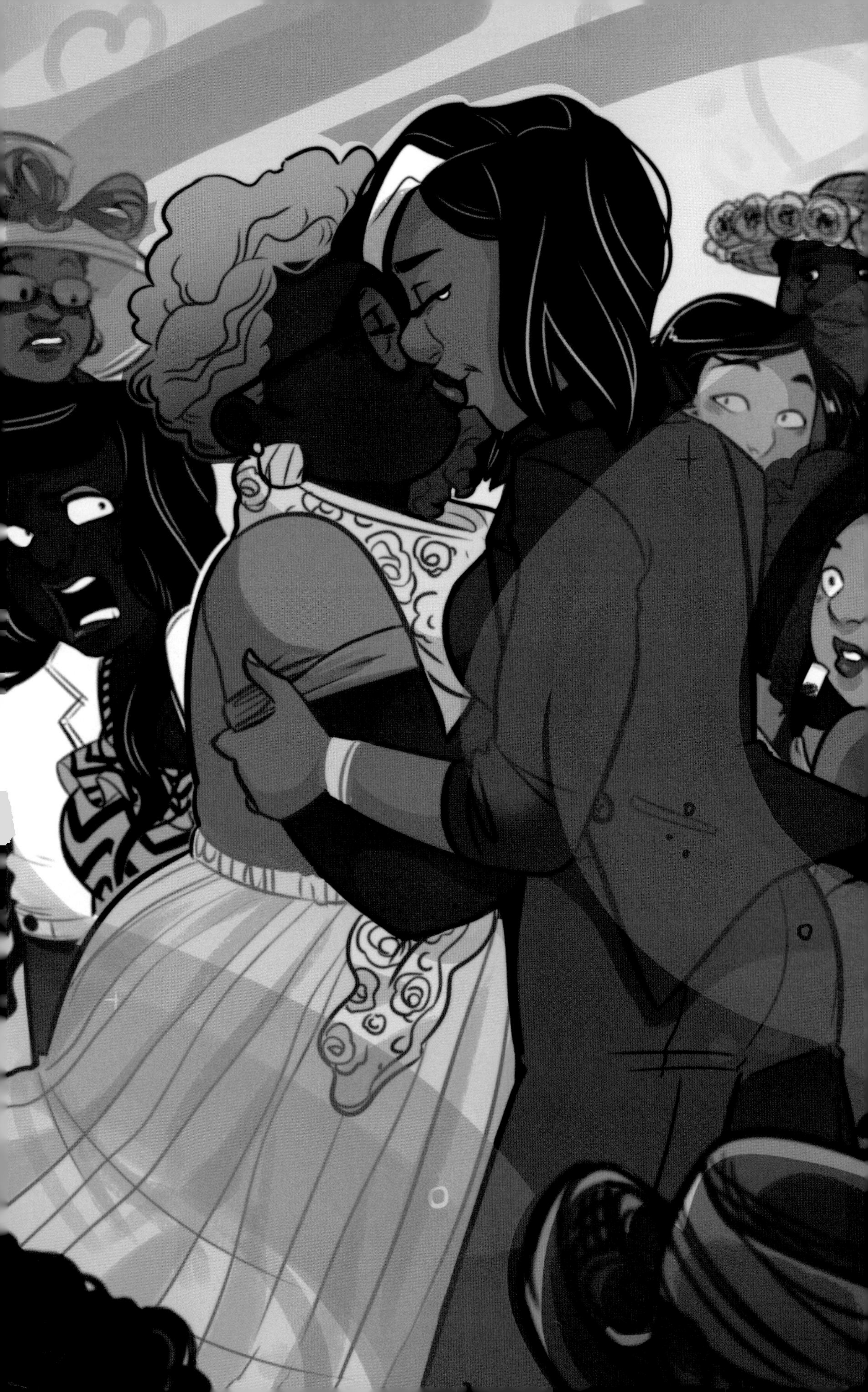

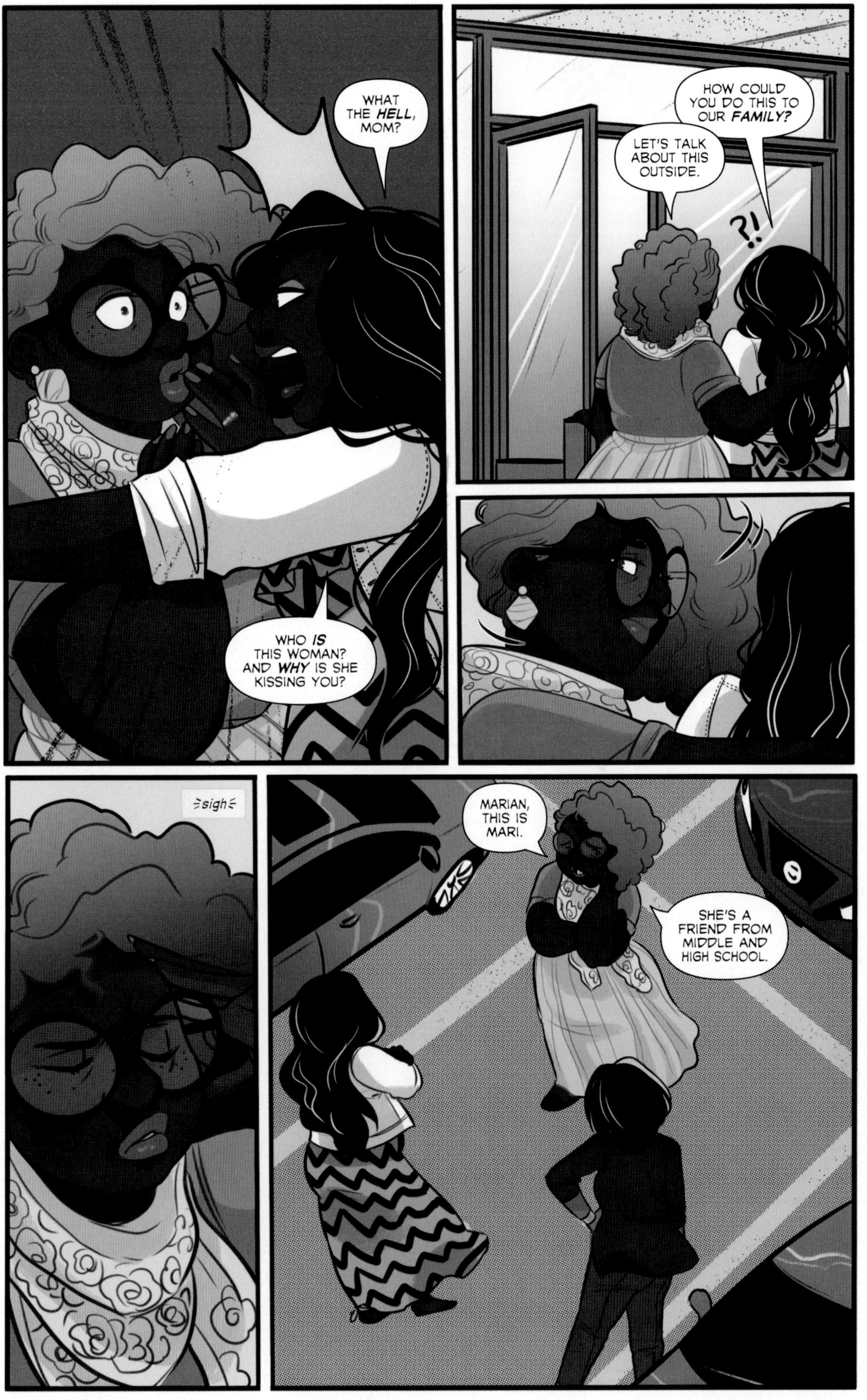

WHAT THE *HELL*, MOM?
WHO *IS* THIS WOMAN? AND *WHY* IS SHE KISSING YOU?
HOW COULD YOU DO THIS TO OUR *FAMILY?*
LET'S TALK ABOUT THIS OUTSIDE.
?!
sigh
MARIAN, THIS IS MARI.
SHE'S A FRIEND FROM MIDDLE AND HIGH SCHOOL.

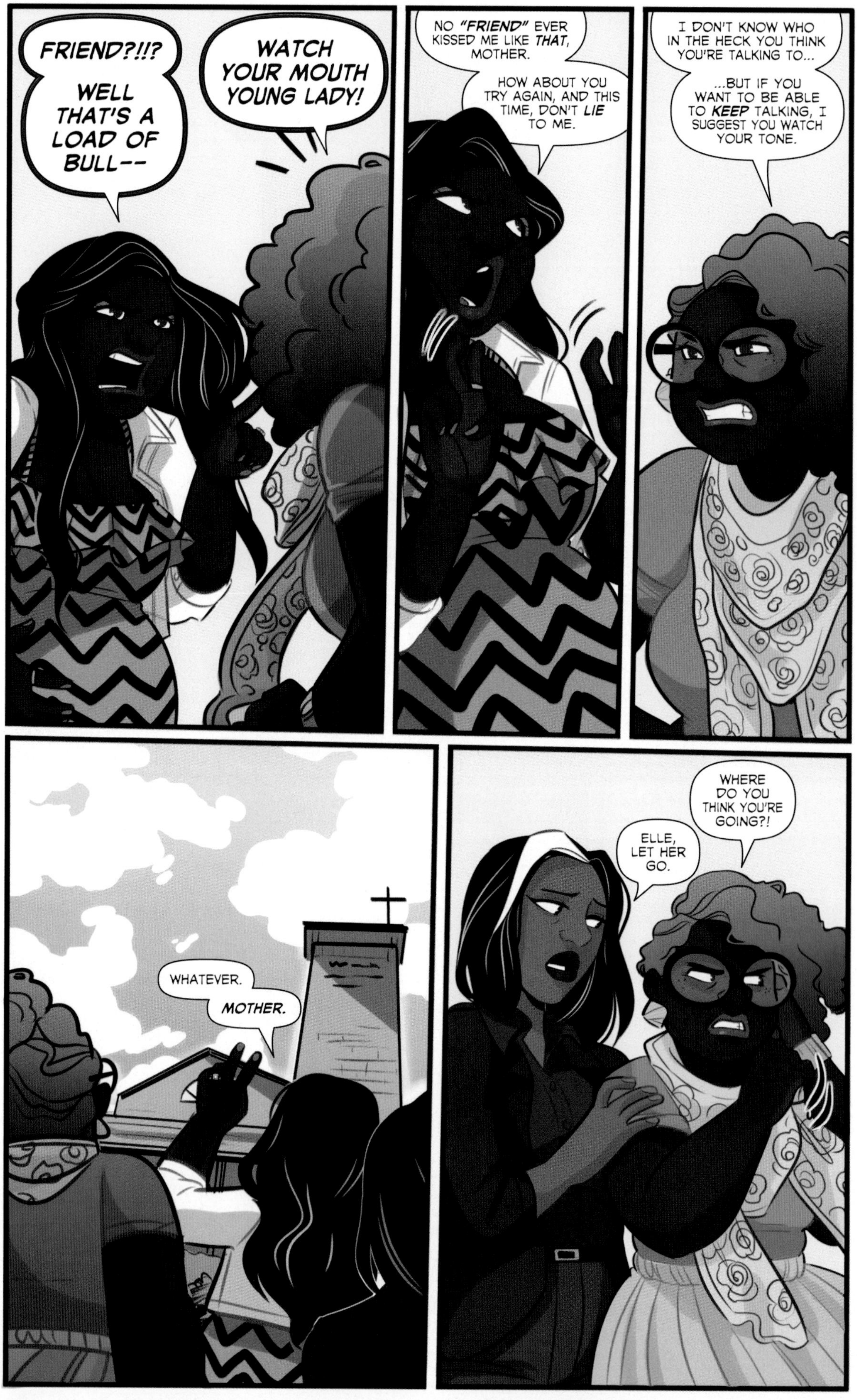
FRIEND?!!? WELL THAT'S A LOAD OF BULL--
WATCH YOUR MOUTH YOUNG LADY!
NO "FRIEND" EVER KISSED ME LIKE THAT, MOTHER.
HOW ABOUT YOU TRY AGAIN, AND THIS TIME, DON'T LIE TO ME.
I DON'T KNOW WHO IN THE HECK YOU THINK YOU'RE TALKING TO...
...BUT IF YOU WANT TO BE ABLE TO KEEP TALKING, I SUGGEST YOU WATCH YOUR TONE.
WHATEVER.
MOTHER.
WHERE DO YOU THINK YOU'RE GOING?!
ELLE, LET HER GO.

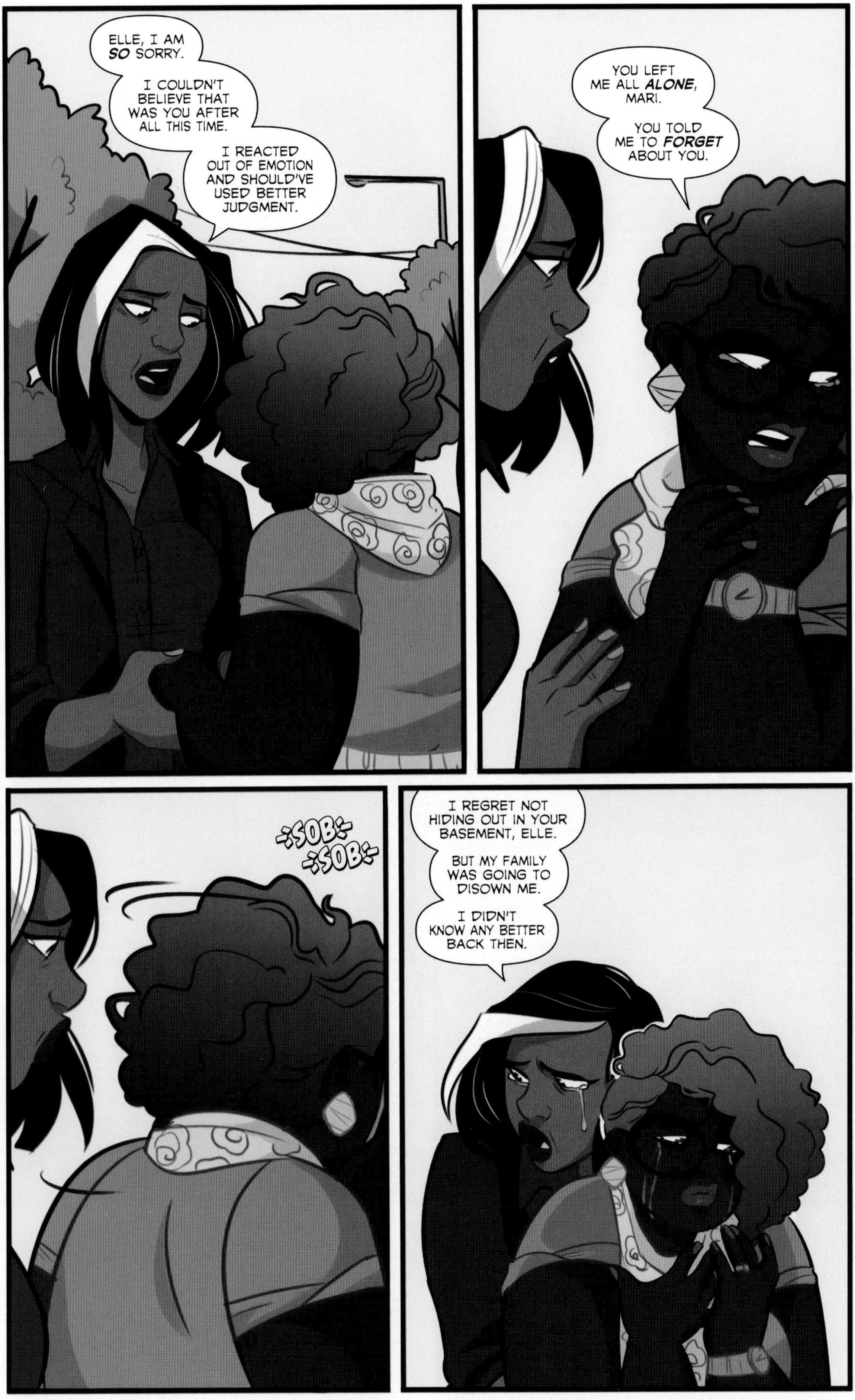
ELLE, I AM **SO** SORRY.
I COULDN'T BELIEVE THAT WAS YOU AFTER ALL THIS TIME.
I REACTED OUT OF EMOTION AND SHOULD'VE USED BETTER JUDGMENT.
YOU LEFT ME ALL **ALONE**, MARI.
YOU TOLD ME TO **FORGET** ABOUT YOU.
SOB
SOB
I REGRET NOT HIDING OUT IN YOUR BASEMENT, ELLE.
BUT MY FAMILY WAS GOING TO DISOWN ME.
I DIDN'T KNOW ANY BETTER BACK THEN.

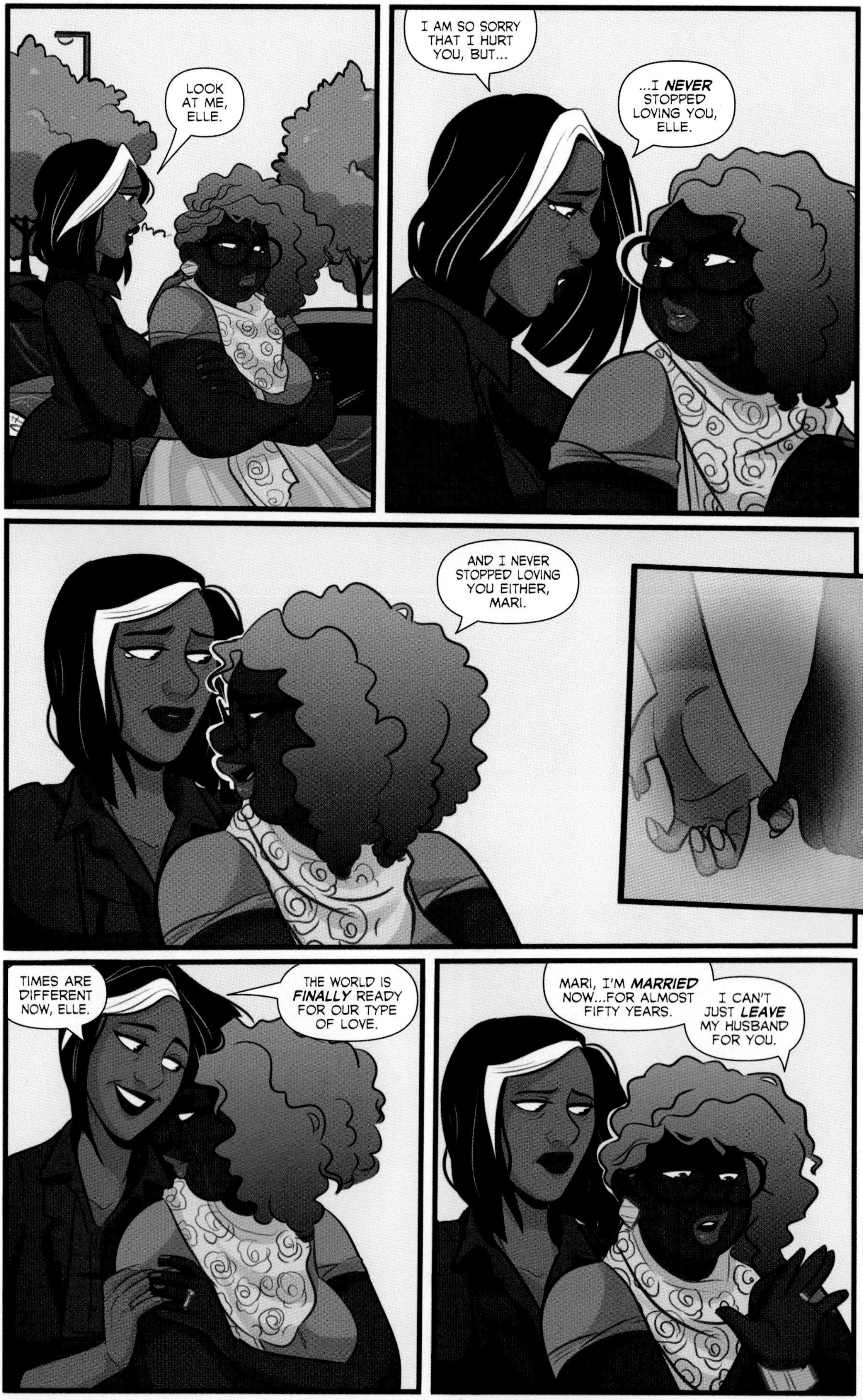
LOOK AT ME, ELLE.
I AM SO SORRY THAT I HURT YOU, BUT...
...I **NEVER** STOPPED LOVING YOU, ELLE.
AND I NEVER STOPPED LOVING YOU EITHER, MARI.
TIMES ARE DIFFERENT NOW, ELLE.
THE WORLD IS **FINALLY** READY FOR OUR TYPE OF LOVE.
MARI, I'M **MARRIED** NOW...FOR ALMOST FIFTY YEARS.
I CAN'T JUST **LEAVE** MY HUSBAND FOR YOU.

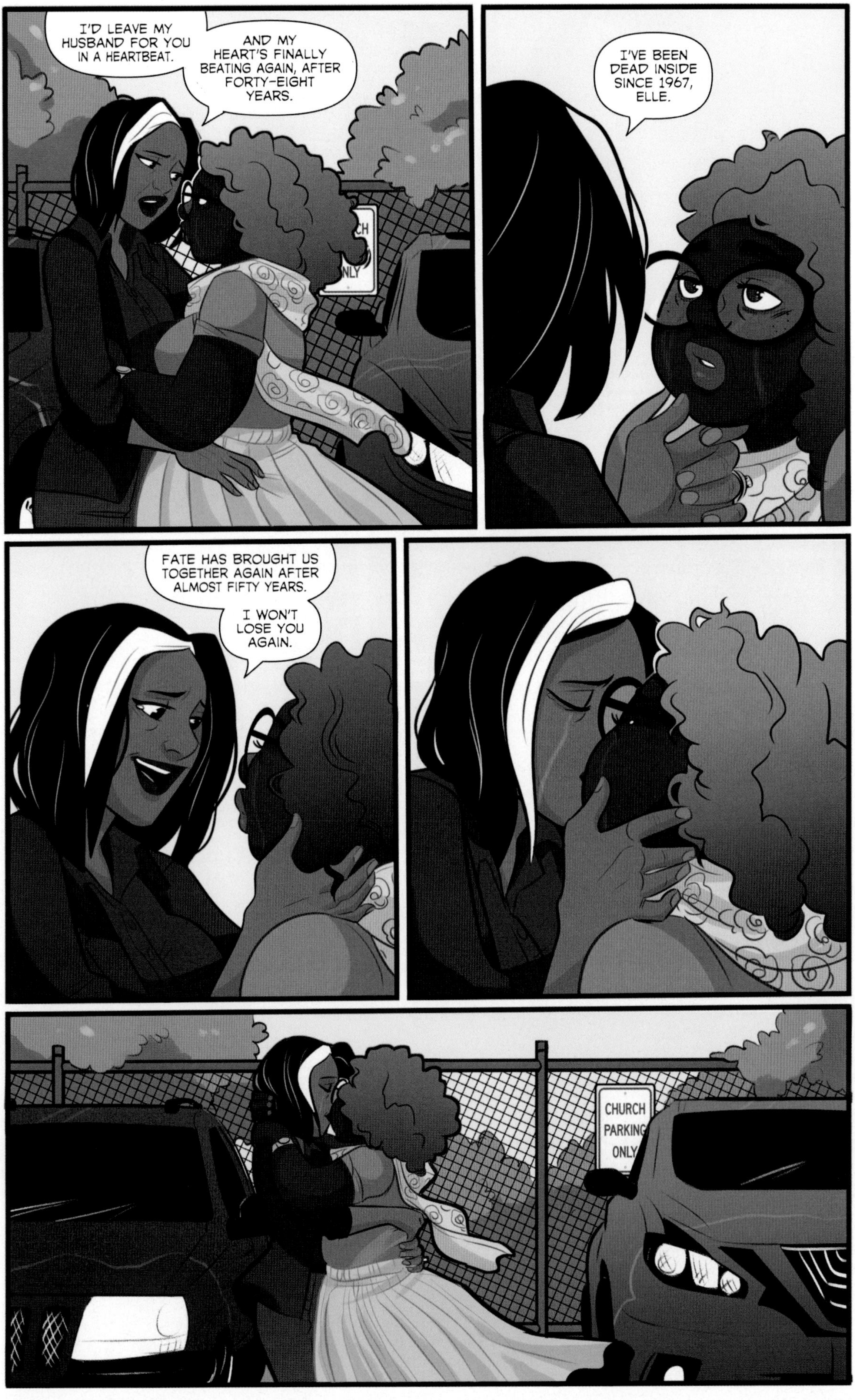
I'D LEAVE MY HUSBAND FOR YOU IN A HEARTBEAT.
AND MY HEART'S FINALLY BEATING AGAIN, AFTER FORTY-EIGHT YEARS.
CH
NLY
I'VE BEEN DEAD INSIDE SINCE 1967, ELLE.
FATE HAS BROUGHT US TOGETHER AGAIN AFTER ALMOST FIFTY YEARS.
I WON'T LOSE YOU AGAIN.
CHURCH PARKING ONLY

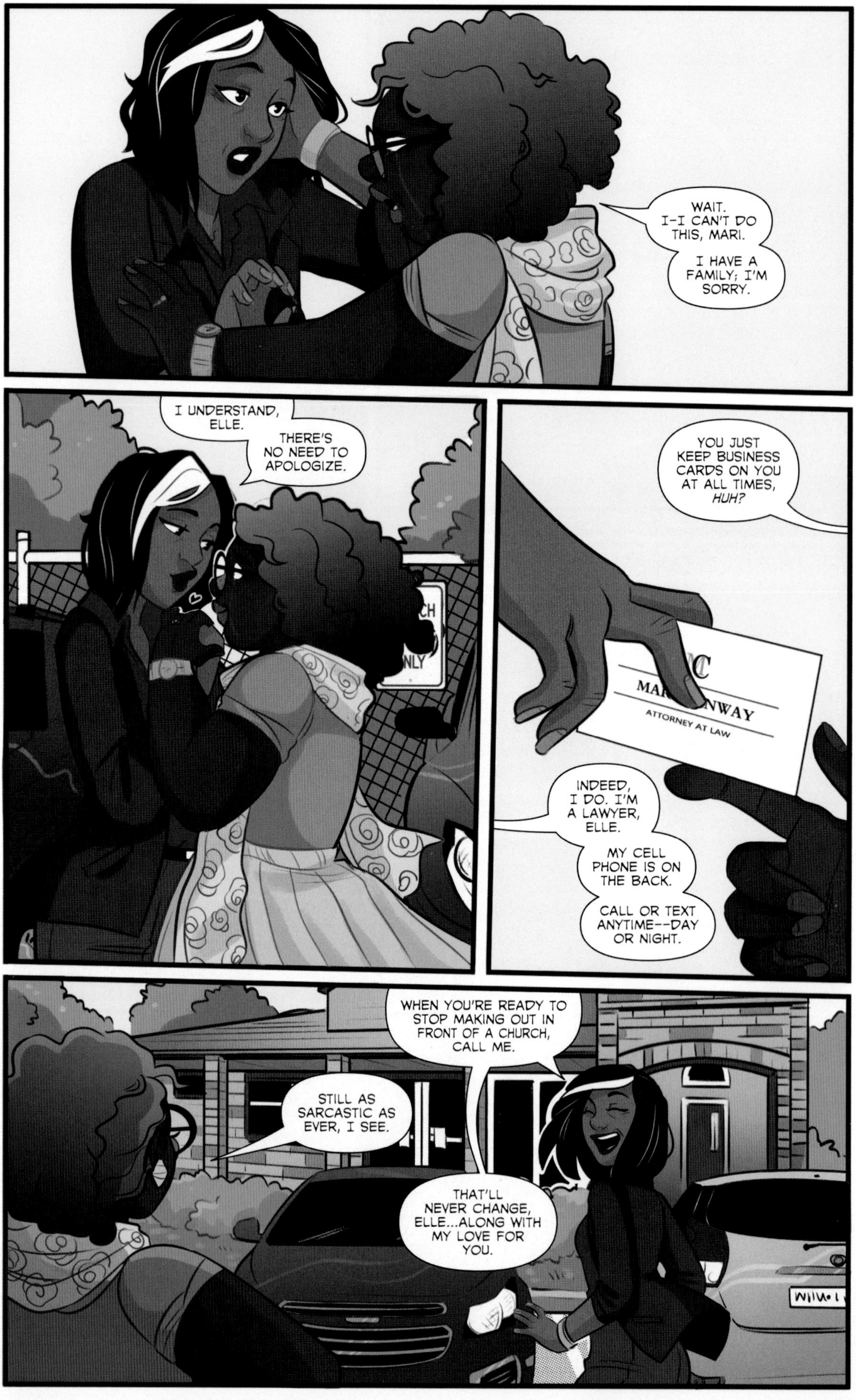
WAIT. I-I CAN'T DO THIS, MARI.
I HAVE A FAMILY; I'M SORRY.
I UNDERSTAND, ELLE.
THERE'S NO NEED TO APOLOGIZE.
YOU JUST KEEP BUSINESS CARDS ON YOU AT ALL TIMES, *HUH?*
ATTORNEY AT LAW
INDEED, I DO. I'M A LAWYER, ELLE.
MY CELL PHONE IS ON THE BACK.
CALL OR TEXT ANYTIME--DAY OR NIGHT.
WHEN YOU'RE READY TO STOP MAKING OUT IN FRONT OF A CHURCH, CALL ME.
STILL AS SARCASTIC AS EVER, I SEE.
THAT'LL NEVER CHANGE, ELLE...ALONG WITH MY LOVE FOR YOU.

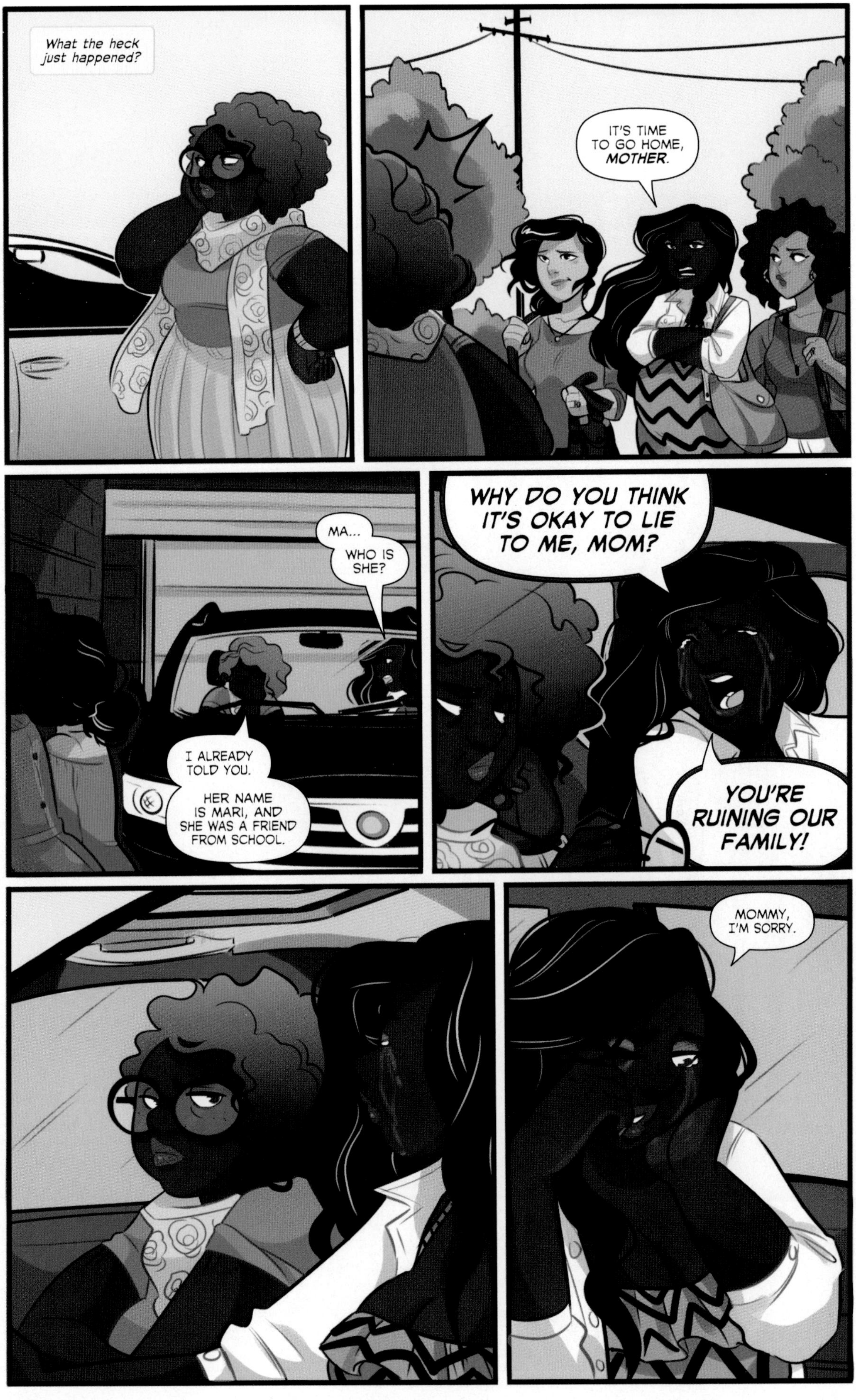
What the heck just happened?
IT'S TIME TO GO HOME, *MOTHER*.
MA...
WHO IS SHE?
I ALREADY TOLD YOU.
HER NAME IS MARI, AND SHE WAS A FRIEND FROM SCHOOL.
WHY DO YOU THINK IT'S OKAY TO LIE TO ME, MOM?
YOU'RE RUINING OUR FAMILY!
MOMMY, I'M SORRY.

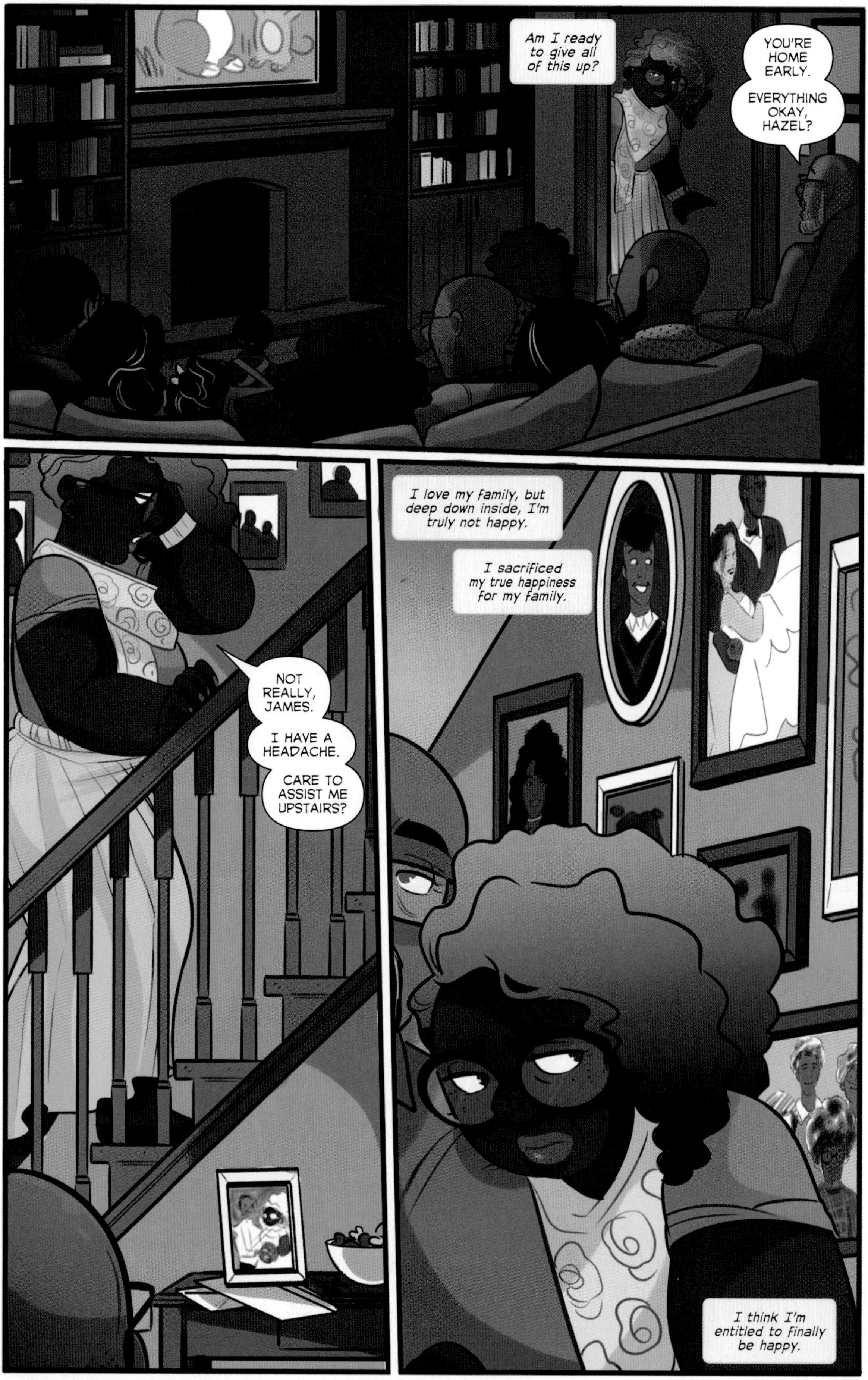
Am I ready to give all of this up?
YOU'RE HOME EARLY.
EVERYTHING OKAY, HAZEL?
NOT REALLY, JAMES.
I HAVE A HEADACHE.
CARE TO ASSIST ME UPSTAIRS?
I love my family, but deep down inside, I'm truly not happy.
I sacrificed my true happiness for my family.
I think I'm entitled to finally be happy.

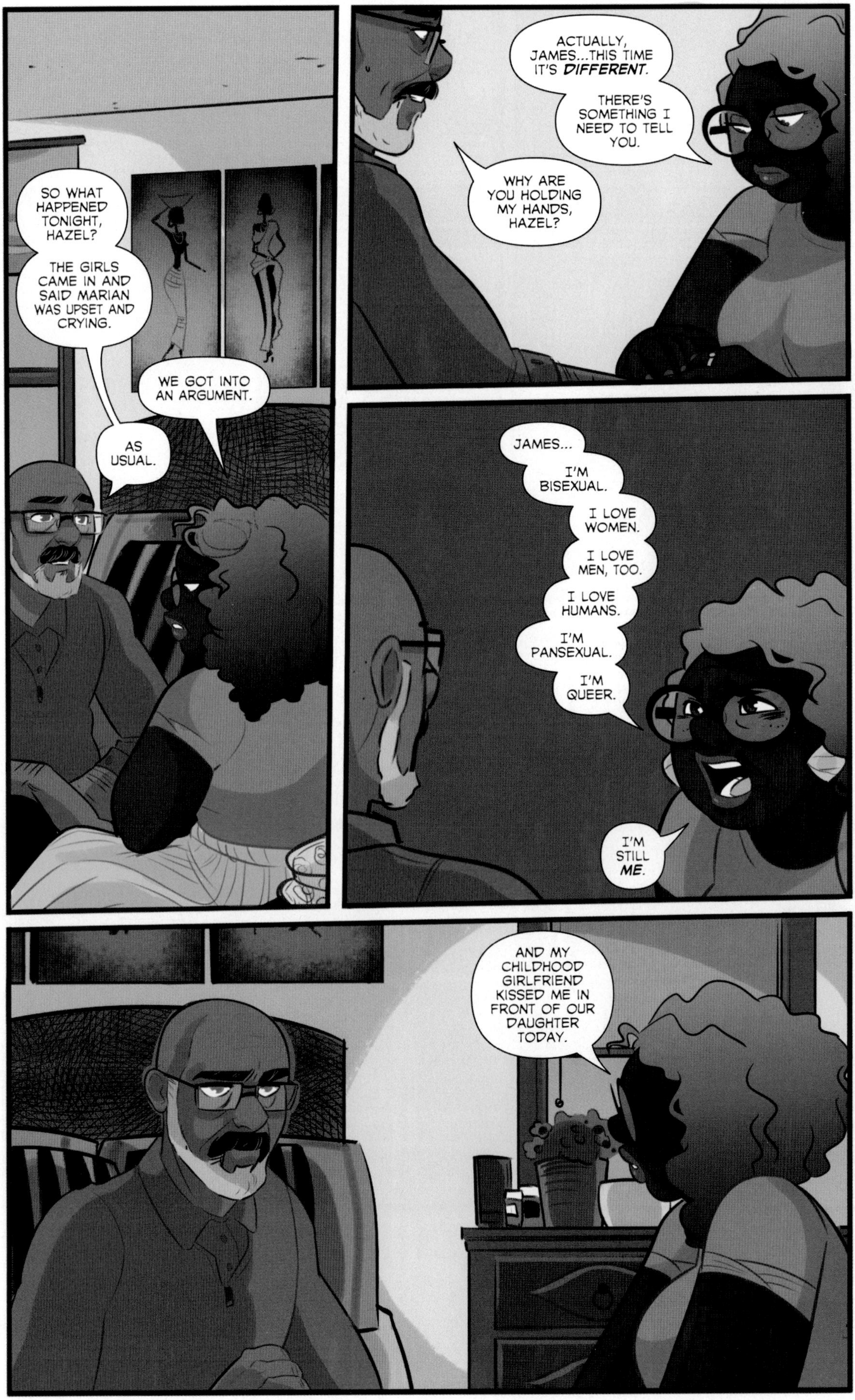
SO WHAT HAPPENED TONIGHT, HAZEL?
THE GIRLS CAME IN AND SAID MARIAN WAS UPSET AND CRYING.
WE GOT INTO AN ARGUMENT.
AS USUAL.
ACTUALLY, JAMES...THIS TIME IT'S *DIFFERENT*.
THERE'S SOMETHING I NEED TO TELL YOU.
WHY ARE YOU HOLDING MY HANDS, HAZEL?
JAMES...
I'M BISEXUAL.
I LOVE WOMEN.
I LOVE MEN, TOO.
I LOVE HUMANS.
I'M PANSEXUAL.
I'M QUEER.
I'M STILL *ME*.
AND MY CHILDHOOD GIRLFRIEND KISSED ME IN FRONT OF OUR DAUGHTER TODAY.

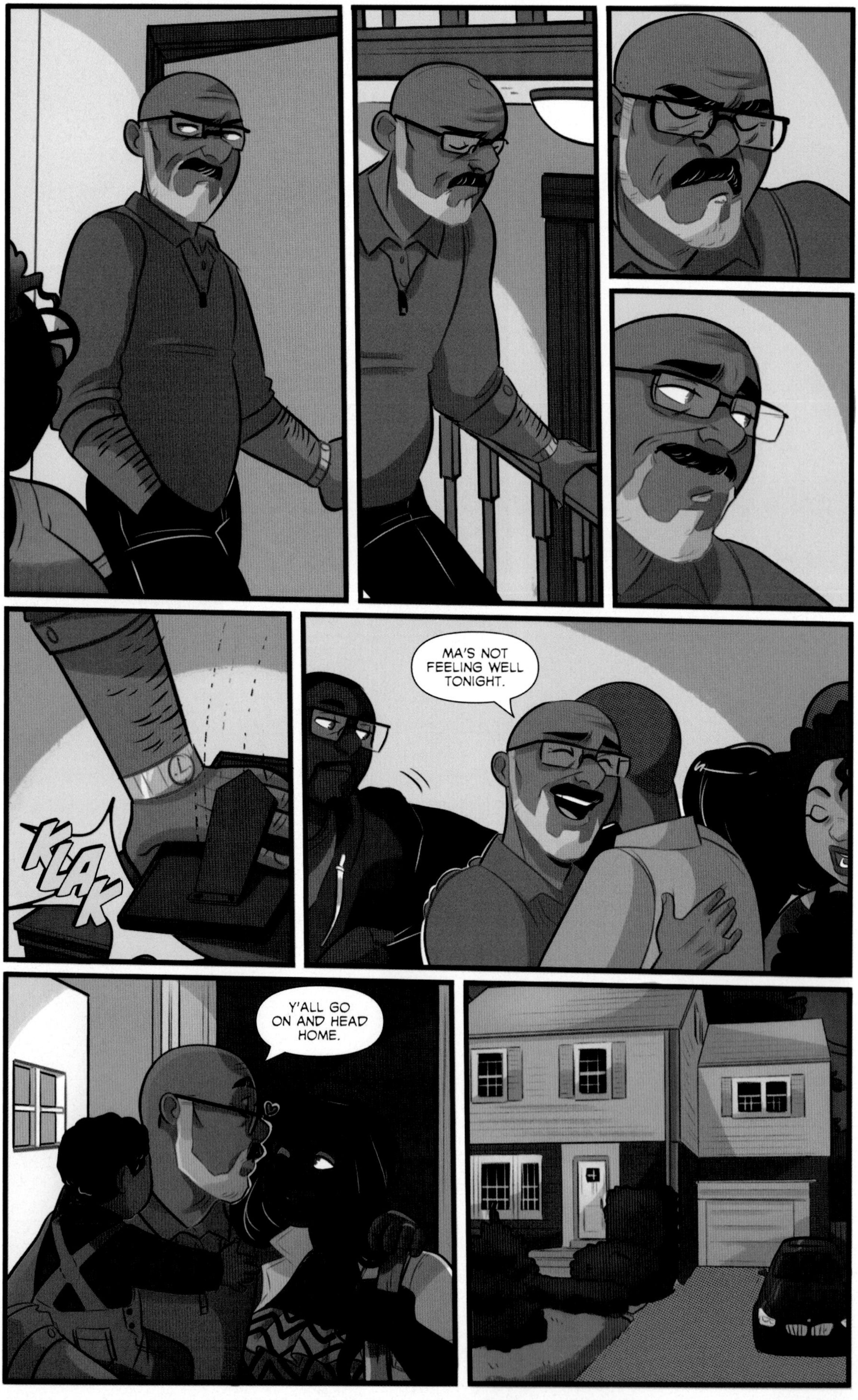
KLAK
MA'S NOT FEELING WELL TONIGHT.
Y'ALL GO ON AND HEAD HOME.

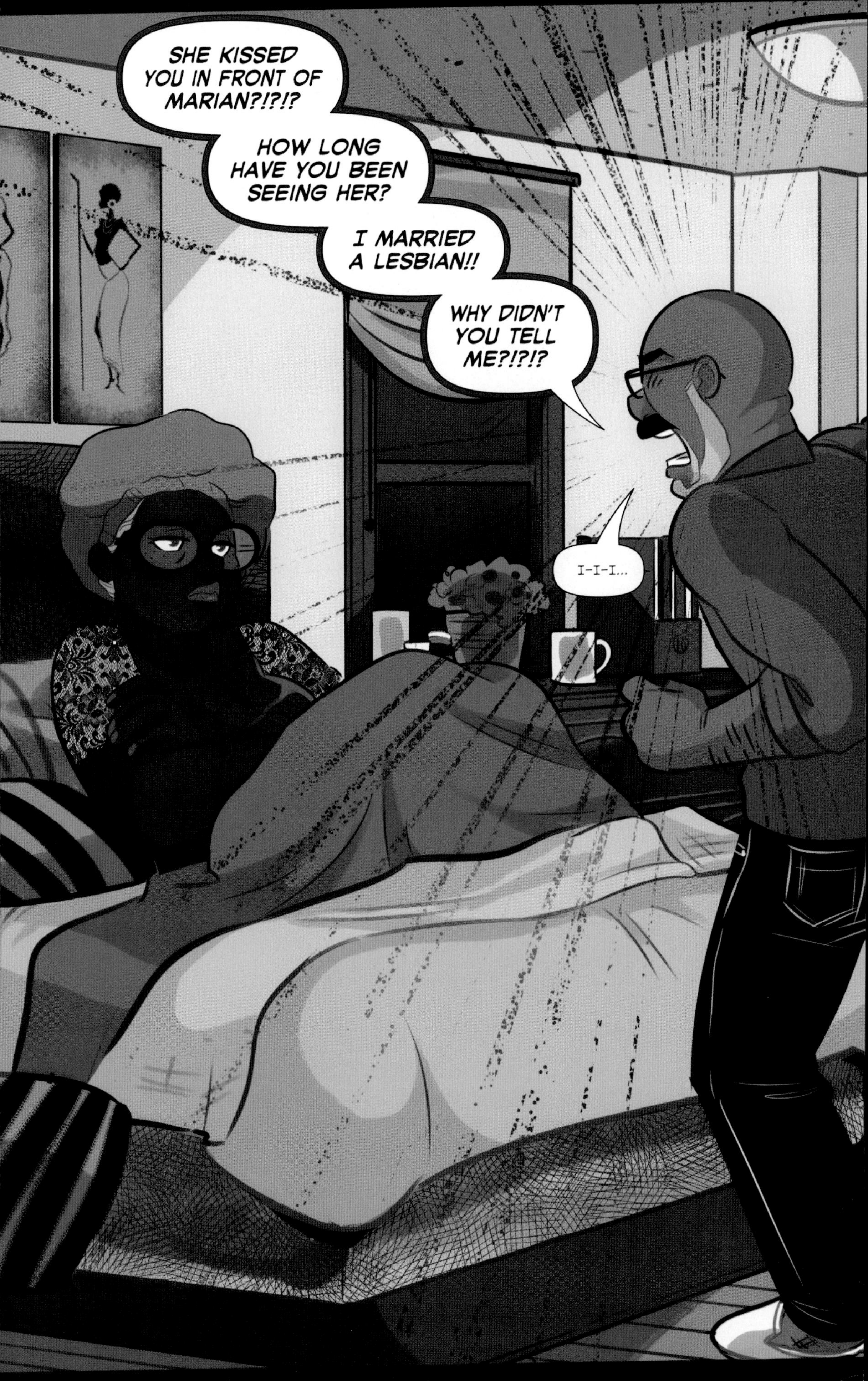
SHE KISSED YOU IN FRONT OF MARIAN?!?!?
HOW LONG HAVE YOU BEEN SEEING HER?
I MARRIED A LESBIAN!!
WHY DIDN'T YOU TELL ME?!?!?
I-I-I...

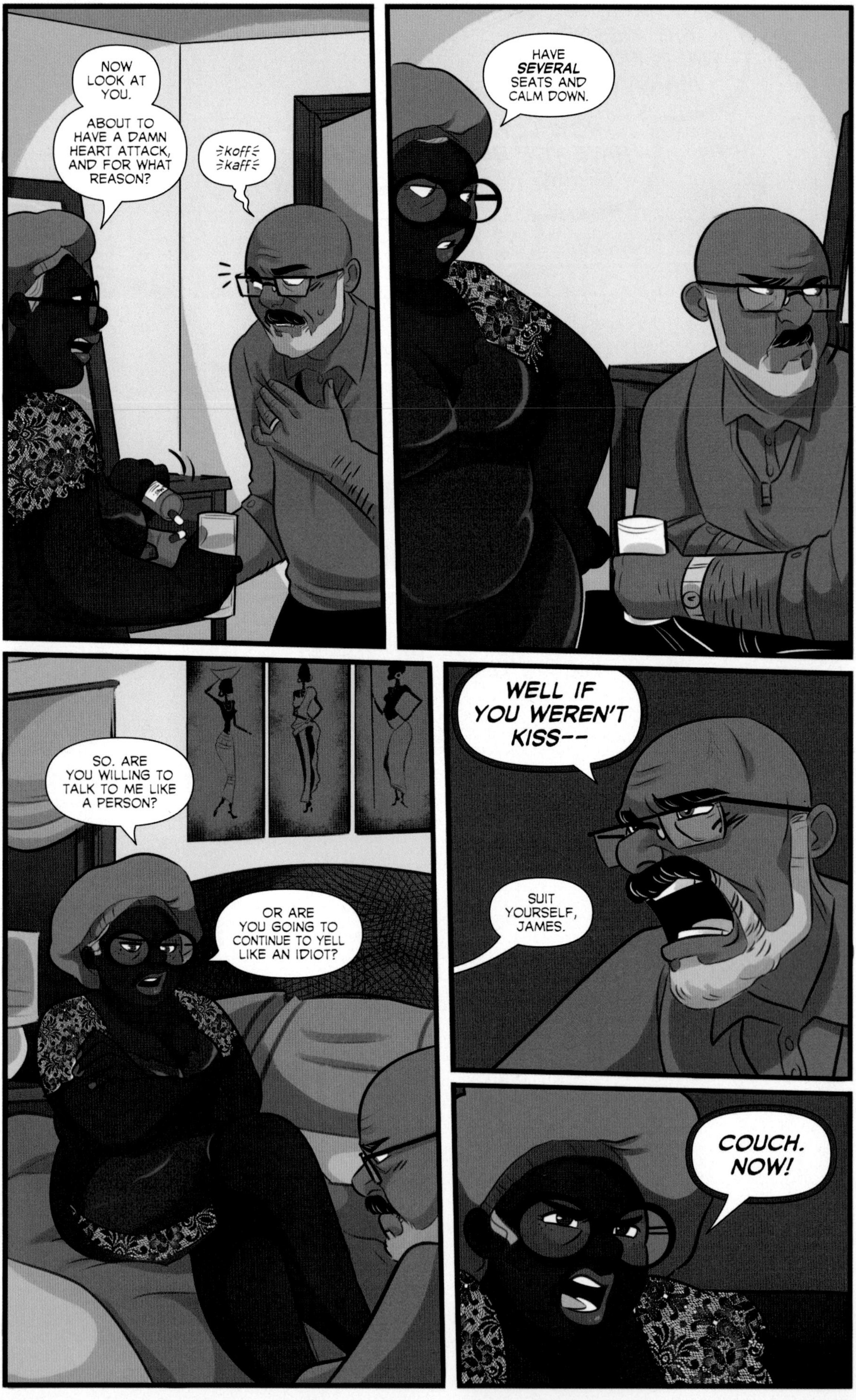
NOW LOOK AT YOU.
ABOUT TO HAVE A DAMN HEART ATTACK, AND FOR WHAT REASON?
koff kaff
HAVE SEVERAL SEATS AND CALM DOWN.
SO. ARE YOU WILLING TO TALK TO ME LIKE A PERSON?
OR ARE YOU GOING TO CONTINUE TO YELL LIKE AN IDIOT?
WELL IF YOU WEREN'T KISS--
SUIT YOURSELF, JAMES.
COUCH. NOW!

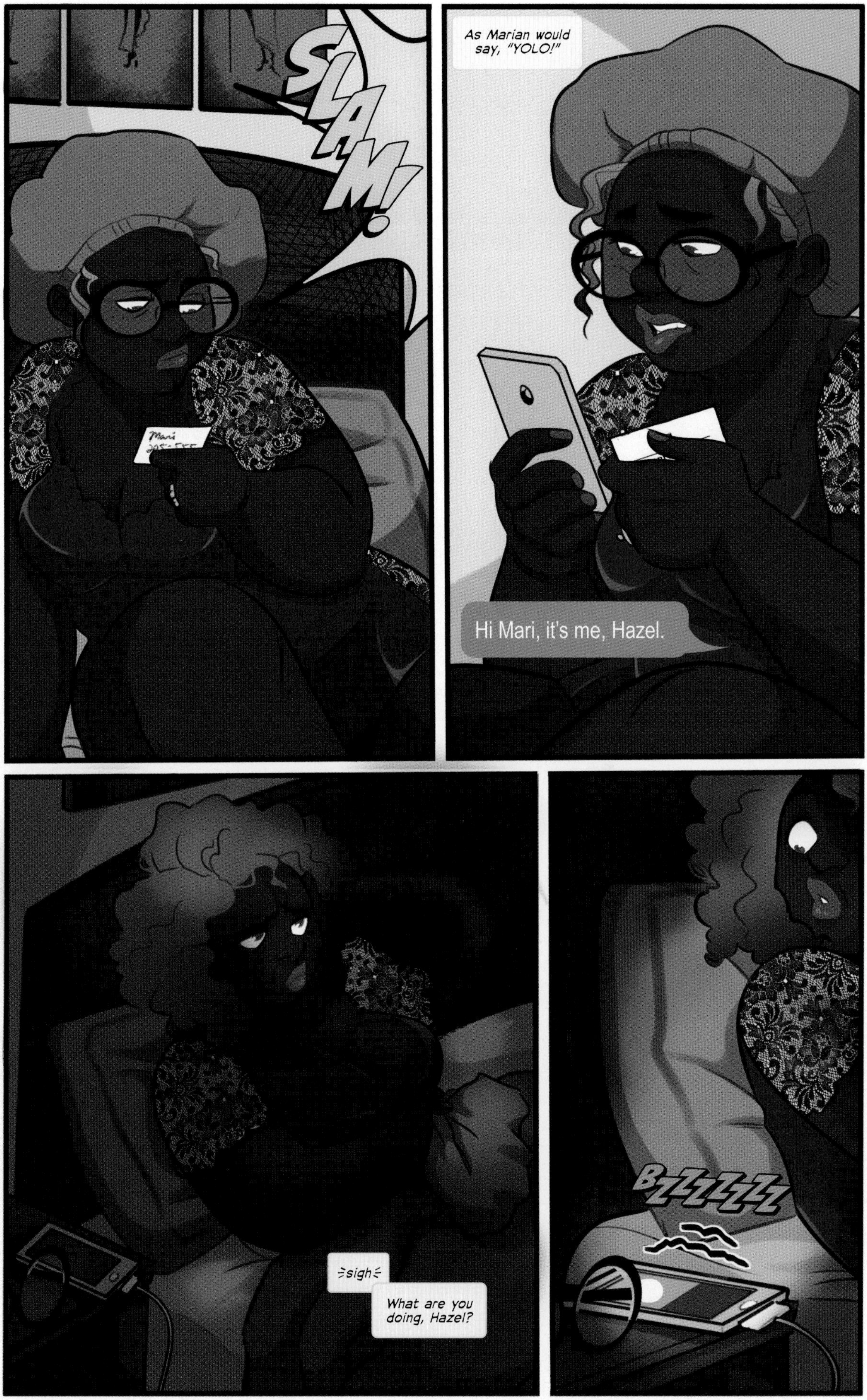
SLAM!
As Marian would say, "YOLO!"
Hi Mari, it's me, Hazel.
sigh
What are you doing, Hazel?
BZZZZZZ

Hi Mari, it's me, Hazel.
Elle. I still can't believe today happened.
I've been pinching myself, it feels like a dream.
I'm not dreaming, Mari.
That kiss was definitely not a dream.
I've had dreams of kissing you, and it was never like that.
Mari

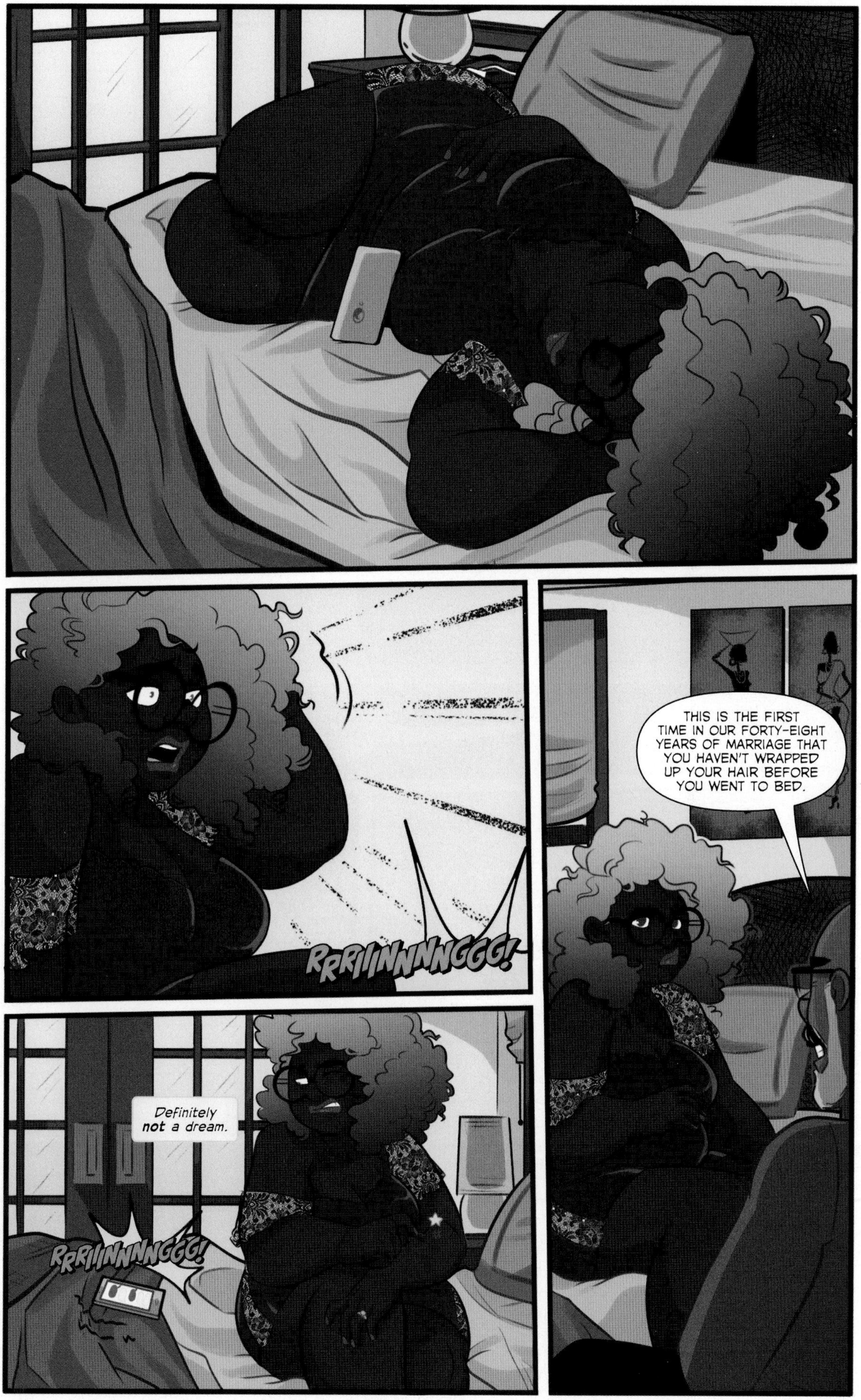
RRRIIINNNNGGG!
THIS IS THE FIRST TIME IN OUR FORTY-EIGHT YEARS OF MARRIAGE THAT YOU HAVEN'T WRAPPED UP YOUR HAIR BEFORE YOU WENT TO BED.
Definitely **not** a dream.
RRRIIINNNNGGG!

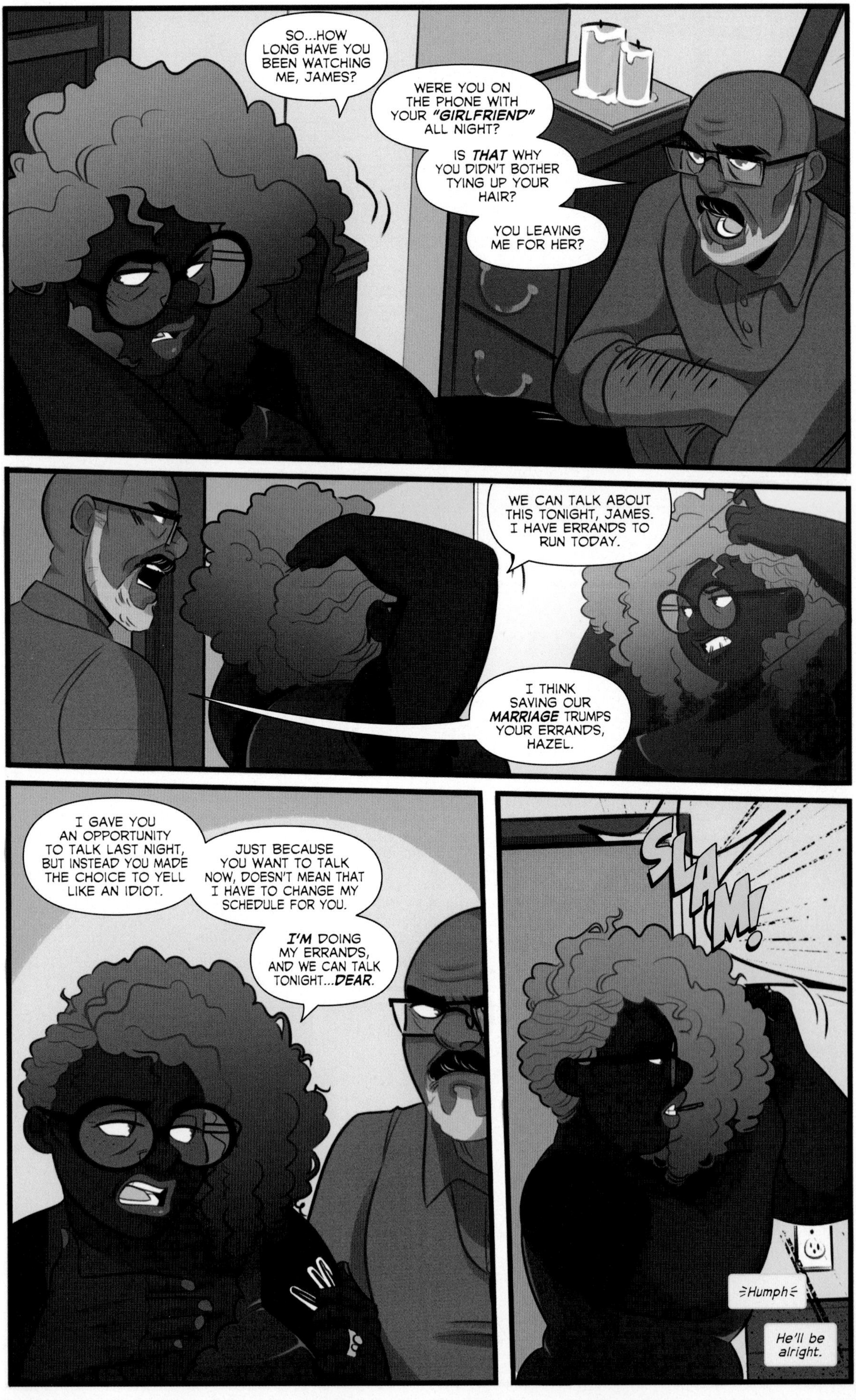

SO...HOW LONG HAVE YOU BEEN WATCHING ME, JAMES?
WERE YOU ON THE PHONE WITH YOUR "GIRLFRIEND" ALL NIGHT?
IS THAT WHY YOU DIDN'T BOTHER TYING UP YOUR HAIR?
YOU LEAVING ME FOR HER?
WE CAN TALK ABOUT THIS TONIGHT, JAMES. I HAVE ERRANDS TO RUN TODAY.
I THINK SAVING OUR MARRIAGE TRUMPS YOUR ERRANDS, HAZEL.
I GAVE YOU AN OPPORTUNITY TO TALK LAST NIGHT, BUT INSTEAD YOU MADE THE CHOICE TO YELL LIKE AN IDIOT.
JUST BECAUSE YOU WANT TO TALK NOW, DOESN'T MEAN THAT I HAVE TO CHANGE MY SCHEDULE FOR YOU.
I'M DOING MY ERRANDS, AND WE CAN TALK TONIGHT...DEAR.
SLAM!
Humph
He'll be alright.

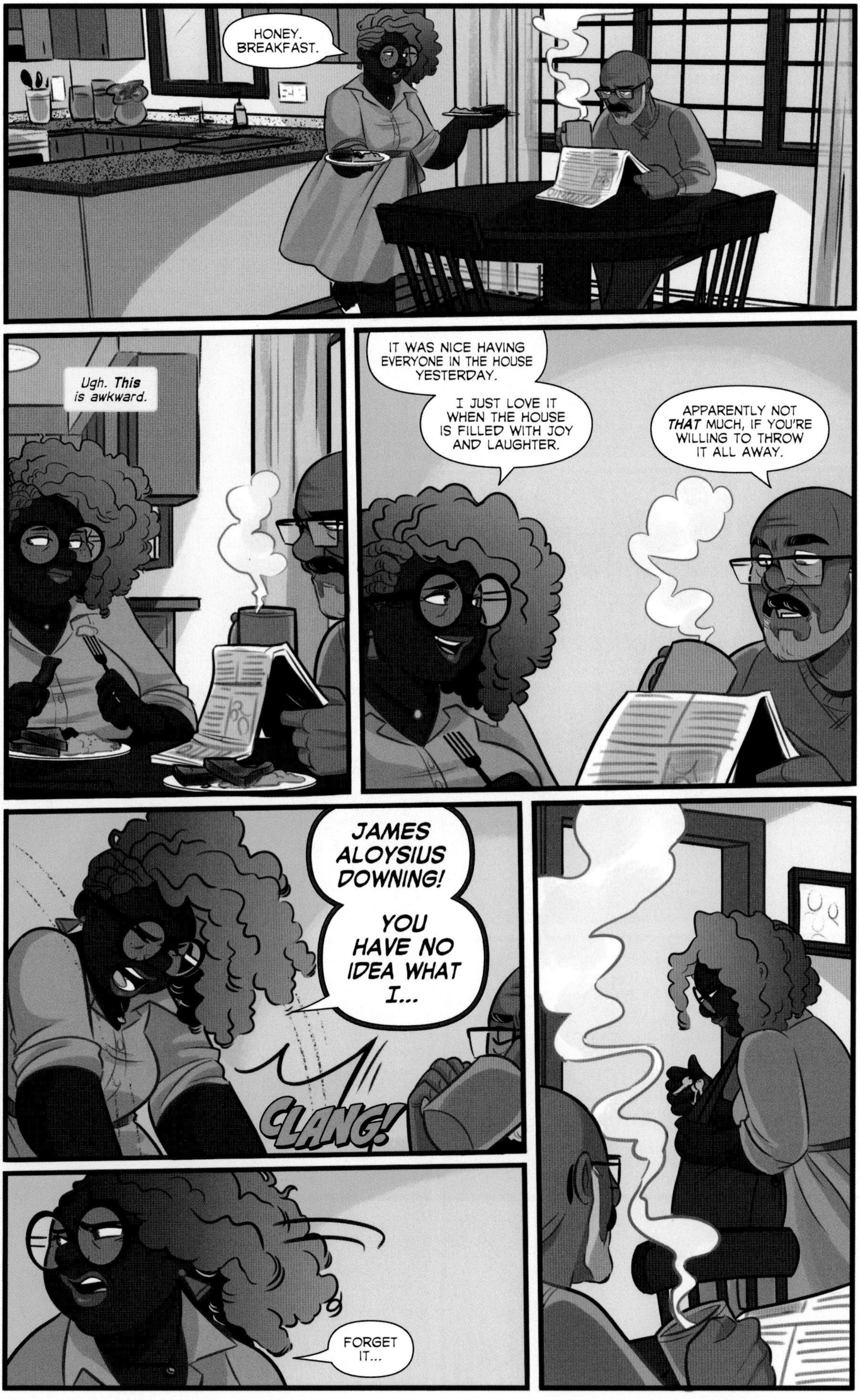
HONEY. BREAKFAST.
Ugh. This is awkward.
IT WAS NICE HAVING EVERYONE IN THE HOUSE YESTERDAY.
I JUST LOVE IT WHEN THE HOUSE IS FILLED WITH JOY AND LAUGHTER.
APPARENTLY NOT THAT MUCH, IF YOU'RE WILLING TO THROW IT ALL AWAY.
JAMES ALOYSIUS DOWNING!
YOU HAVE NO IDEA WHAT I...
CLANG!
FORGET IT...

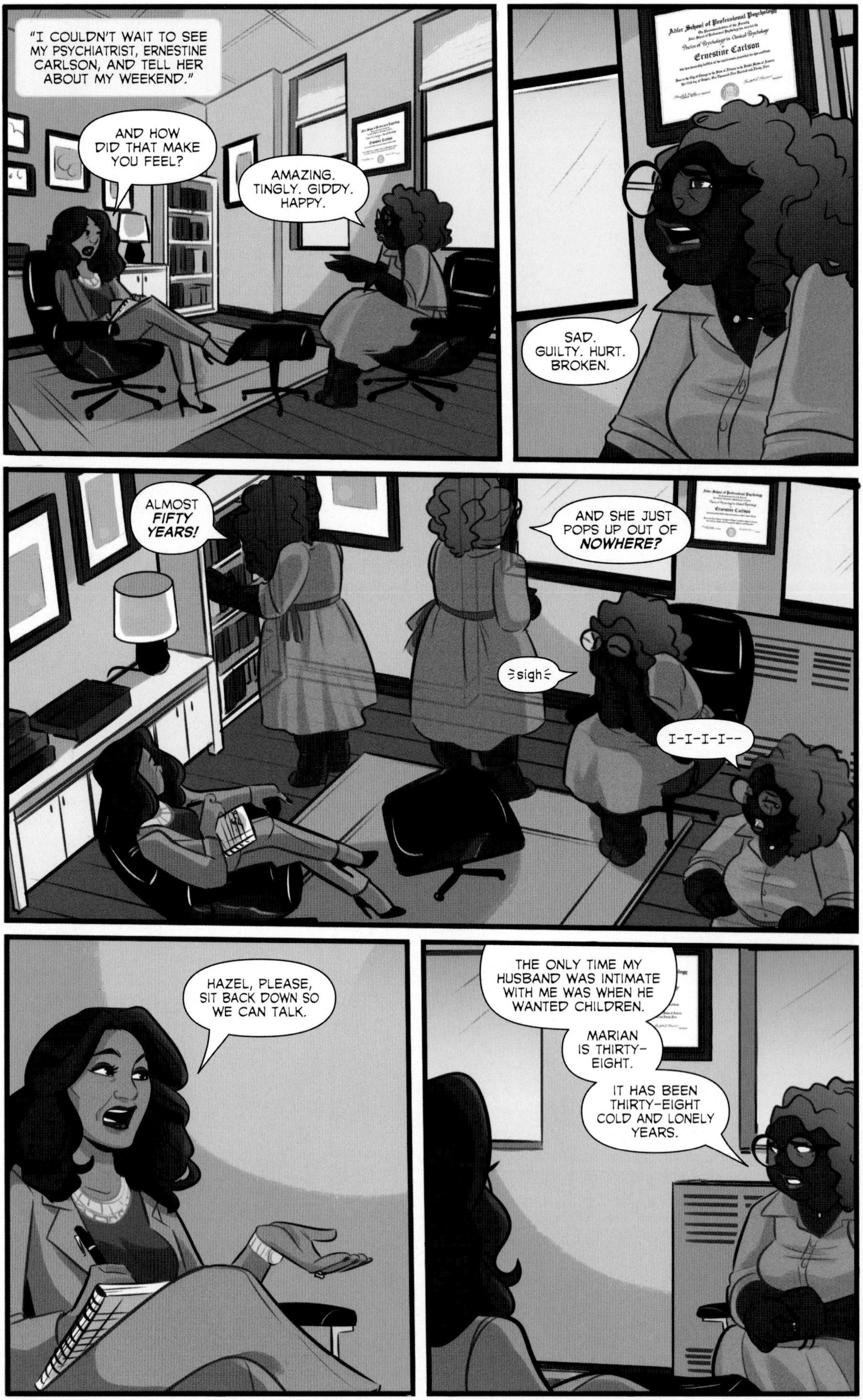
"I COULDN'T WAIT TO SEE MY PSYCHIATRIST, ERNESTINE CARLSON, AND TELL HER ABOUT MY WEEKEND."
AND HOW DID THAT MAKE YOU FEEL?
AMAZING. TINGLY. GIDDY. HAPPY.
SAD. GUILTY. HURT. BROKEN.
ALMOST *FIFTY YEARS!*
AND SHE JUST POPS UP OUT OF *NOWHERE?*
sigh
I-I-I-I--
HAZEL, PLEASE, SIT BACK DOWN SO WE CAN TALK.
THE ONLY TIME MY HUSBAND WAS INTIMATE WITH ME WAS WHEN HE WANTED CHILDREN.
MARIAN IS THIRTY-EIGHT.
IT HAS BEEN THIRTY-EIGHT COLD AND LONELY YEARS.

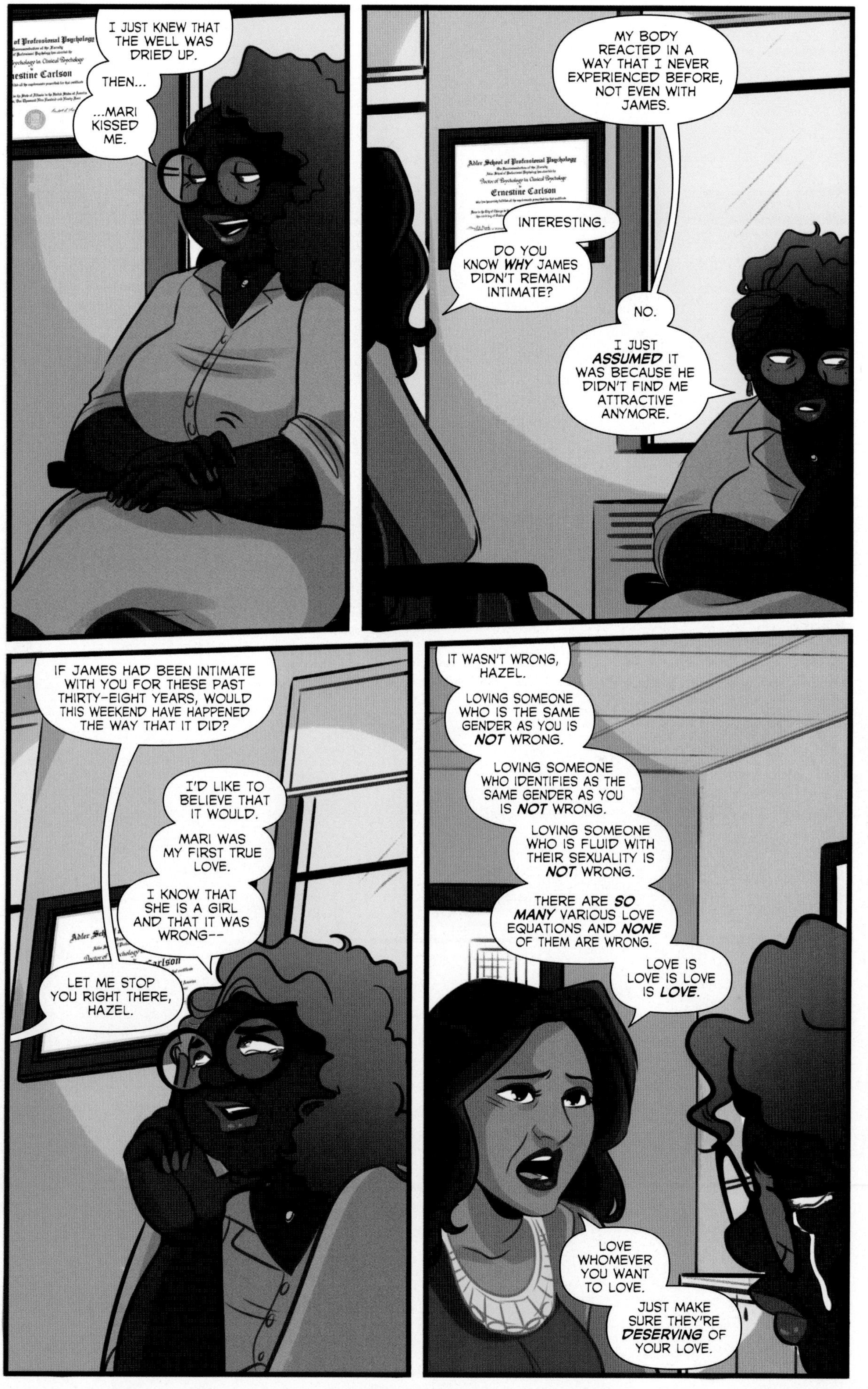
I JUST KNEW THAT THE WELL WAS DRIED UP.
THEN...
...MARI KISSED ME.
MY BODY REACTED IN A WAY THAT I NEVER EXPERIENCED BEFORE, NOT EVEN WITH JAMES.
Adler School of Professional Psychology
Doctor of Psychology in Clinical Psychology
Ernestine Carlson
INTERESTING.
DO YOU KNOW *WHY* JAMES DIDN'T REMAIN INTIMATE?
NO.
I JUST *ASSUMED* IT WAS BECAUSE HE DIDN'T FIND ME ATTRACTIVE ANYMORE.
IF JAMES HAD BEEN INTIMATE WITH YOU FOR THESE PAST THIRTY-EIGHT YEARS, WOULD THIS WEEKEND HAVE HAPPENED THE WAY THAT IT DID?
I'D LIKE TO BELIEVE THAT IT WOULD.
MARI WAS MY FIRST TRUE LOVE.
I KNOW THAT SHE IS A GIRL AND THAT IT WAS WRONG--
LET ME STOP YOU RIGHT THERE, HAZEL.
IT WASN'T WRONG, HAZEL.
LOVING SOMEONE WHO IS THE SAME GENDER AS YOU IS *NOT* WRONG.
LOVING SOMEONE WHO IDENTIFIES AS THE SAME GENDER AS YOU IS *NOT* WRONG.
LOVING SOMEONE WHO IS FLUID WITH THEIR SEXUALITY IS *NOT* WRONG.
THERE ARE *SO MANY* VARIOUS LOVE EQUATIONS AND *NONE* OF THEM ARE WRONG.
LOVE IS LOVE IS LOVE IS *LOVE*.
LOVE WHOMEVER YOU WANT TO LOVE.
JUST MAKE SURE THEY'RE *DESERVING* OF YOUR LOVE.

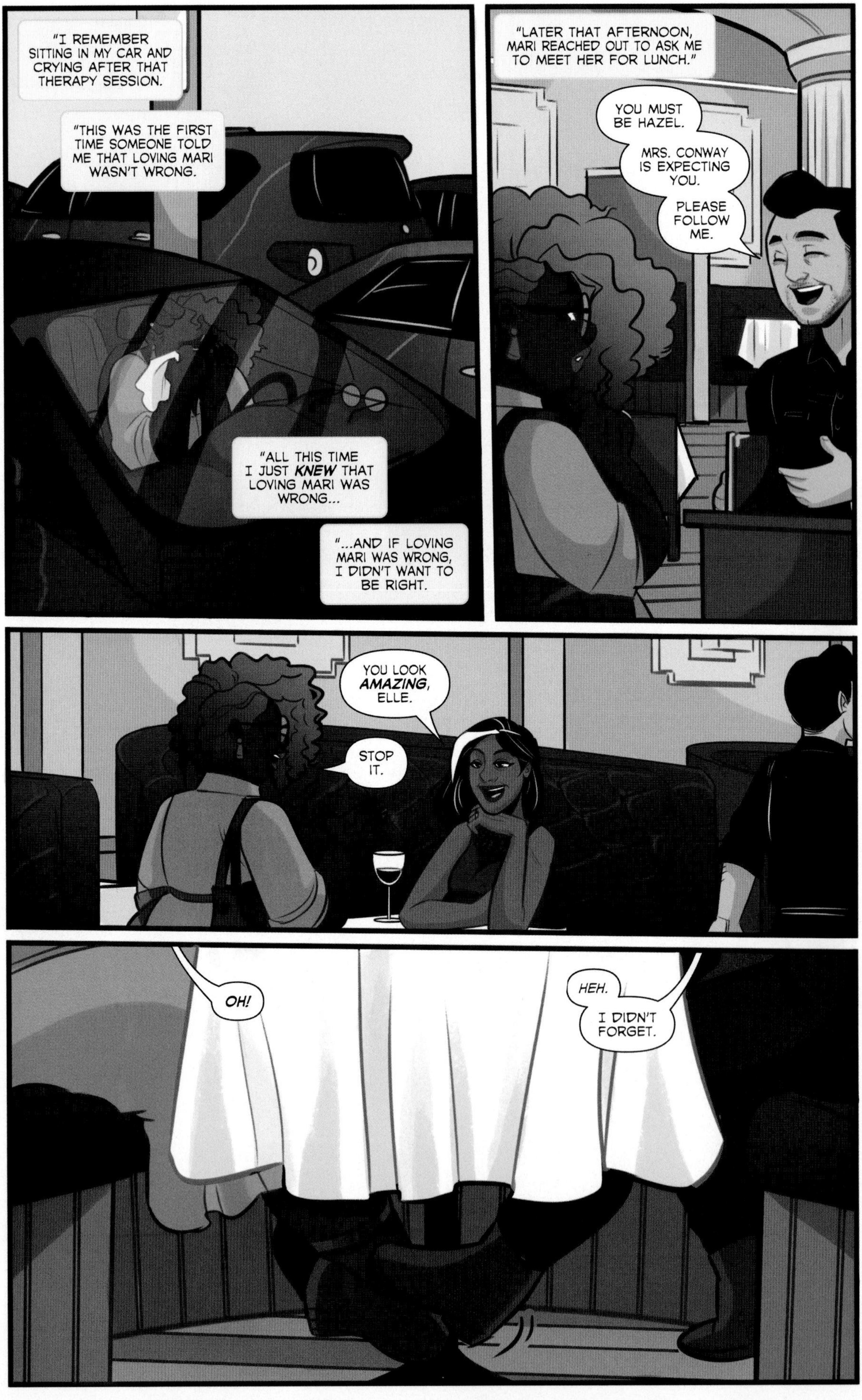
"I REMEMBER SITTING IN MY CAR AND CRYING AFTER THAT THERAPY SESSION.
"THIS WAS THE FIRST TIME SOMEONE TOLD ME THAT LOVING MARI WASN'T WRONG.
"ALL THIS TIME I JUST *KNEW* THAT LOVING MARI WAS WRONG...
"...AND IF LOVING MARI WAS WRONG, I DIDN'T WANT TO BE RIGHT.
"LATER THAT AFTERNOON, MARI REACHED OUT TO ASK ME TO MEET HER FOR LUNCH."
YOU MUST BE HAZEL.
MRS. CONWAY IS EXPECTING YOU.
PLEASE FOLLOW ME.
YOU LOOK *AMAZING*, ELLE.
STOP IT.
OH!
HEH.
I DIDN'T FORGET.

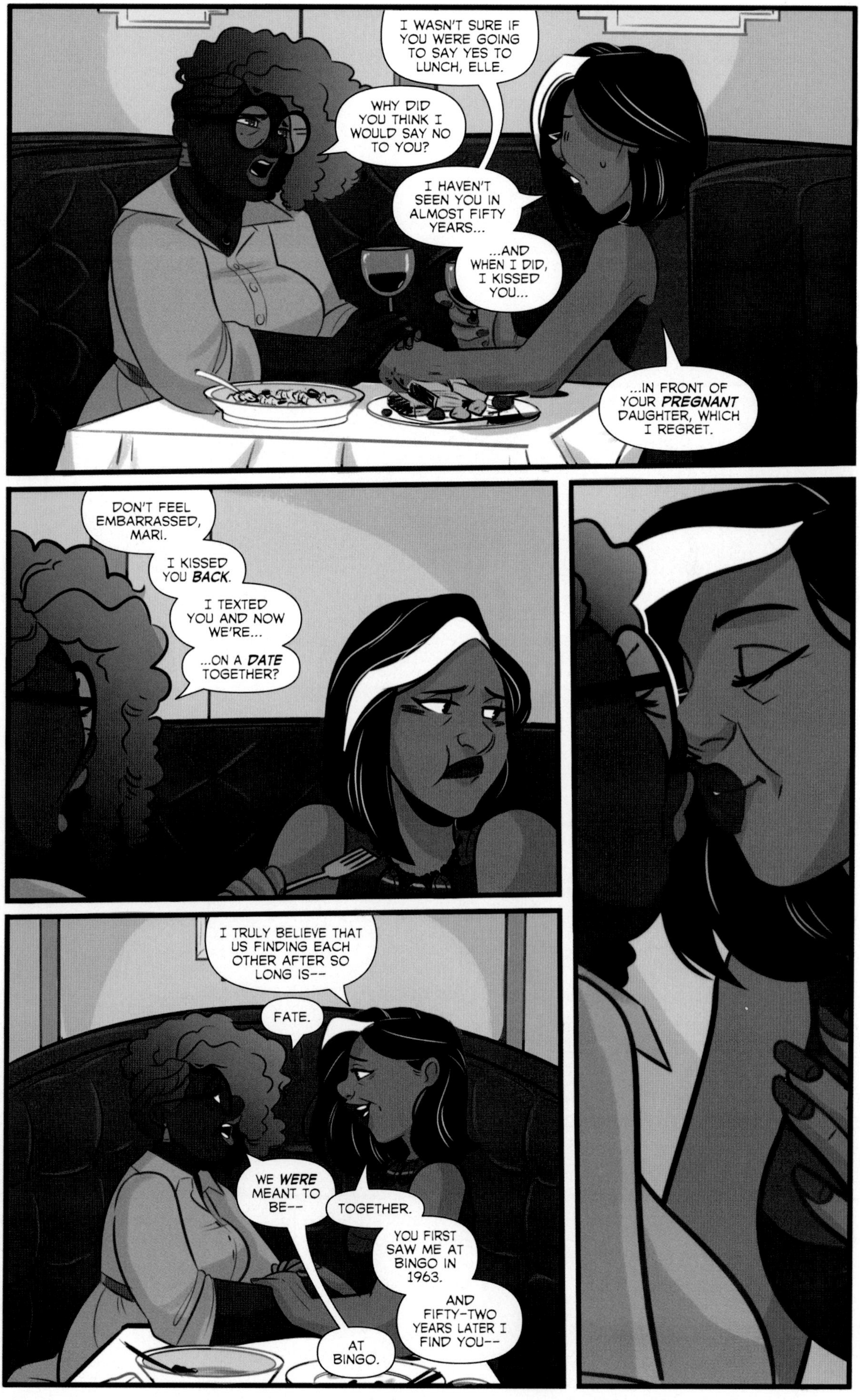
I WASN'T SURE IF YOU WERE GOING TO SAY YES TO LUNCH, ELLE.
WHY DID YOU THINK I WOULD SAY NO TO YOU?
I HAVEN'T SEEN YOU IN ALMOST FIFTY YEARS...
...AND WHEN I DID, I KISSED YOU...
...IN FRONT OF YOUR *PREGNANT* DAUGHTER, WHICH I REGRET.
DON'T FEEL EMBARRASSED, MARI.
I KISSED YOU *BACK*.
I TEXTED YOU AND NOW WE'RE...
...ON A *DATE* TOGETHER?
I TRULY BELIEVE THAT US FINDING EACH OTHER AFTER SO LONG IS--
FATE.
WE *WERE* MEANT TO BE--
TOGETHER.
YOU FIRST SAW ME AT BINGO IN 1963.
AND FIFTY-TWO YEARS LATER I FIND YOU--
AT BINGO.

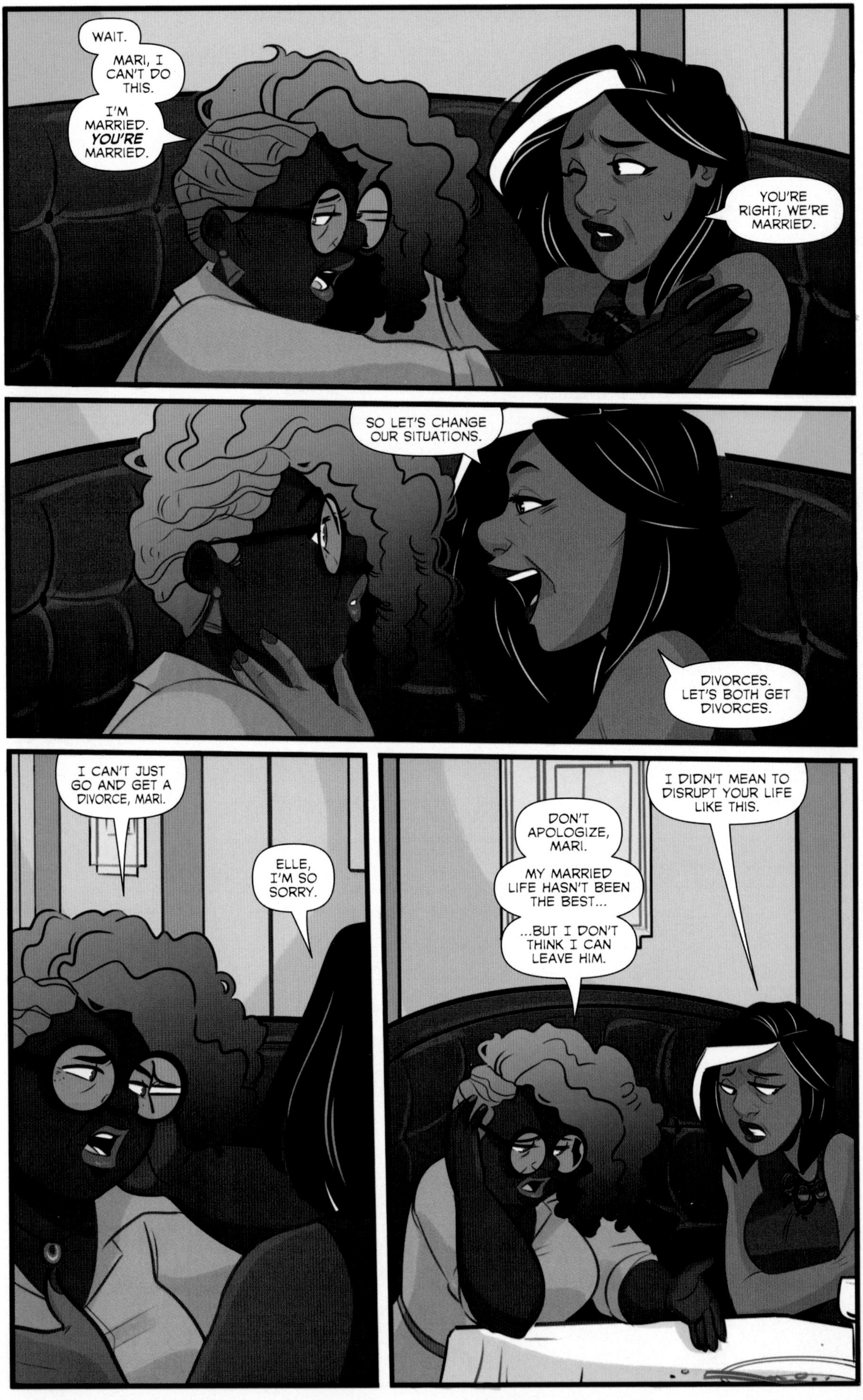
WAIT.
MARI, I CAN'T DO THIS.
I'M MARRIED. YOU'RE MARRIED.
YOU'RE RIGHT; WE'RE MARRIED.
SO LET'S CHANGE OUR SITUATIONS.
DIVORCES. LET'S BOTH GET DIVORCES.
I CAN'T JUST GO AND GET A DIVORCE, MARI.
ELLE, I'M SO SORRY.
I DIDN'T MEAN TO DISRUPT YOUR LIFE LIKE THIS.
DON'T APOLOGIZE, MARI.
MY MARRIED LIFE HASN'T BEEN THE BEST...
...BUT I DON'T THINK I CAN LEAVE HIM.

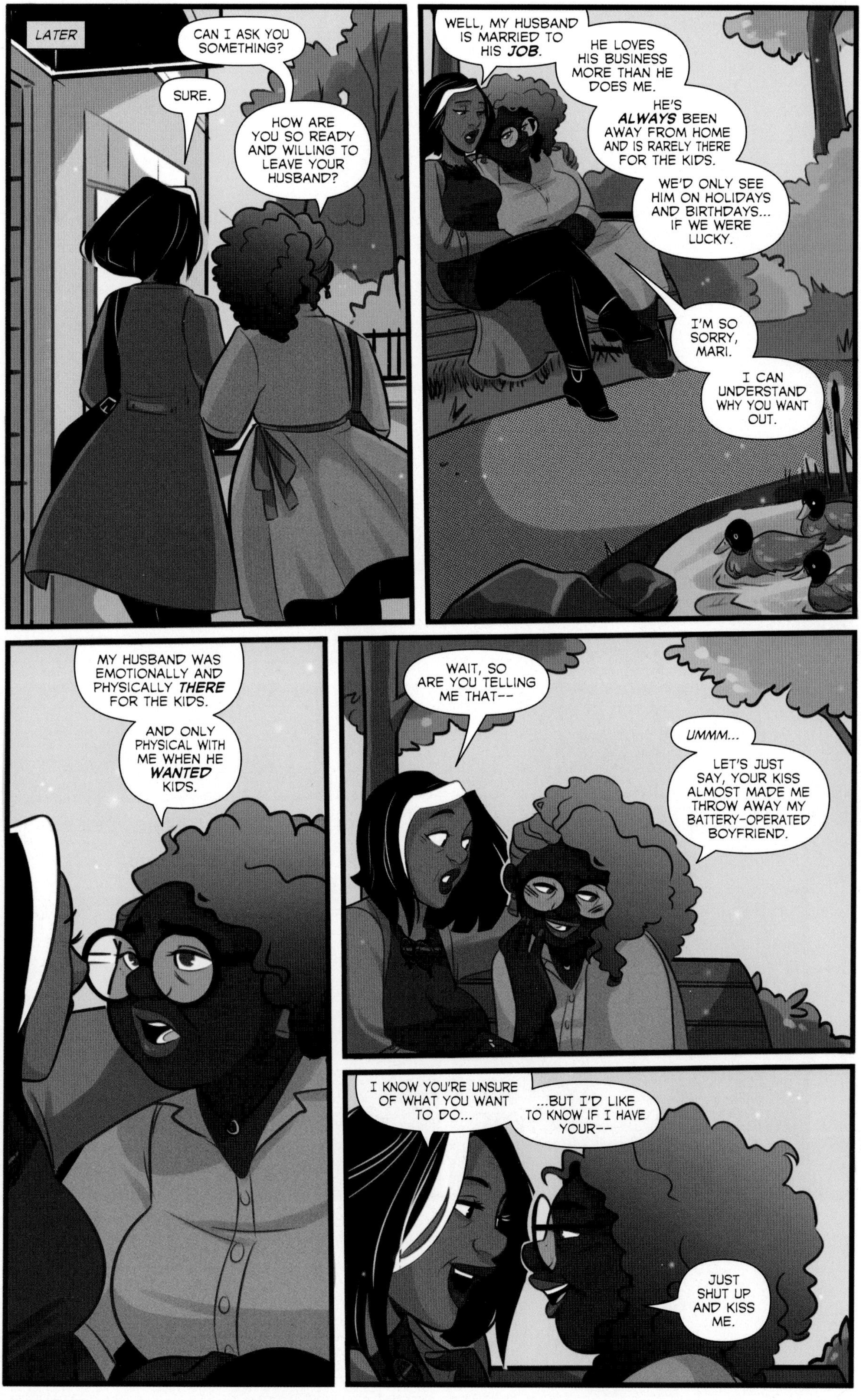
LATER
CAN I ASK YOU SOMETHING?
SURE.
HOW ARE YOU SO READY AND WILLING TO LEAVE YOUR HUSBAND?
WELL, MY HUSBAND IS MARRIED TO HIS *JOB*.
HE LOVES HIS BUSINESS MORE THAN HE DOES ME.
HE'S ***ALWAYS*** BEEN AWAY FROM HOME AND IS RARELY THERE FOR THE KIDS.
WE'D ONLY SEE HIM ON HOLIDAYS AND BIRTHDAYS... IF WE WERE LUCKY.
I'M SO SORRY, MARI.
I CAN UNDERSTAND WHY YOU WANT OUT.
MY HUSBAND WAS EMOTIONALLY AND PHYSICALLY ***THERE*** FOR THE KIDS.
AND ONLY PHYSICAL WITH ME WHEN HE ***WANTED*** KIDS.
WAIT, SO ARE YOU TELLING ME THAT--
UMMM...
LET'S JUST SAY, YOUR KISS ALMOST MADE ME THROW AWAY MY BATTERY-OPERATED BOYFRIEND.
I KNOW YOU'RE UNSURE OF WHAT YOU WANT TO DO...
...BUT I'D LIKE TO KNOW IF I HAVE YOUR--
JUST SHUT UP AND KISS ME.

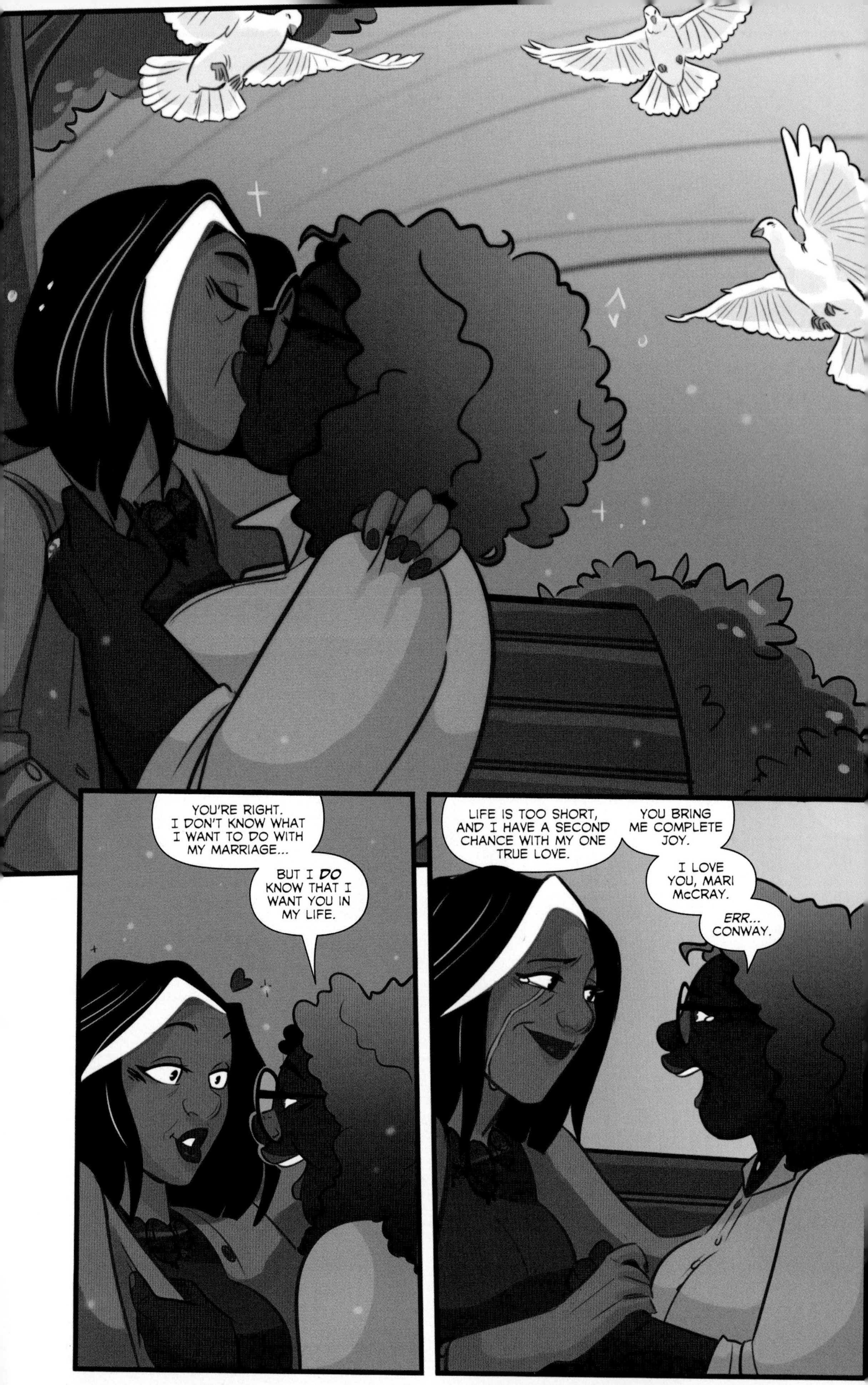
YOU'RE RIGHT. I DON'T KNOW WHAT I WANT TO DO WITH MY MARRIAGE...
BUT I *DO* KNOW THAT I WANT YOU IN MY LIFE.
LIFE IS TOO SHORT, AND I HAVE A SECOND CHANCE WITH MY ONE TRUE LOVE.
YOU BRING ME COMPLETE JOY.
I LOVE YOU, MARI McCRAY.
ERR... CONWAY.

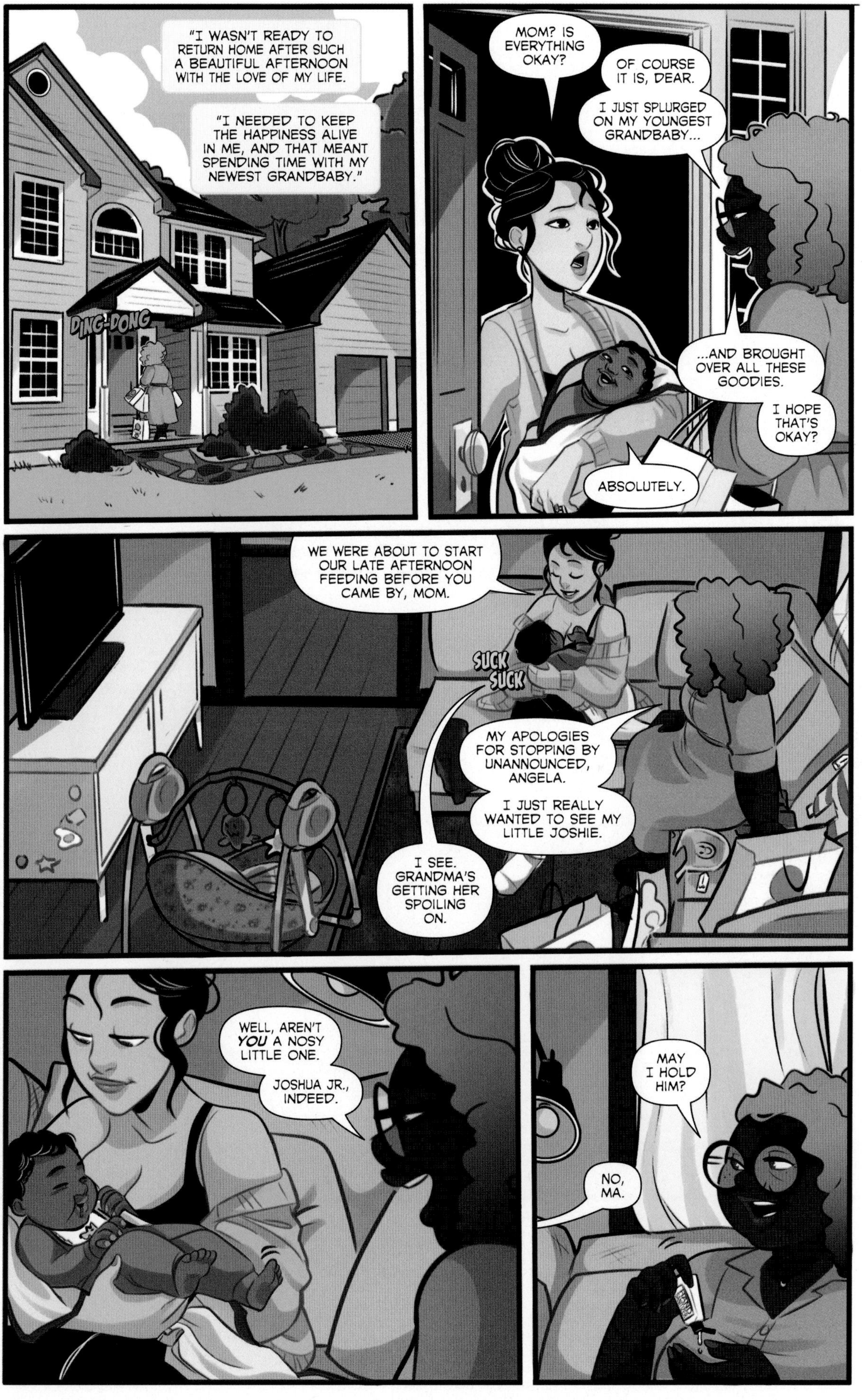
"I WASN'T READY TO RETURN HOME AFTER SUCH A BEAUTIFUL AFTERNOON WITH THE LOVE OF MY LIFE.
"I NEEDED TO KEEP THE HAPPINESS ALIVE IN ME, AND THAT MEANT SPENDING TIME WITH MY NEWEST GRANDBABY."
DING-DONG
MOM? IS EVERYTHING OKAY?
OF COURSE IT IS, DEAR.
I JUST SPLURGED ON MY YOUNGEST GRANDBABY...
...AND BROUGHT OVER ALL THESE GOODIES.
I HOPE THAT'S OKAY?
ABSOLUTELY.
WE WERE ABOUT TO START OUR LATE AFTERNOON FEEDING BEFORE YOU CAME BY, MOM.
SUCK SUCK
MY APOLOGIES FOR STOPPING BY UNANNOUNCED, ANGELA.
I JUST REALLY WANTED TO SEE MY LITTLE JOSHIE.
I SEE. GRANDMA'S GETTING HER SPOILING ON.
WELL, AREN'T *YOU* A NOSY LITTLE ONE.
JOSHUA JR., INDEED.
MAY I HOLD HIM?
NO, MA.

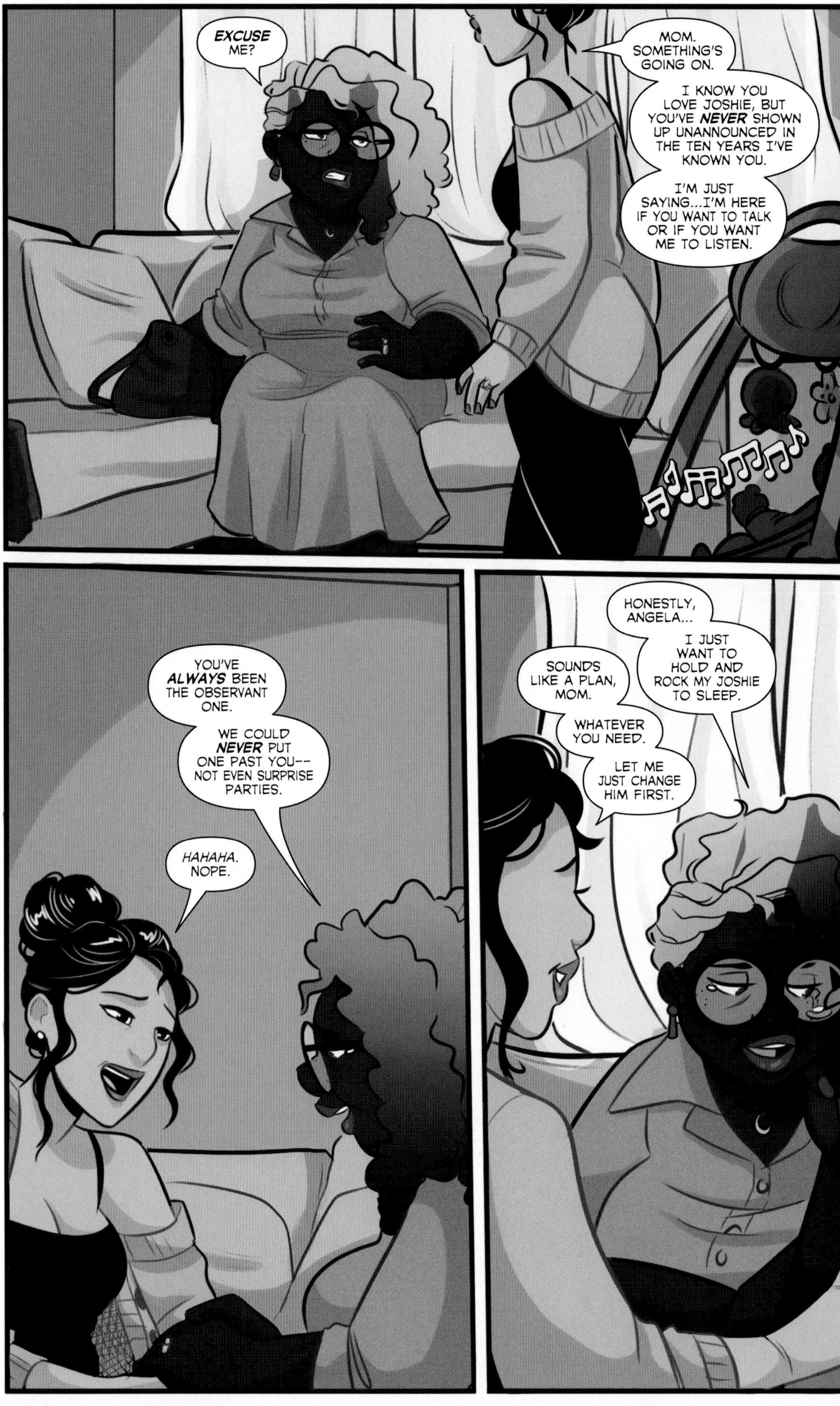
EXCUSE ME?
MOM. SOMETHING'S GOING ON.
I KNOW YOU LOVE JOSHIE, BUT YOU'VE NEVER SHOWN UP UNANNOUNCED IN THE TEN YEARS I'VE KNOWN YOU.
I'M JUST SAYING...I'M HERE IF YOU WANT TO TALK OR IF YOU WANT ME TO LISTEN.
YOU'VE ALWAYS BEEN THE OBSERVANT ONE.
WE COULD NEVER PUT ONE PAST YOU--NOT EVEN SURPRISE PARTIES.
HAHAHA. NOPE.
HONESTLY, ANGELA...
I JUST WANT TO HOLD AND ROCK MY JOSHIE TO SLEEP.
SOUNDS LIKE A PLAN, MOM.
WHATEVER YOU NEED.
LET ME JUST CHANGE HIM FIRST.

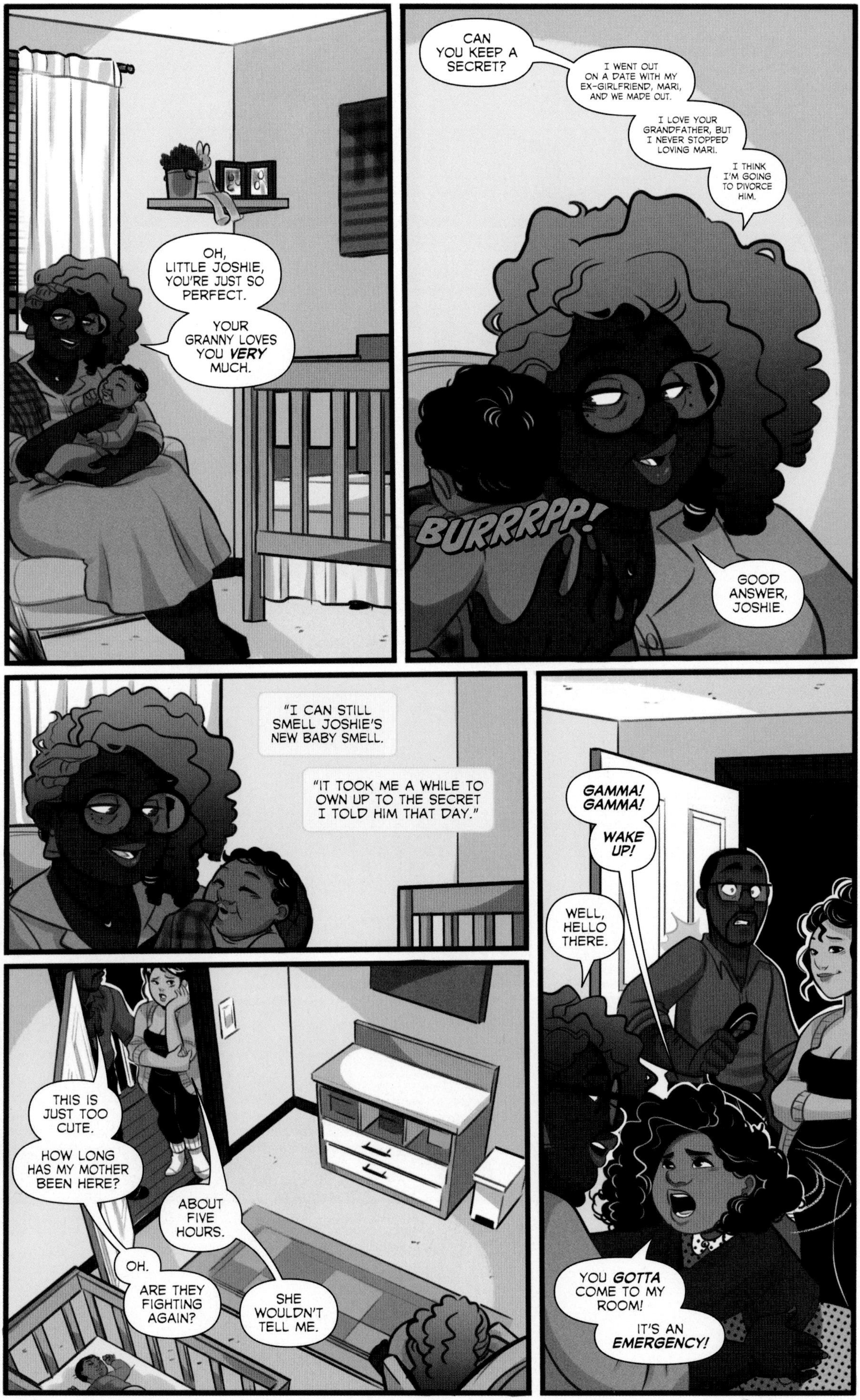
OH, LITTLE JOSHIE, YOU'RE JUST SO PERFECT.
YOUR GRANNY LOVES YOU *VERY* MUCH.
CAN YOU KEEP A SECRET?
I WENT OUT ON A DATE WITH MY EX-GIRLFRIEND, MARI, AND WE MADE OUT.
I LOVE YOUR GRANDFATHER, BUT I NEVER STOPPED LOVING MARI.
I THINK I'M GOING TO DIVORCE HIM.
BURRRPP!
GOOD ANSWER, JOSHIE.
"I CAN STILL SMELL JOSHIE'S NEW BABY SMELL.
"IT TOOK ME A WHILE TO OWN UP TO THE SECRET I TOLD HIM THAT DAY."
THIS IS JUST TOO CUTE.
HOW LONG HAS MY MOTHER BEEN HERE?
ABOUT FIVE HOURS.
OH.
ARE THEY FIGHTING AGAIN?
SHE WOULDN'T TELL ME.
GAMMA! GAMMA!
WAKE UP!
WELL, HELLO THERE.
YOU *GOTTA* COME TO MY ROOM!
IT'S AN *EMERGENCY!*

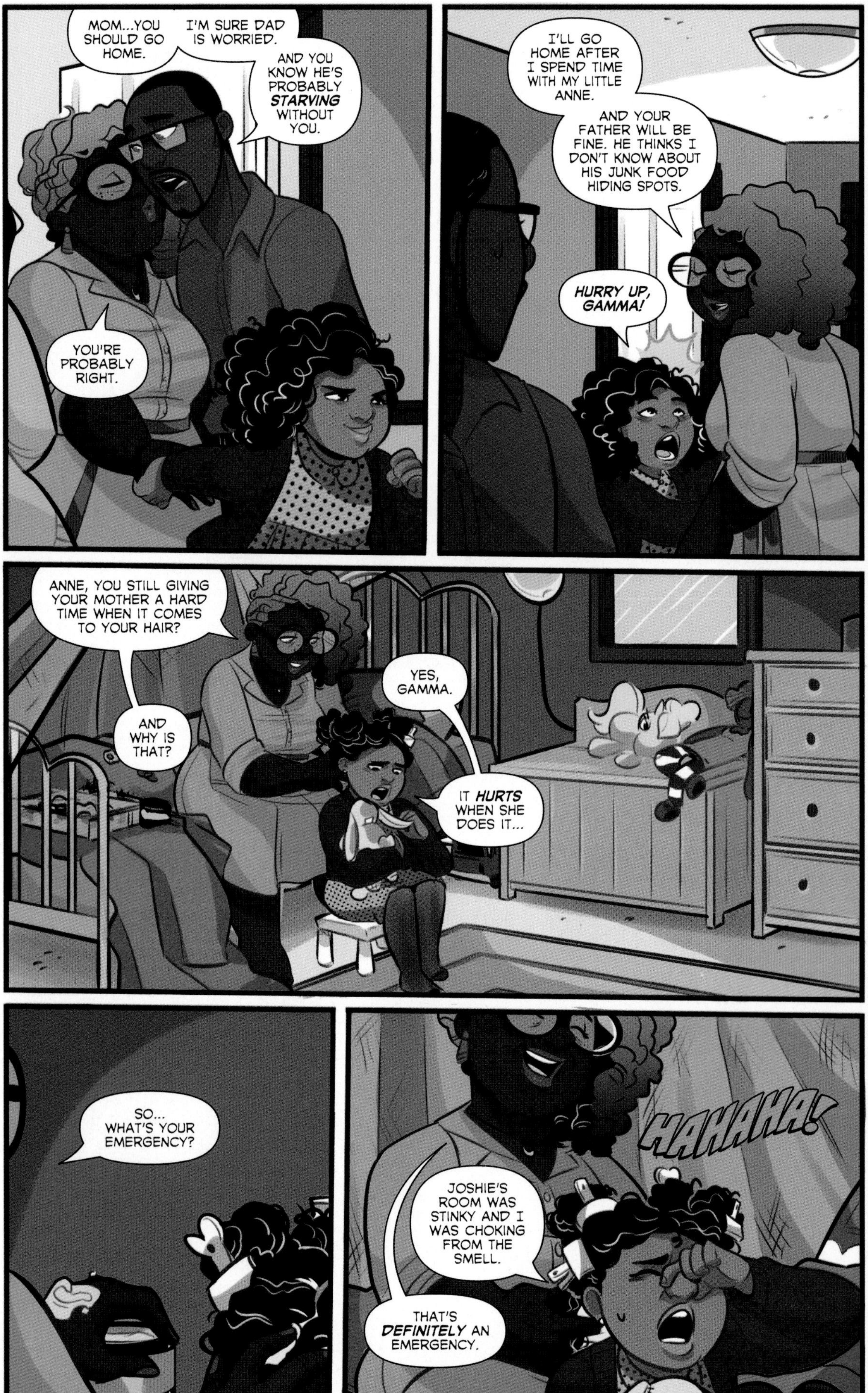
MOM...YOU SHOULD GO HOME.
I'M SURE DAD IS WORRIED.
AND YOU KNOW HE'S PROBABLY **STARVING** WITHOUT YOU.
YOU'RE PROBABLY RIGHT.
I'LL GO HOME AFTER I SPEND TIME WITH MY LITTLE ANNE.
AND YOUR FATHER WILL BE FINE. HE THINKS I DON'T KNOW ABOUT HIS JUNK FOOD HIDING SPOTS.
HURRY UP, GAMMA!
ANNE, YOU STILL GIVING YOUR MOTHER A HARD TIME WHEN IT COMES TO YOUR HAIR?
YES, GAMMA.
AND WHY IS THAT?
IT **HURTS** WHEN SHE DOES IT...
SO... WHAT'S YOUR EMERGENCY?
HAHAHA!
JOSHIE'S ROOM WAS STINKY AND I WAS CHOKING FROM THE SMELL.
THAT'S **DEFINITELY** AN EMERGENCY.

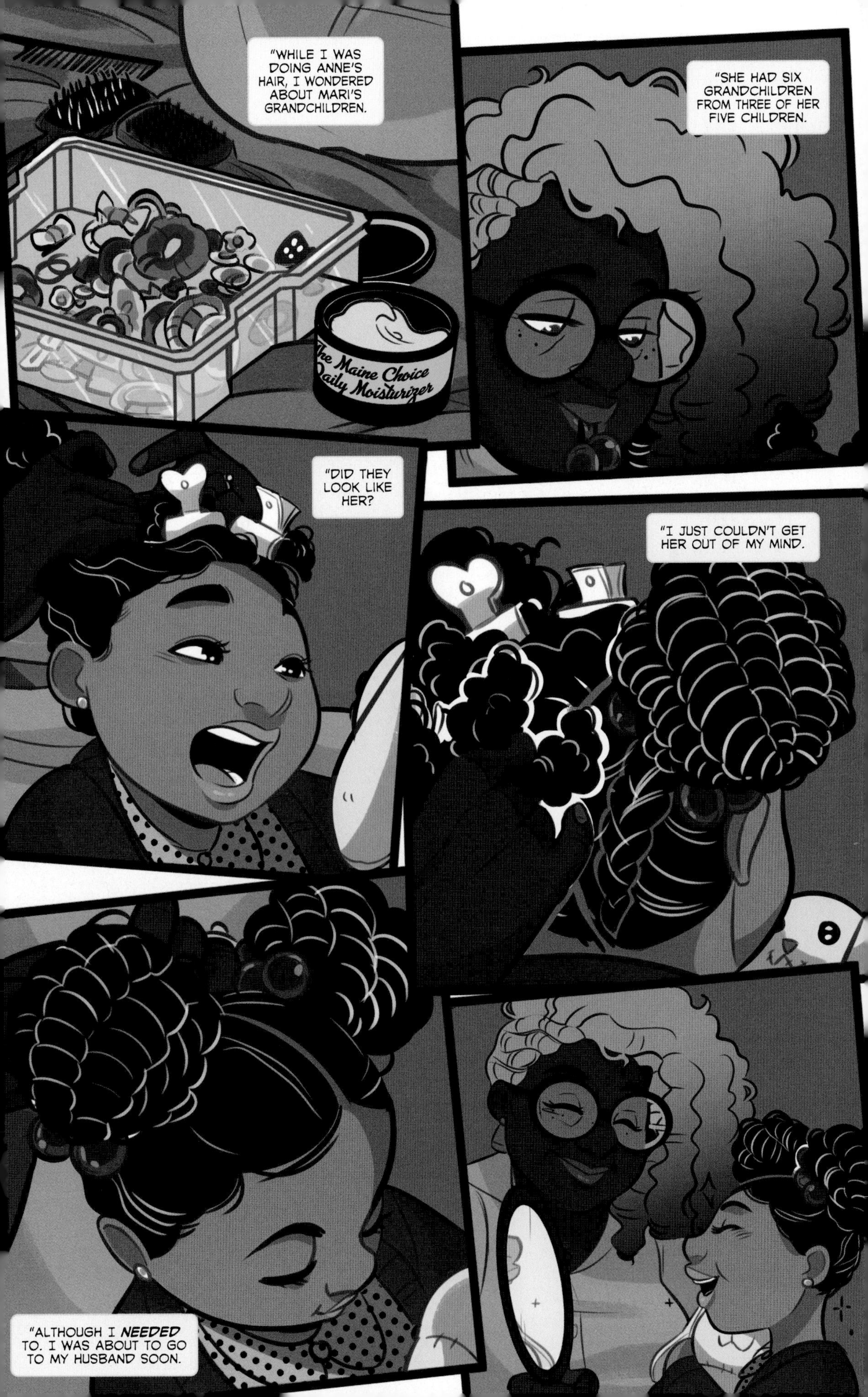
"WHILE I WAS DOING ANNE'S HAIR, I WONDERED ABOUT MARI'S GRANDCHILDREN.
The Maine Choice Daily Moisturizer
"SHE HAD SIX GRANDCHILDREN FROM THREE OF HER FIVE CHILDREN.
"DID THEY LOOK LIKE HER?
"I JUST COULDN'T GET HER OUT OF MY MIND.
"ALTHOUGH I *NEEDED* TO. I WAS ABOUT TO GO TO MY HUSBAND SOON.

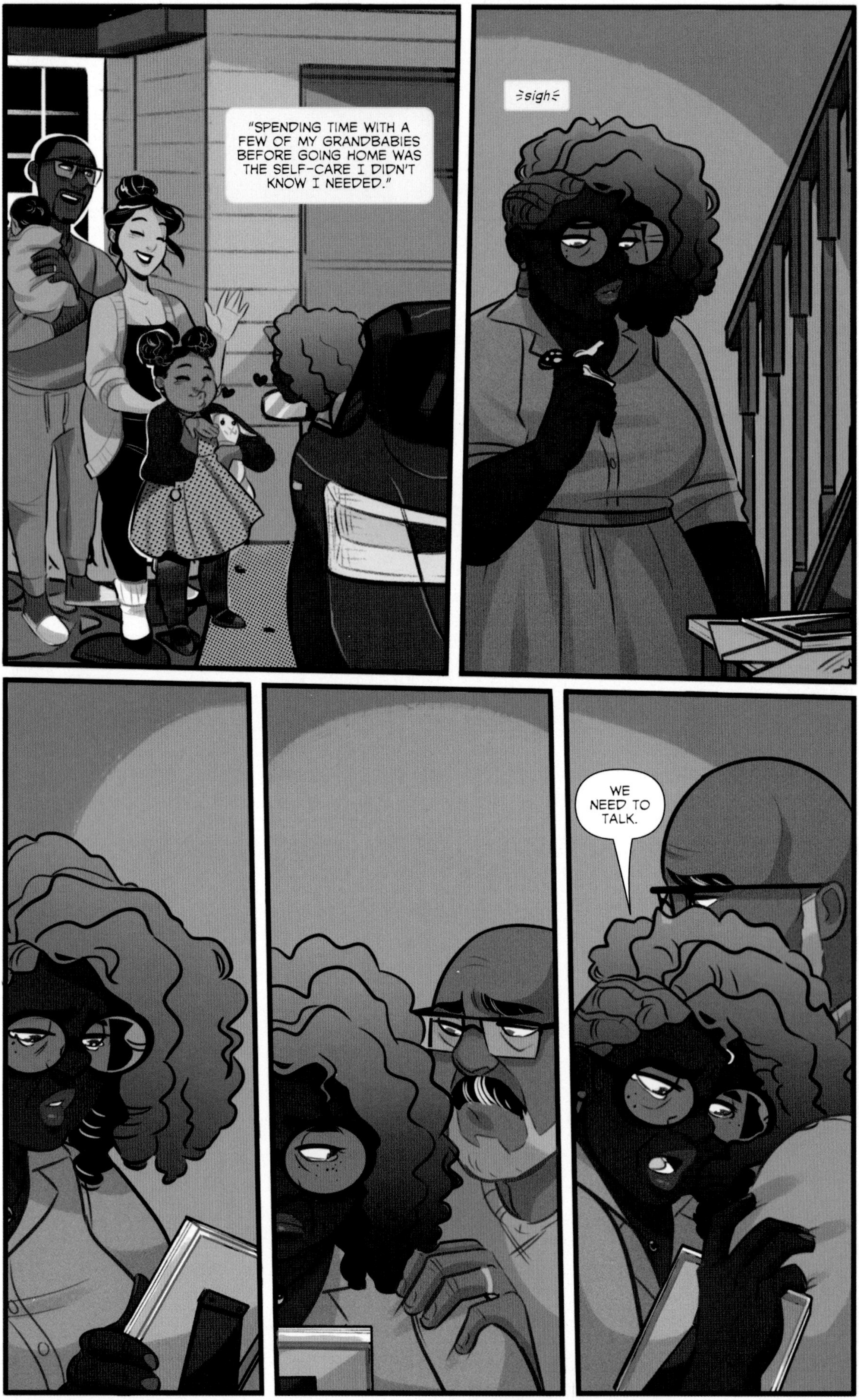
"SPENDING TIME WITH A FEW OF MY GRANDBABIES BEFORE GOING HOME WAS THE SELF-CARE I DIDN'T KNOW I NEEDED."
sigh
WE NEED TO TALK.

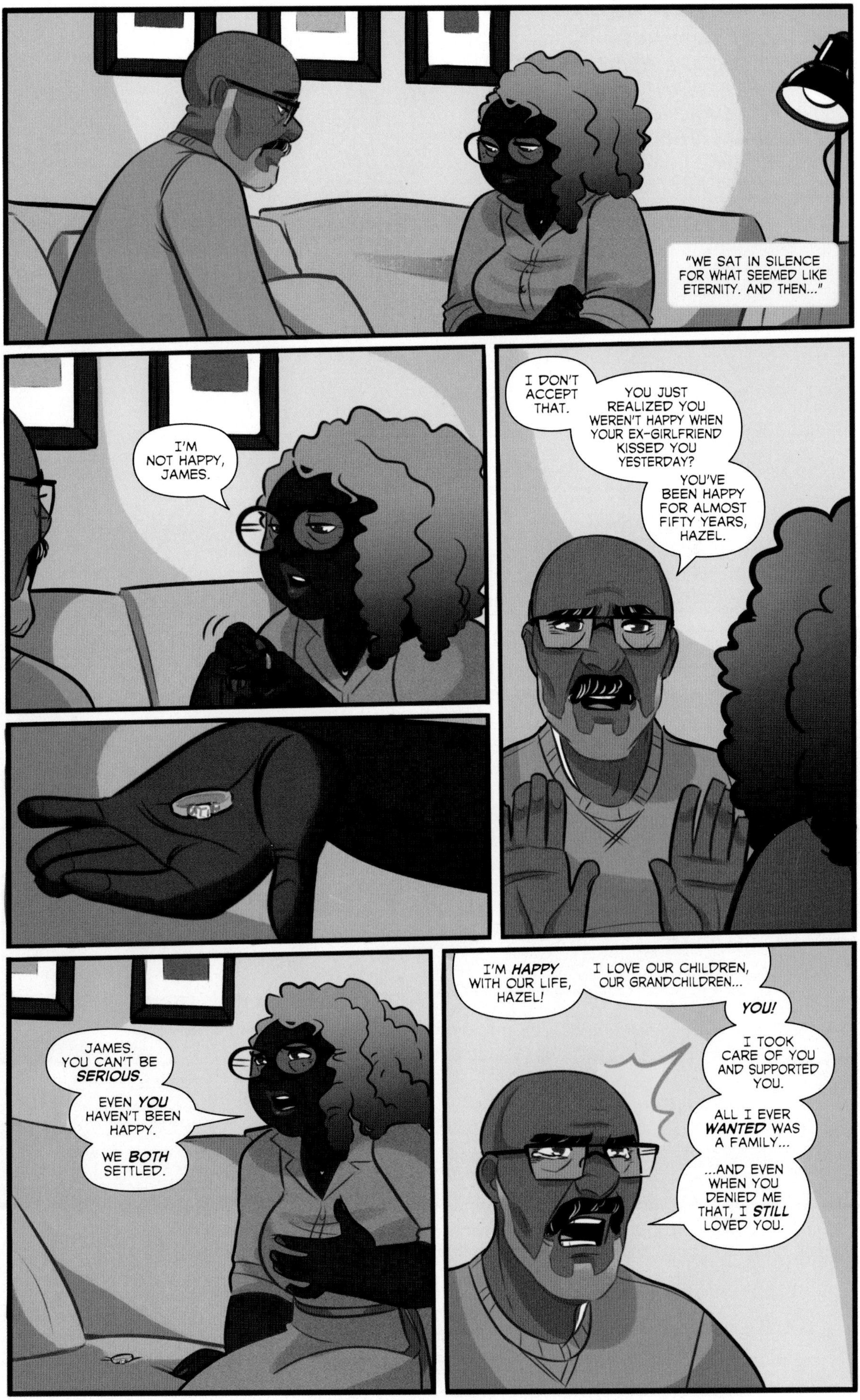
"WE SAT IN SILENCE FOR WHAT SEEMED LIKE ETERNITY. AND THEN..."
I'M NOT HAPPY, JAMES.
I DON'T ACCEPT THAT.
YOU JUST REALIZED YOU WEREN'T HAPPY WHEN YOUR EX-GIRLFRIEND KISSED YOU YESTERDAY?
YOU'VE BEEN HAPPY FOR ALMOST FIFTY YEARS, HAZEL.
JAMES. YOU CAN'T BE SERIOUS.
EVEN YOU HAVEN'T BEEN HAPPY.
WE BOTH SETTLED.
I'M HAPPY WITH OUR LIFE, HAZEL!
I LOVE OUR CHILDREN, OUR GRANDCHILDREN...
YOU!
I TOOK CARE OF YOU AND SUPPORTED YOU.
ALL I EVER WANTED WAS A FAMILY...
...AND EVEN WHEN YOU DENIED ME THAT, I STILL LOVED YOU.

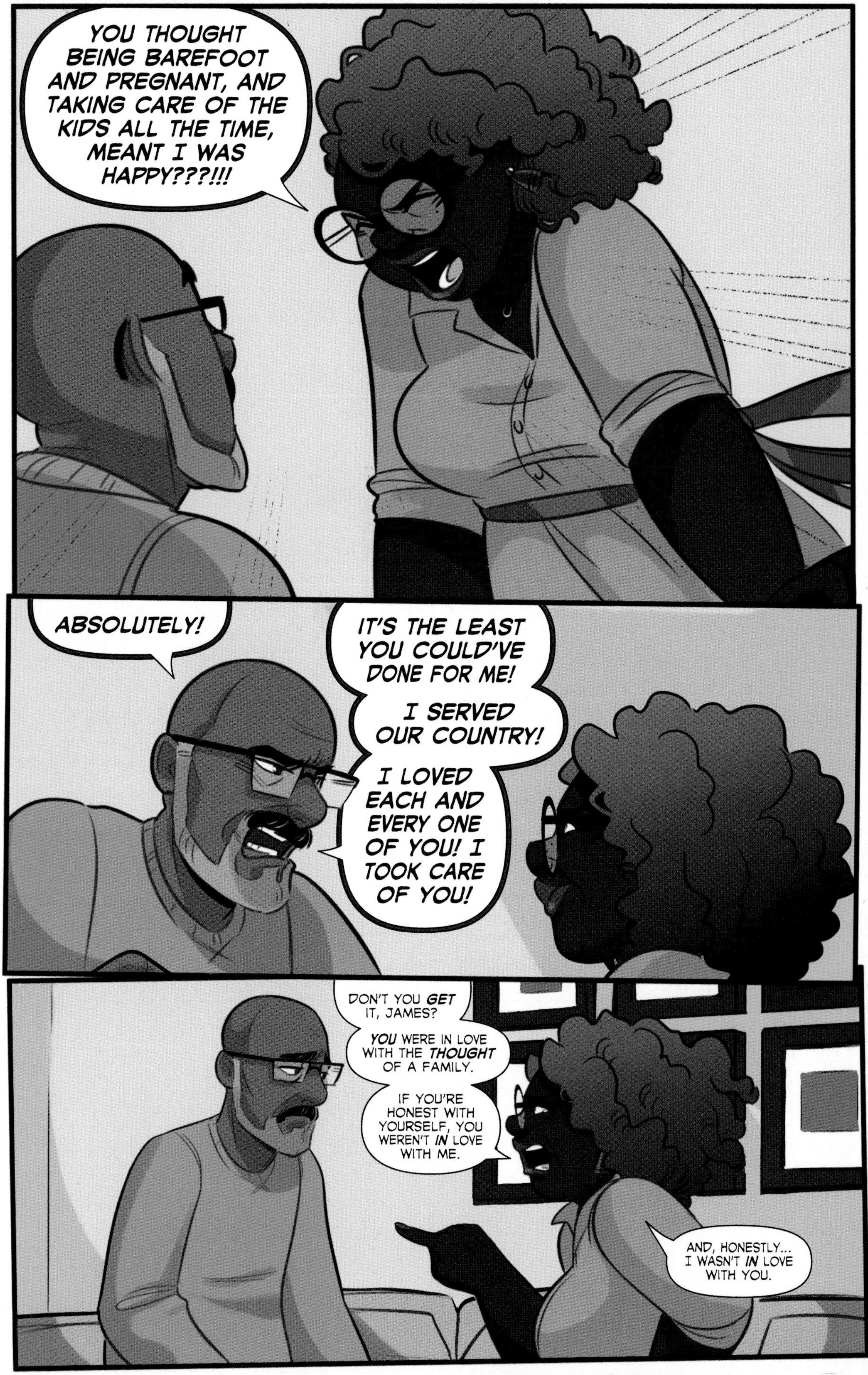
YOU THOUGHT BEING BAREFOOT AND PREGNANT, AND TAKING CARE OF THE KIDS ALL THE TIME, MEANT I WAS HAPPY???!!!
ABSOLUTELY!
IT'S THE LEAST YOU COULD'VE DONE FOR ME!
I SERVED OUR COUNTRY!
I LOVED EACH AND EVERY ONE OF YOU! I TOOK CARE OF YOU!
DON'T YOU GET IT, JAMES?
YOU WERE IN LOVE WITH THE THOUGHT OF A FAMILY.
IF YOU'RE HONEST WITH YOURSELF, YOU WEREN'T IN LOVE WITH ME.
AND, HONESTLY... I WASN'T IN LOVE WITH YOU.

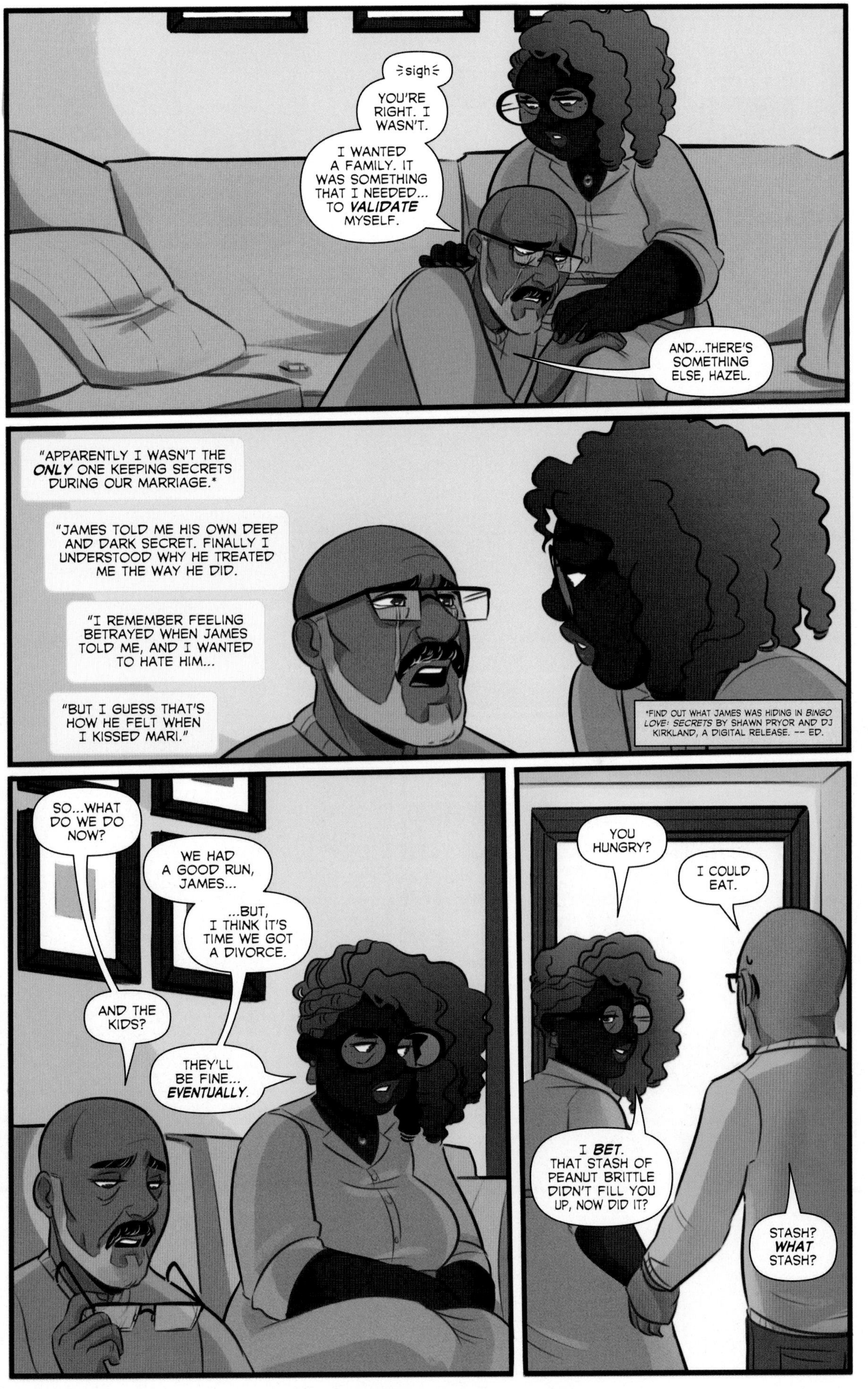
sigh
YOU'RE RIGHT. I WASN'T.
I WANTED A FAMILY. IT WAS SOMETHING THAT I NEEDED... TO VALIDATE MYSELF.
AND...THERE'S SOMETHING ELSE, HAZEL.
"APPARENTLY I WASN'T THE ONLY ONE KEEPING SECRETS DURING OUR MARRIAGE.*
"JAMES TOLD ME HIS OWN DEEP AND DARK SECRET. FINALLY I UNDERSTOOD WHY HE TREATED ME THE WAY HE DID.
"I REMEMBER FEELING BETRAYED WHEN JAMES TOLD ME, AND I WANTED TO HATE HIM...
"BUT I GUESS THAT'S HOW HE FELT WHEN I KISSED MARI."
*FIND OUT WHAT JAMES WAS HIDING IN BINGO LOVE: SECRETS BY SHAWN PRYOR AND DJ KIRKLAND, A DIGITAL RELEASE. -- ED.
SO...WHAT DO WE DO NOW?
WE HAD A GOOD RUN, JAMES...
...BUT, I THINK IT'S TIME WE GOT A DIVORCE.
AND THE KIDS?
THEY'LL BE FINE... EVENTUALLY.
YOU HUNGRY?
I COULD EAT.
I BET. THAT STASH OF PEANUT BRITTLE DIDN'T FILL YOU UP, NOW DID IT?
STASH? WHAT STASH?

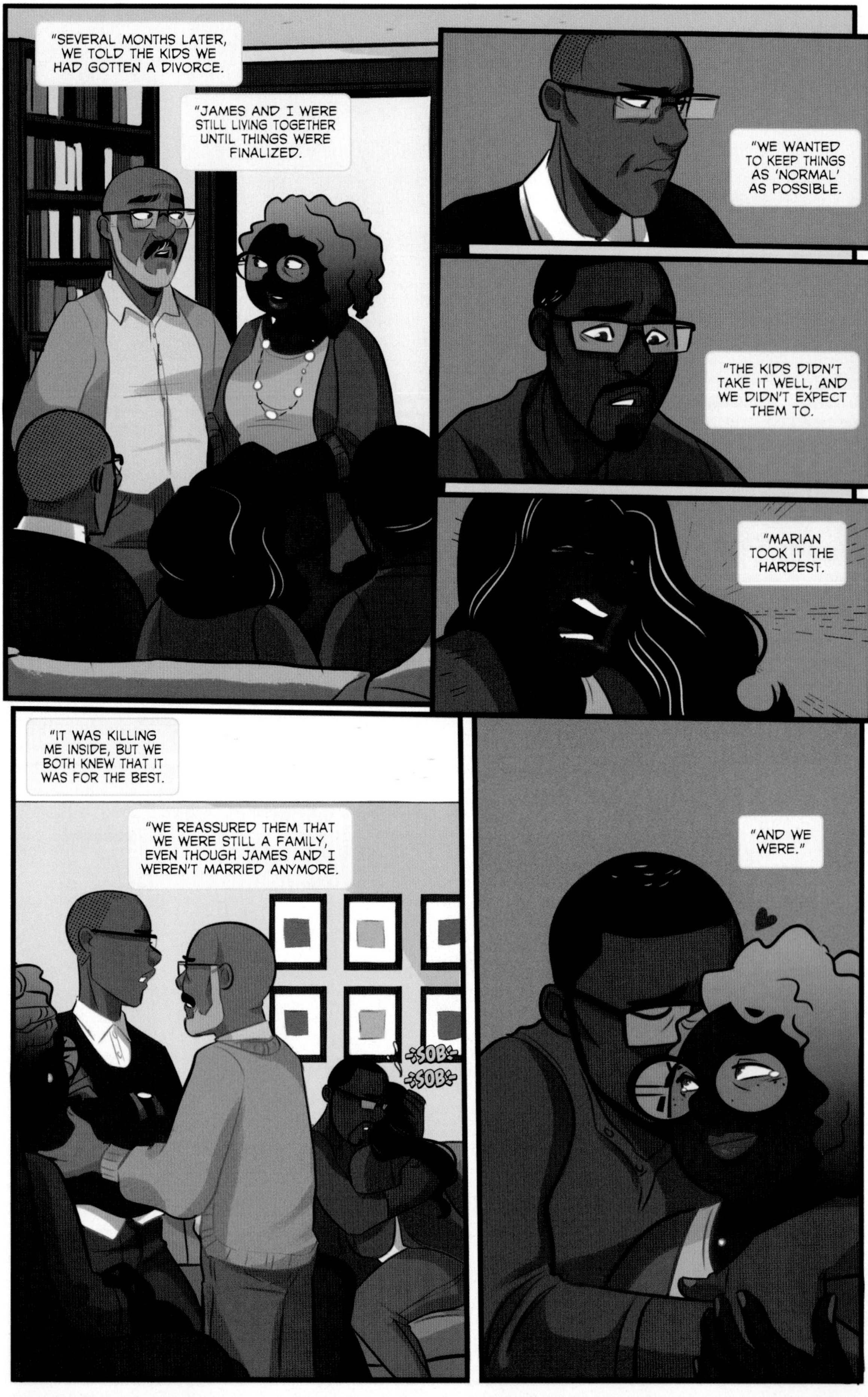
"SEVERAL MONTHS LATER, WE TOLD THE KIDS WE HAD GOTTEN A DIVORCE.
"JAMES AND I WERE STILL LIVING TOGETHER UNTIL THINGS WERE FINALIZED.
"WE WANTED TO KEEP THINGS AS 'NORMAL' AS POSSIBLE.
"THE KIDS DIDN'T TAKE IT WELL, AND WE DIDN'T EXPECT THEM TO.
"MARIAN TOOK IT THE HARDEST.
"IT WAS KILLING ME INSIDE, BUT WE BOTH KNEW THAT IT WAS FOR THE BEST.
"WE REASSURED THEM THAT WE WERE STILL A FAMILY, EVEN THOUGH JAMES AND I WEREN'T MARRIED ANYMORE.
SOB
SOB
"AND WE WERE."

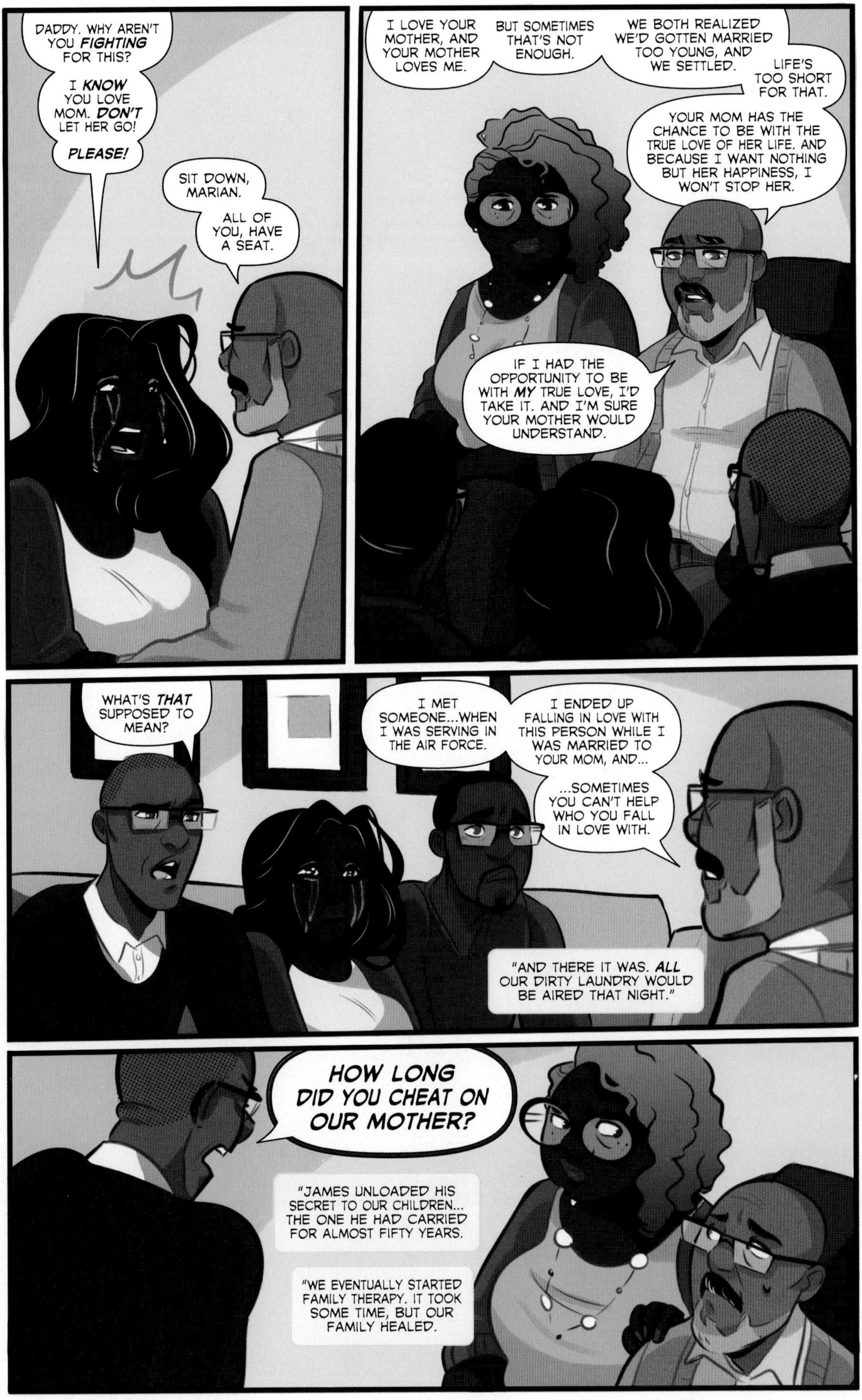
DADDY. WHY AREN'T YOU FIGHTING FOR THIS?
I KNOW YOU LOVE MOM. DON'T LET HER GO!
PLEASE!
SIT DOWN, MARIAN.
ALL OF YOU, HAVE A SEAT.
I LOVE YOUR MOTHER, AND YOUR MOTHER LOVES ME.
BUT SOMETIMES THAT'S NOT ENOUGH.
WE BOTH REALIZED WE'D GOTTEN MARRIED TOO YOUNG, AND WE SETTLED.
LIFE'S TOO SHORT FOR THAT.
YOUR MOM HAS THE CHANCE TO BE WITH THE TRUE LOVE OF HER LIFE. AND BECAUSE I WANT NOTHING BUT HER HAPPINESS, I WON'T STOP HER.
IF I HAD THE OPPORTUNITY TO BE WITH MY TRUE LOVE, I'D TAKE IT. AND I'M SURE YOUR MOTHER WOULD UNDERSTAND.
WHAT'S THAT SUPPOSED TO MEAN?
I MET SOMEONE...WHEN I WAS SERVING IN THE AIR FORCE.
I ENDED UP FALLING IN LOVE WITH THIS PERSON WHILE I WAS MARRIED TO YOUR MOM, AND...
...SOMETIMES YOU CAN'T HELP WHO YOU FALL IN LOVE WITH.
"AND THERE IT WAS. ALL OUR DIRTY LAUNDRY WOULD BE AIRED THAT NIGHT."
HOW LONG DID YOU CHEAT ON OUR MOTHER?
"JAMES UNLOADED HIS SECRET TO OUR CHILDREN... THE ONE HE HAD CARRIED FOR ALMOST FIFTY YEARS.
"WE EVENTUALLY STARTED FAMILY THERAPY. IT TOOK SOME TIME, BUT OUR FAMILY HEALED.

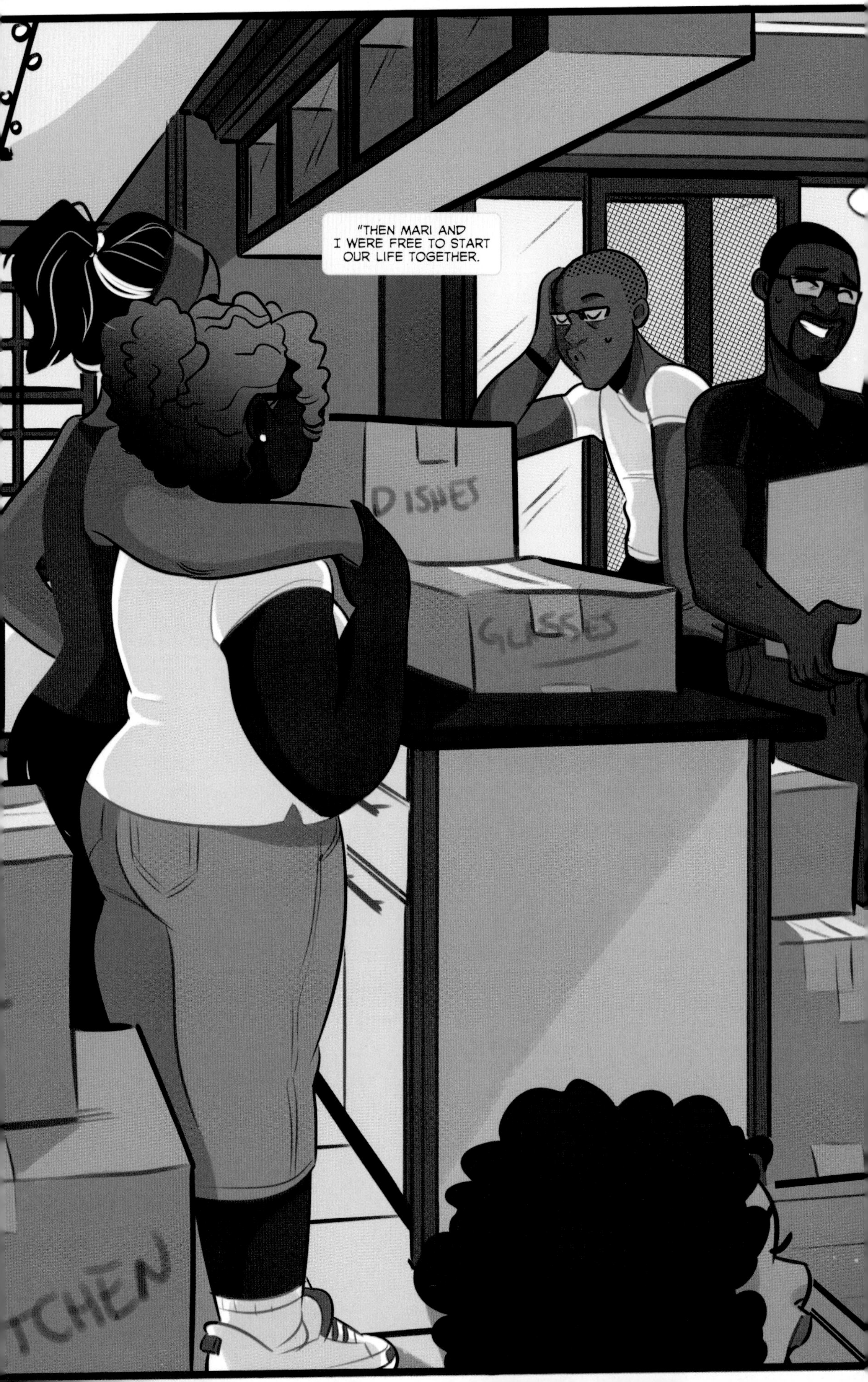
"THEN MARI AND I WERE FREE TO START OUR LIFE TOGETHER.
DISHES
GLASSES

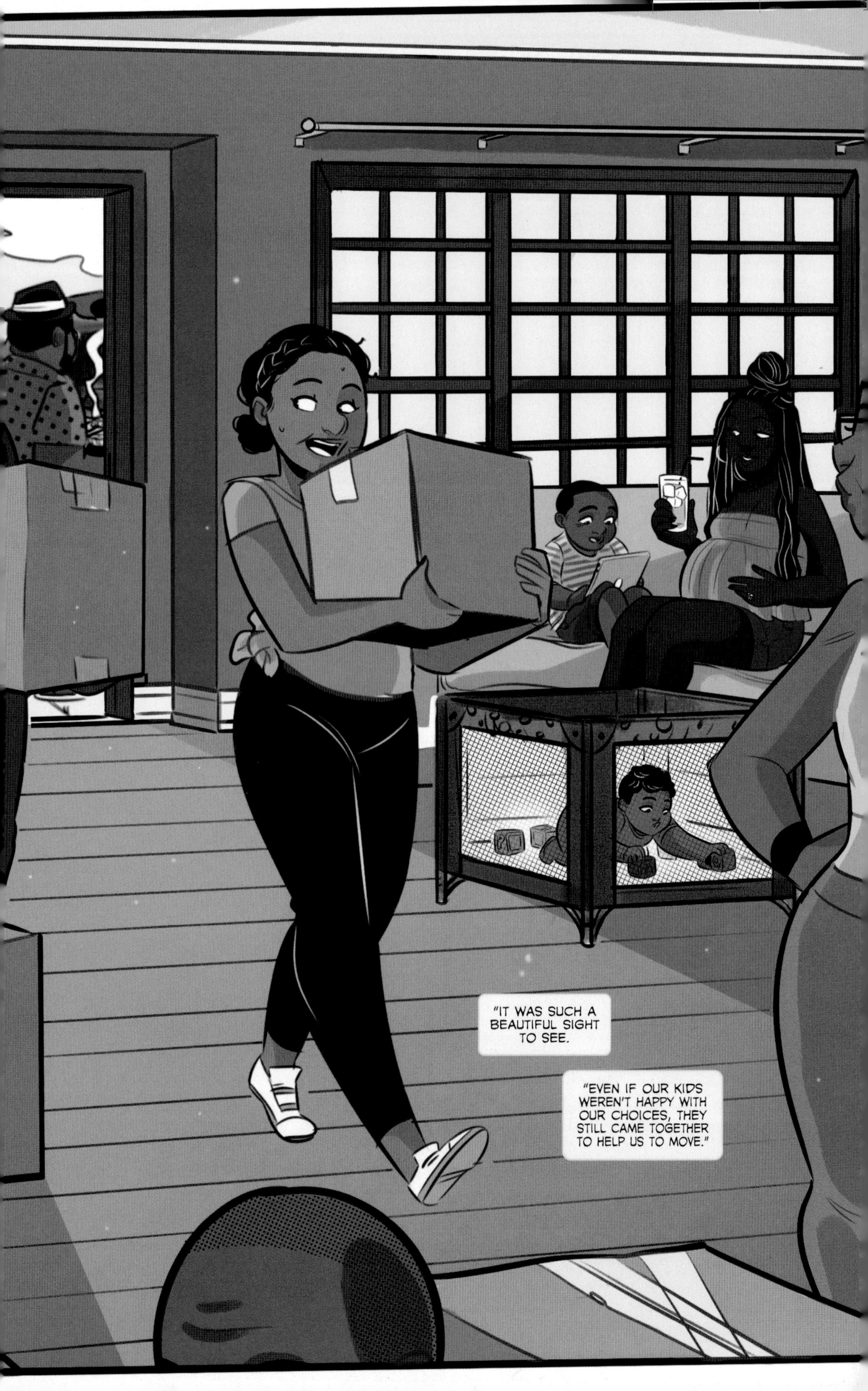
"IT WAS SUCH A BEAUTIFUL SIGHT TO SEE.
"EVEN IF OUR KIDS WEREN'T HAPPY WITH OUR CHOICES, THEY STILL CAME TOGETHER TO HELP US TO MOVE."

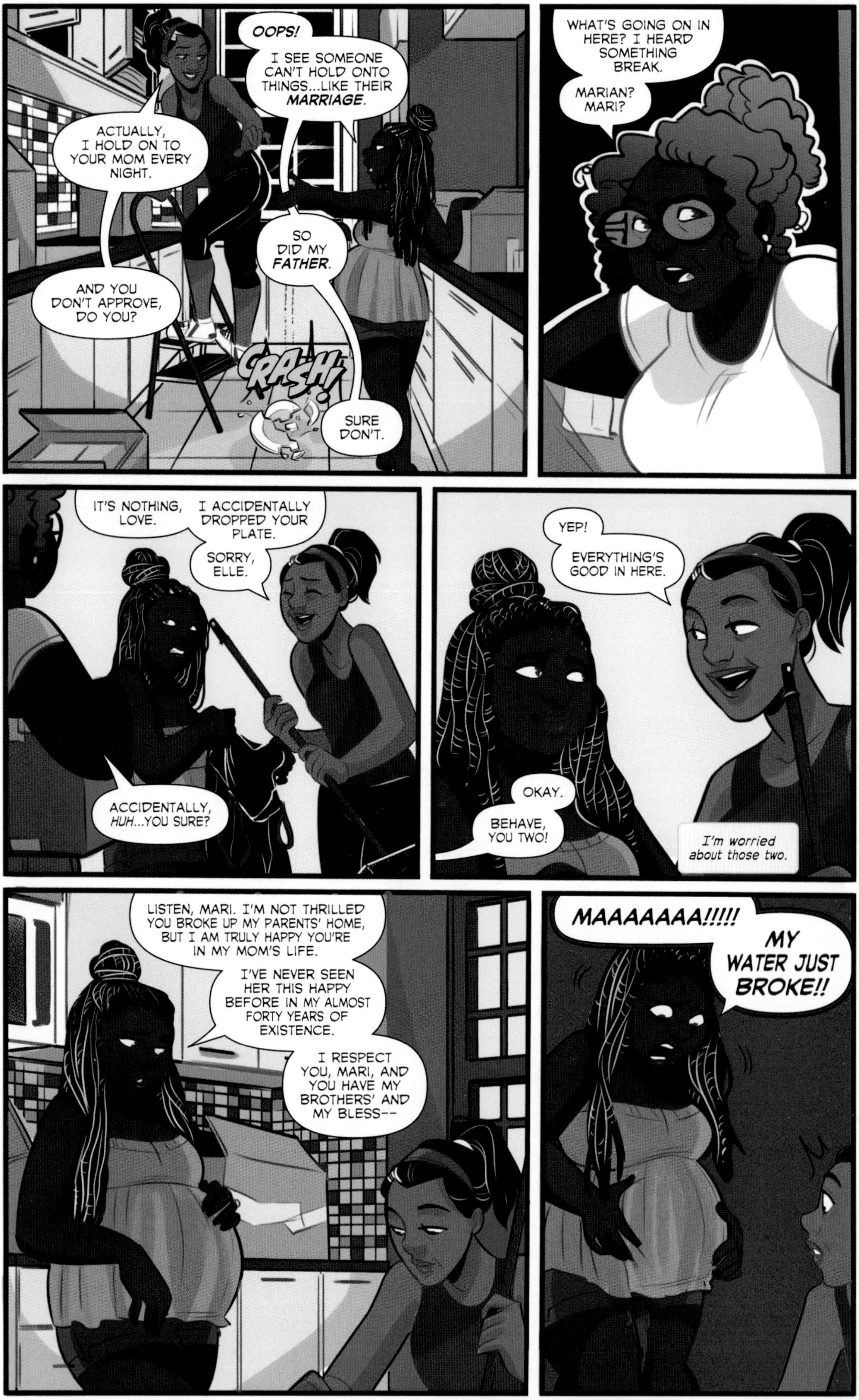
OOPS!
I SEE SOMEONE CAN'T HOLD ONTO THINGS...LIKE THEIR *MARRIAGE*.
ACTUALLY, I HOLD ON TO YOUR MOM EVERY NIGHT.
SO DID MY *FATHER*.
AND YOU DON'T APPROVE, DO YOU?
CRASH!
SURE DON'T.
WHAT'S GOING ON IN HERE? I HEARD SOMETHING BREAK.
MARIAN? MARI?
IT'S NOTHING, LOVE.
I ACCIDENTALLY DROPPED YOUR PLATE.
SORRY, ELLE.
ACCIDENTALLY, *HUH*...YOU SURE?
YEP!
EVERYTHING'S GOOD IN HERE.
OKAY.
BEHAVE, YOU TWO!
I'm worried about those two.
LISTEN, MARI. I'M NOT THRILLED YOU BROKE UP MY PARENTS' HOME, BUT I AM TRULY HAPPY YOU'RE IN MY MOM'S LIFE.
I'VE NEVER SEEN HER THIS HAPPY BEFORE IN MY ALMOST FORTY YEARS OF EXISTENCE.
I RESPECT YOU, MARI, AND YOU HAVE MY BROTHERS' AND MY BLESS--
MAAAAAAA!!!!!
MY WATER JUST BROKE!!

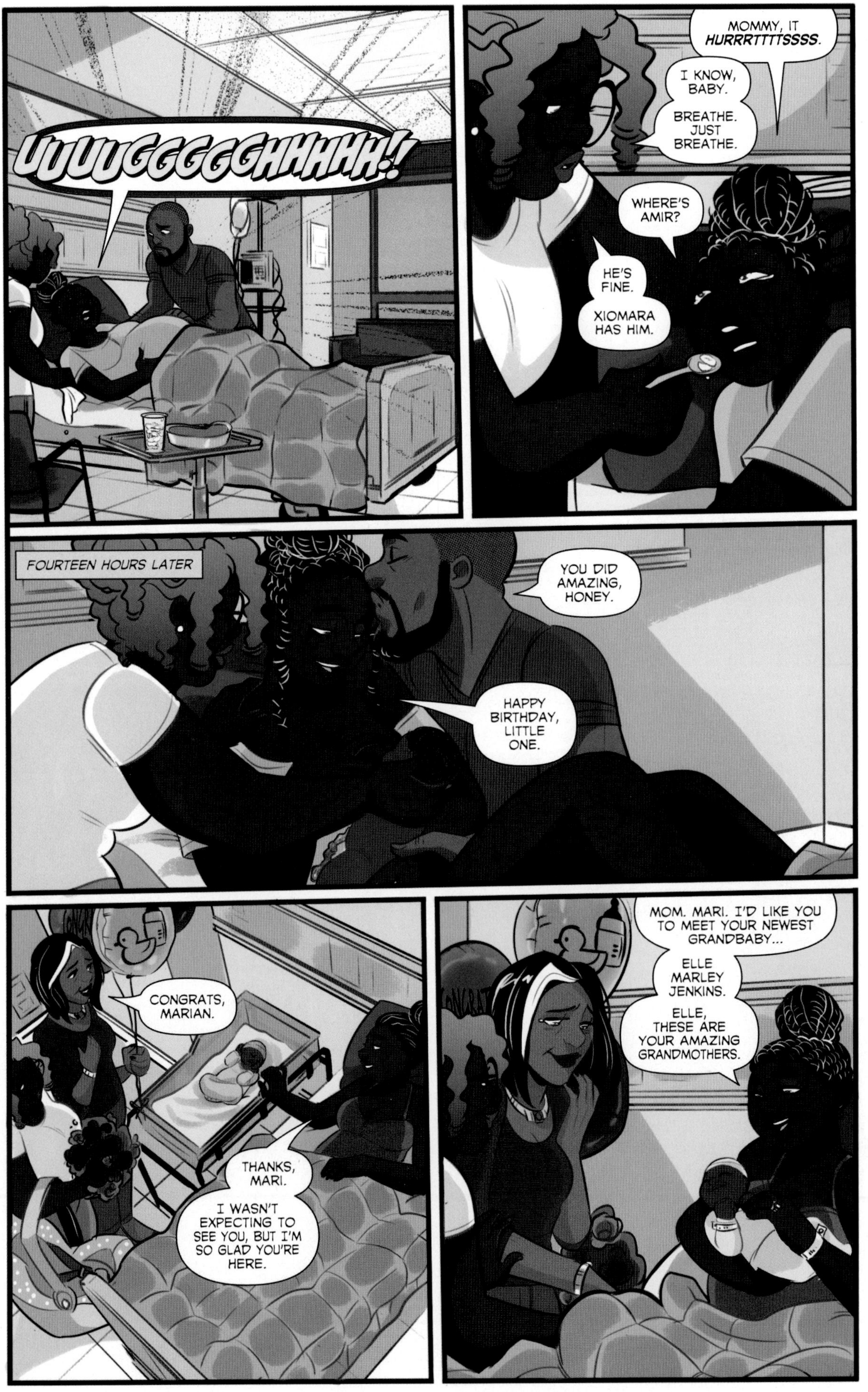
UUUUGGGGGHHHHH!
MOMMY, IT HURRRTTTTSSSS.
I KNOW, BABY.
BREATHE. JUST BREATHE.
WHERE'S AMIR?
HE'S FINE.
XIOMARA HAS HIM.
FOURTEEN HOURS LATER
YOU DID AMAZING, HONEY.
HAPPY BIRTHDAY, LITTLE ONE.
CONGRATS, MARIAN.
THANKS, MARI.
I WASN'T EXPECTING TO SEE YOU, BUT I'M SO GLAD YOU'RE HERE.
MOM. MARI. I'D LIKE YOU TO MEET YOUR NEWEST GRANDBABY...
ELLE MARLEY JENKINS.
ELLE, THESE ARE YOUR AMAZING GRANDMOTHERS.

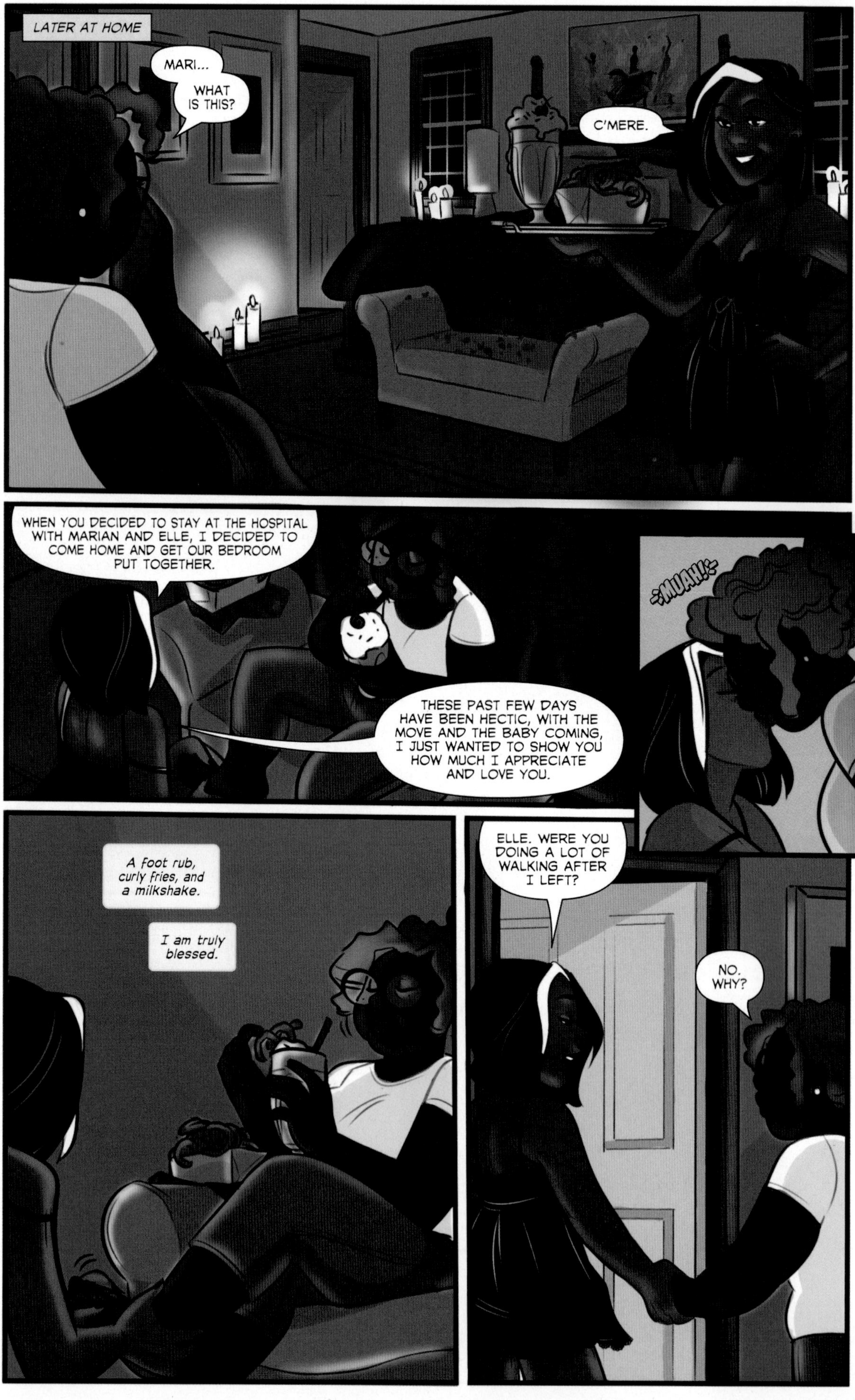
LATER AT HOME
MARI...
WHAT IS THIS?
C'MERE.
WHEN YOU DECIDED TO STAY AT THE HOSPITAL WITH MARIAN AND ELLE, I DECIDED TO COME HOME AND GET OUR BEDROOM PUT TOGETHER.
THESE PAST FEW DAYS HAVE BEEN HECTIC, WITH THE MOVE AND THE BABY COMING, I JUST WANTED TO SHOW YOU HOW MUCH I APPRECIATE AND LOVE YOU.
MUAH!
A foot rub, curly fries, and a milkshake.
I am truly blessed.
ELLE. WERE YOU DOING A LOT OF WALKING AFTER I LEFT?
NO. WHY?

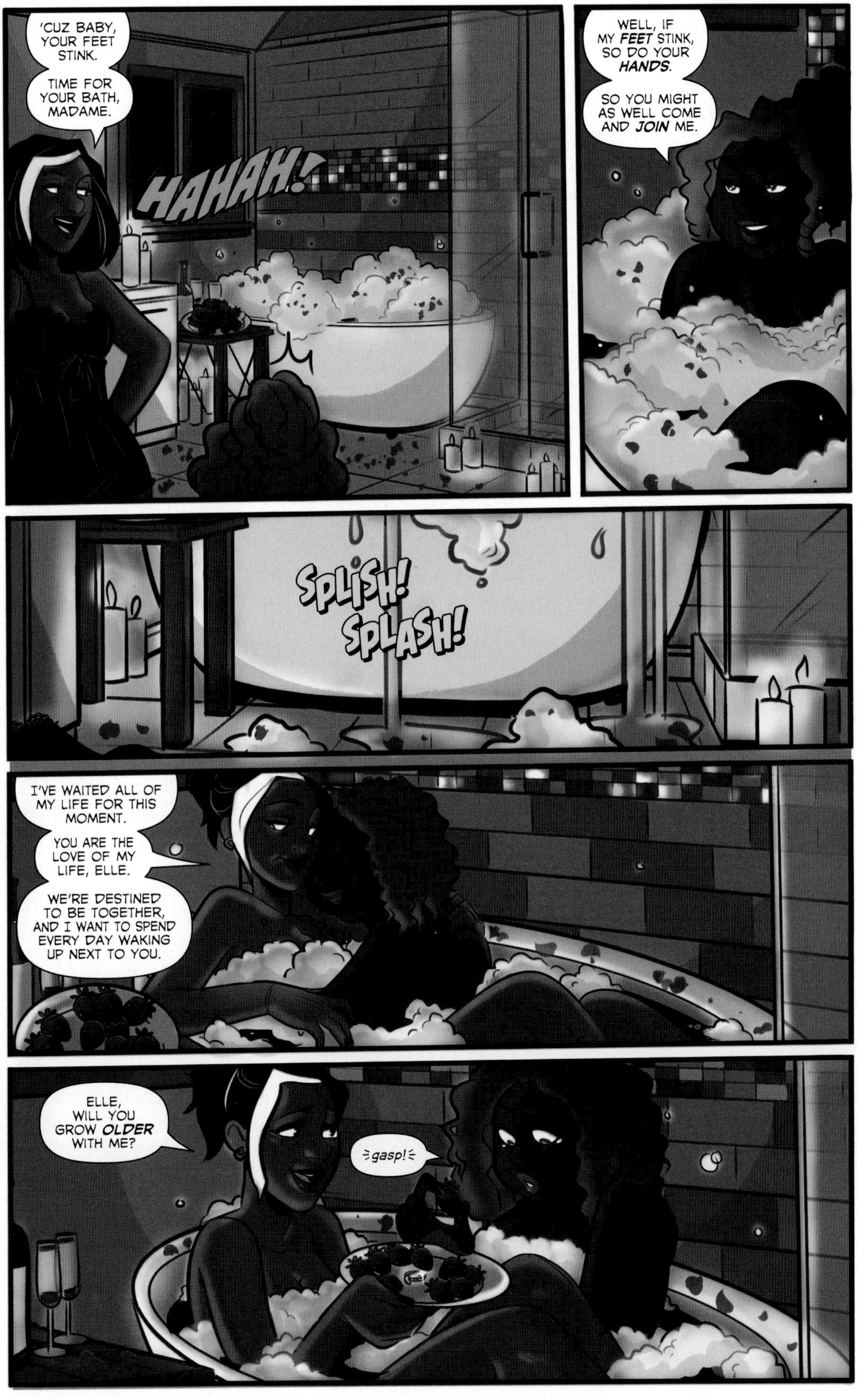
'CUZ BABY, YOUR FEET STINK.
TIME FOR YOUR BATH, MADAME.
HAHAH!
WELL, IF MY FEET STINK, SO DO YOUR HANDS.
SO YOU MIGHT AS WELL COME AND JOIN ME.
SPLISH! SPLASH!
I'VE WAITED ALL OF MY LIFE FOR THIS MOMENT.
YOU ARE THE LOVE OF MY LIFE, ELLE.
WE'RE DESTINED TO BE TOGETHER, AND I WANT TO SPEND EVERY DAY WAKING UP NEXT TO YOU.
ELLE, WILL YOU GROW OLDER WITH ME?
gasp!

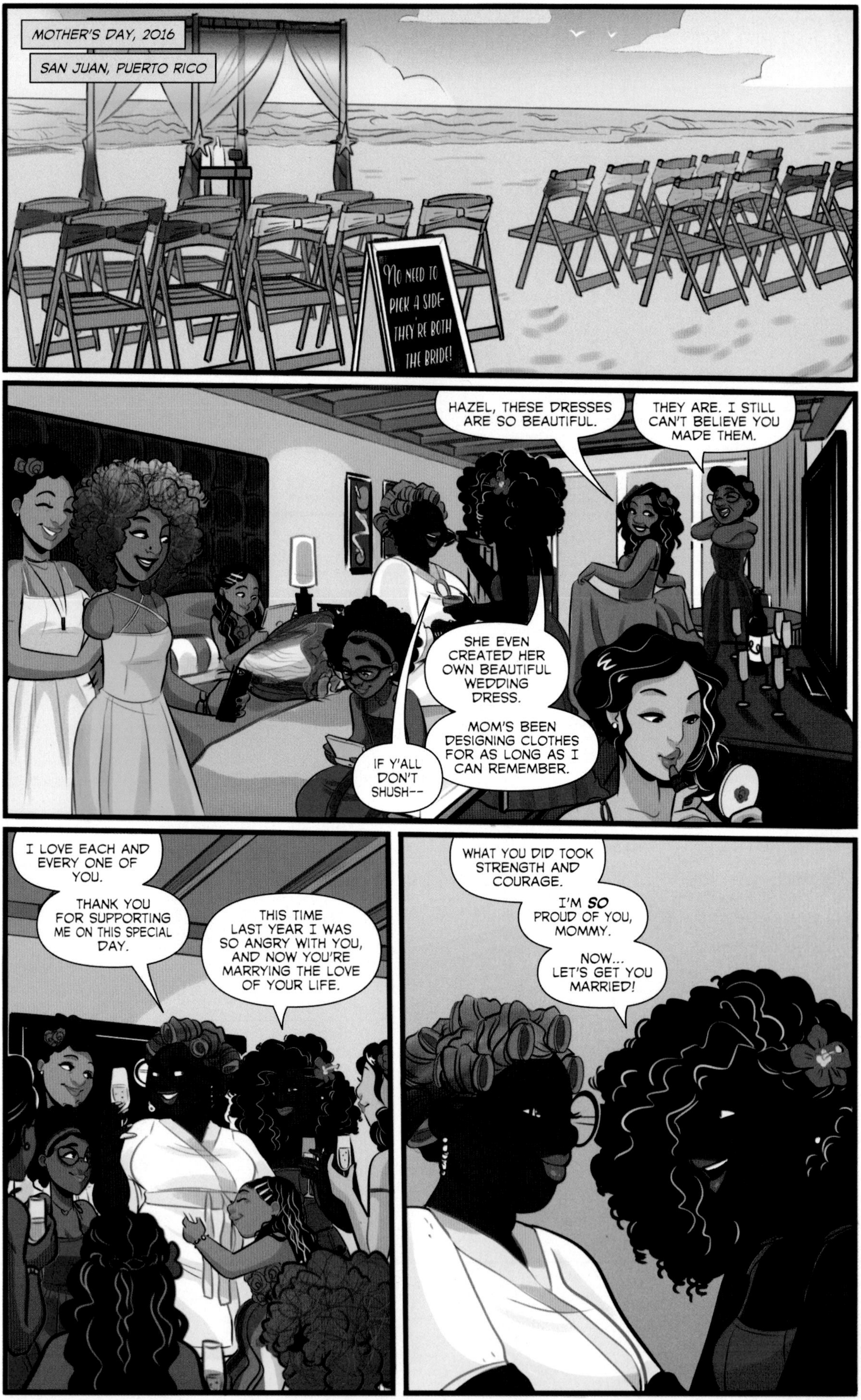
MOTHER'S DAY, 2016
SAN JUAN, PUERTO RICO
No need to pick a side- they're both the bride!
HAZEL, THESE DRESSES ARE SO BEAUTIFUL.
THEY ARE. I STILL CAN'T BELIEVE YOU MADE THEM.
SHE EVEN CREATED HER OWN BEAUTIFUL WEDDING DRESS.
MOM'S BEEN DESIGNING CLOTHES FOR AS LONG AS I CAN REMEMBER.
IF Y'ALL DON'T SHUSH--
I LOVE EACH AND EVERY ONE OF YOU.
THANK YOU FOR SUPPORTING ME ON THIS SPECIAL DAY.
THIS TIME LAST YEAR I WAS SO ANGRY WITH YOU, AND NOW YOU'RE MARRYING THE LOVE OF YOUR LIFE.
WHAT YOU DID TOOK STRENGTH AND COURAGE.
I'M SO PROUD OF YOU, MOMMY.
NOW... LET'S GET YOU MARRIED!

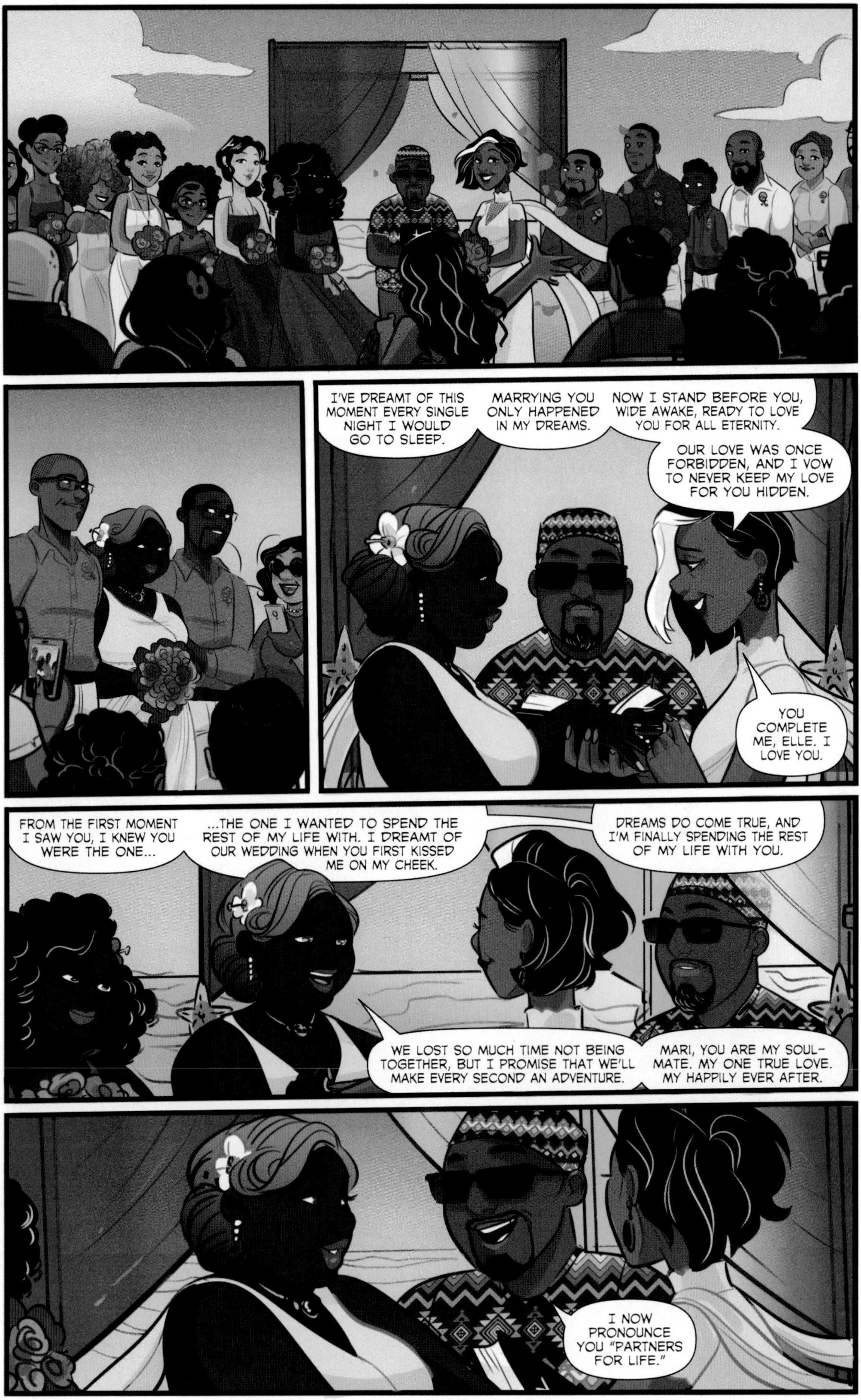
I'VE DREAMT OF THIS MOMENT EVERY SINGLE NIGHT I WOULD GO TO SLEEP.
MARRYING YOU ONLY HAPPENED IN MY DREAMS.
NOW I STAND BEFORE YOU, WIDE AWAKE, READY TO LOVE YOU FOR ALL ETERNITY.
OUR LOVE WAS ONCE FORBIDDEN, AND I VOW TO NEVER KEEP MY LOVE FOR YOU HIDDEN.
YOU COMPLETE ME, ELLE. I LOVE YOU.
FROM THE FIRST MOMENT I SAW YOU, I KNEW YOU WERE THE ONE...
...THE ONE I WANTED TO SPEND THE REST OF MY LIFE WITH. I DREAMT OF OUR WEDDING WHEN YOU FIRST KISSED ME ON MY CHEEK.
DREAMS DO COME TRUE, AND I'M FINALLY SPENDING THE REST OF MY LIFE WITH YOU.
WE LOST SO MUCH TIME NOT BEING TOGETHER, BUT I PROMISE THAT WE'LL MAKE EVERY SECOND AN ADVENTURE.
MARI, YOU ARE MY SOUL-MATE. MY ONE TRUE LOVE. MY HAPPILY EVER AFTER.
I NOW PRONOUNCE YOU "PARTNERS FOR LIFE."

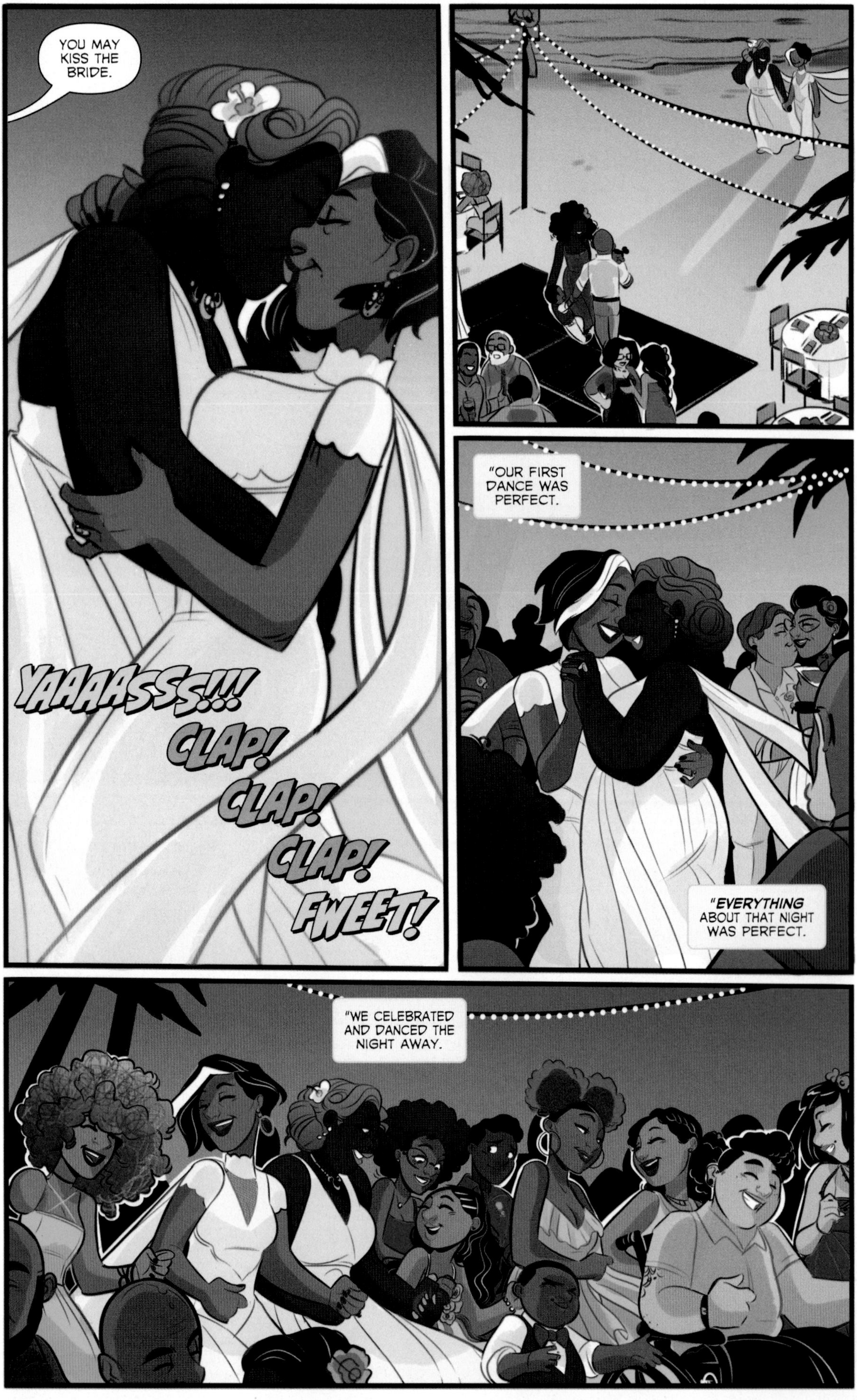
YOU MAY KISS THE BRIDE.
YAAAASSSS!!!
CLAP!
CLAP!
CLAP!
FWEET!
"OUR FIRST DANCE WAS PERFECT.
"EVERYTHING ABOUT THAT NIGHT WAS PERFECT.
"WE CELEBRATED AND DANCED THE NIGHT AWAY.

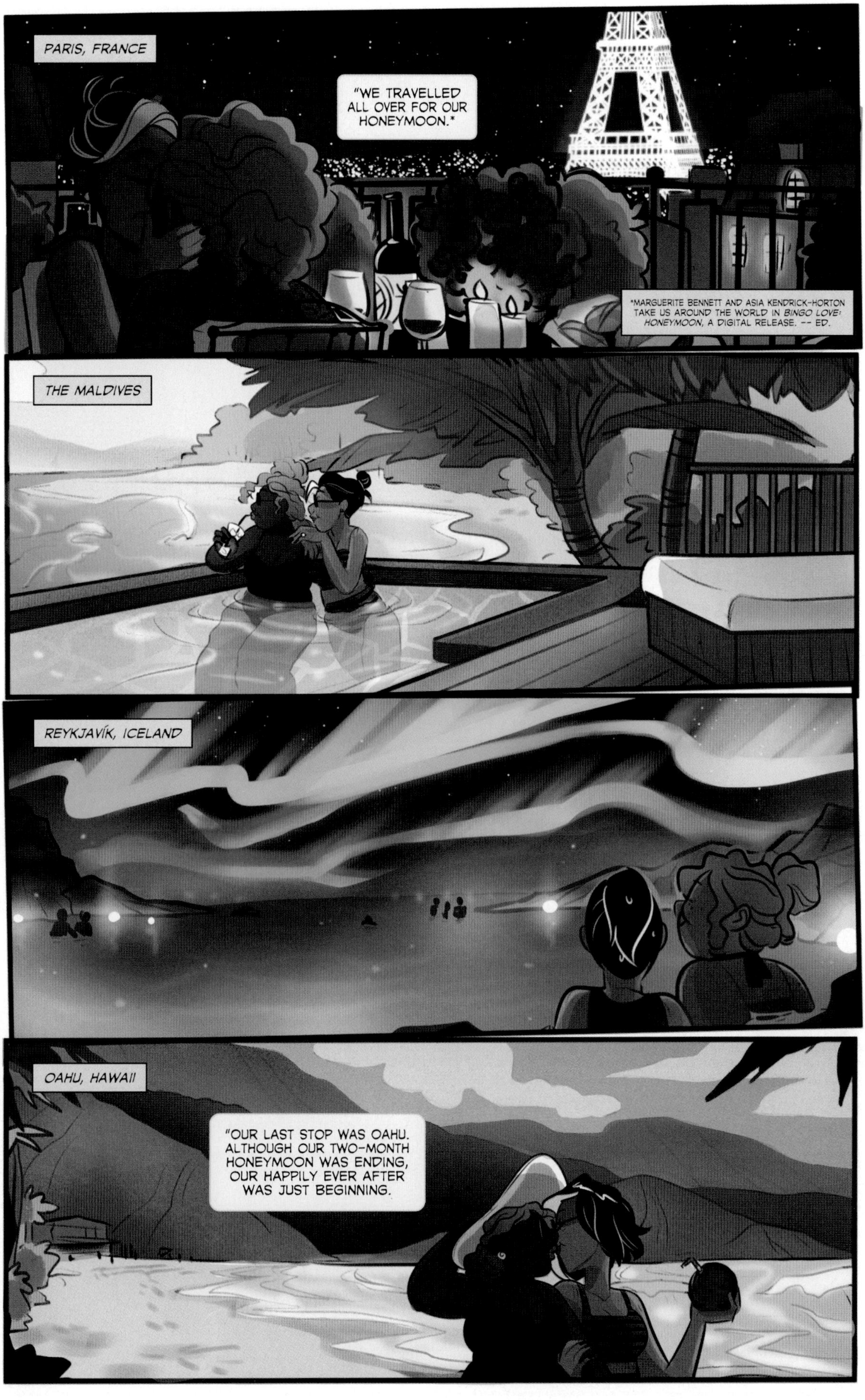
PARIS, FRANCE
"WE TRAVELLED ALL OVER FOR OUR HONEYMOON.*
*MARGUERITE BENNETT AND ASIA KENDRICK-HORTON TAKE US AROUND THE WORLD IN BINGO LOVE: HONEYMOON, A DIGITAL RELEASE. -- ED.
THE MALDIVES
REYKJAVÍK, ICELAND
OAHU, HAWAII
"OUR LAST STOP WAS OAHU. ALTHOUGH OUR TWO-MONTH HONEYMOON WAS ENDING, OUR HAPPILY EVER AFTER WAS JUST BEGINNING.

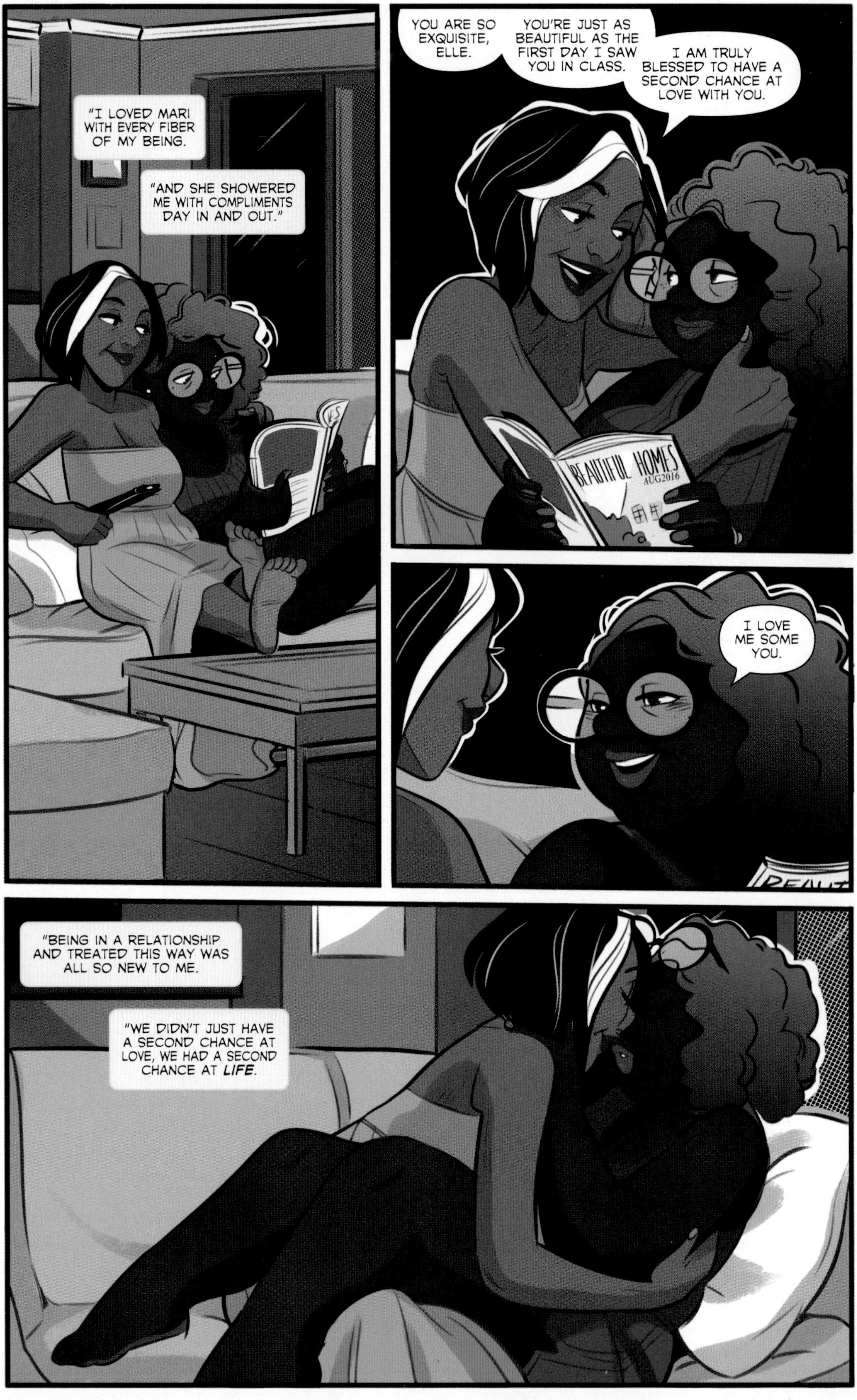
"I LOVED MARI WITH EVERY FIBER OF MY BEING.
"AND SHE SHOWERED ME WITH COMPLIMENTS DAY IN AND OUT."
YOU ARE SO EXQUISITE, ELLE.
YOU'RE JUST AS BEAUTIFUL AS THE FIRST DAY I SAW YOU IN CLASS.
I AM TRULY BLESSED TO HAVE A SECOND CHANCE AT LOVE WITH YOU.
BEAUTIFUL HOMES AUG2016
I LOVE ME SOME YOU.
"BEING IN A RELATIONSHIP AND TREATED THIS WAY WAS ALL SO NEW TO ME.
"WE DIDN'T JUST HAVE A SECOND CHANCE AT LOVE, WE HAD A SECOND CHANCE AT *LIFE*.

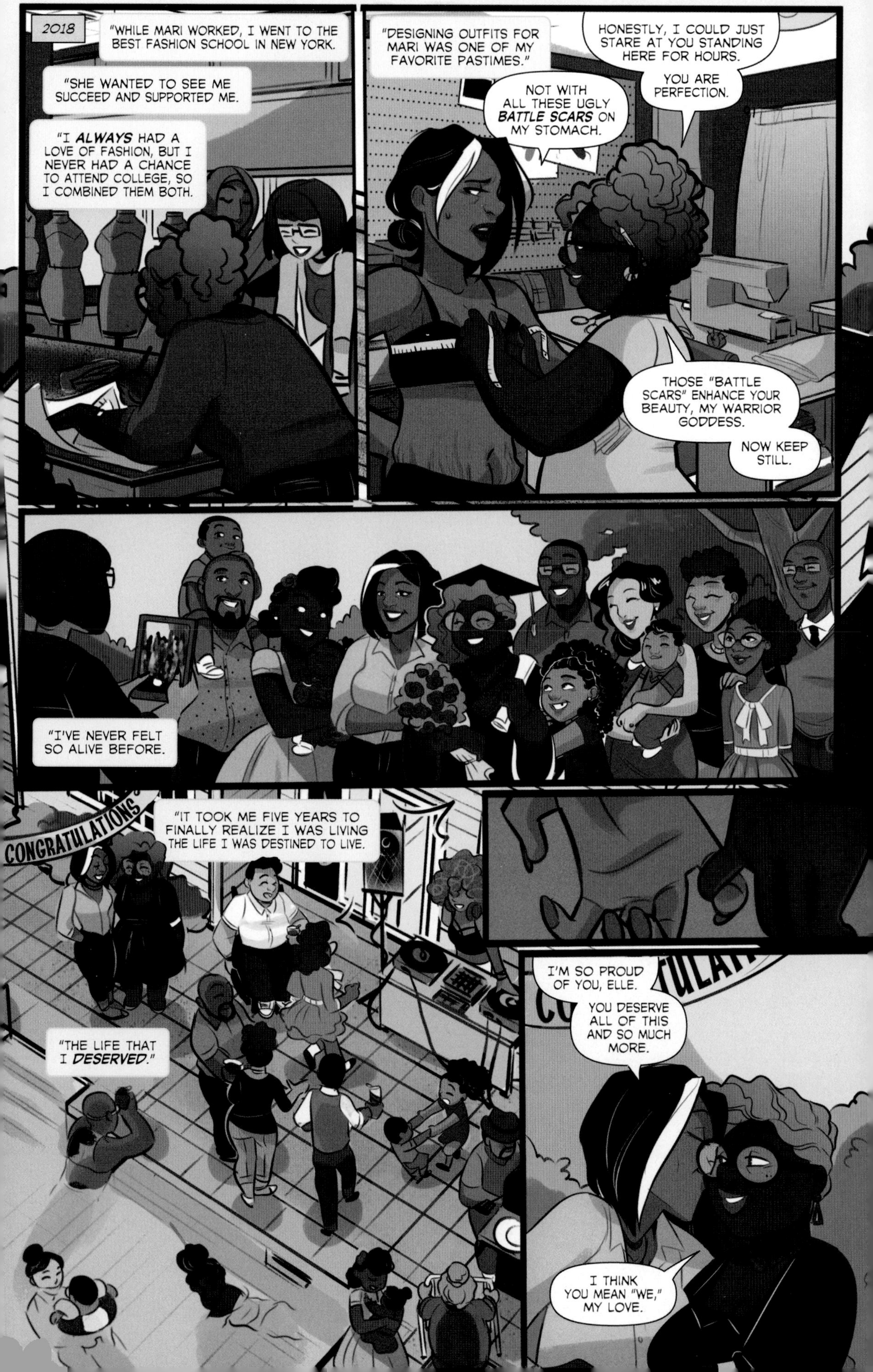
2018
"WHILE MARI WORKED, I WENT TO THE BEST FASHION SCHOOL IN NEW YORK.
"SHE WANTED TO SEE ME SUCCEED AND SUPPORTED ME.
"I **ALWAYS** HAD A LOVE OF FASHION, BUT I NEVER HAD A CHANCE TO ATTEND COLLEGE, SO I COMBINED THEM BOTH.
"DESIGNING OUTFITS FOR MARI WAS ONE OF MY FAVORITE PASTIMES."
HONESTLY, I COULD JUST STARE AT YOU STANDING HERE FOR HOURS.
YOU ARE PERFECTION.
NOT WITH ALL THESE UGLY ***BATTLE SCARS*** ON MY STOMACH.
THOSE "BATTLE SCARS" ENHANCE YOUR BEAUTY, MY WARRIOR GODDESS.
NOW KEEP STILL.
"I'VE NEVER FELT SO ALIVE BEFORE.
CONGRATULATIONS
"IT TOOK ME FIVE YEARS TO FINALLY REALIZE I WAS LIVING THE LIFE I WAS DESTINED TO LIVE.
"THE LIFE THAT I ***DESERVED***."
I'M SO PROUD OF YOU, ELLE.
YOU DESERVE ALL OF THIS AND SO MUCH MORE.
I THINK YOU MEAN "WE," MY LOVE.

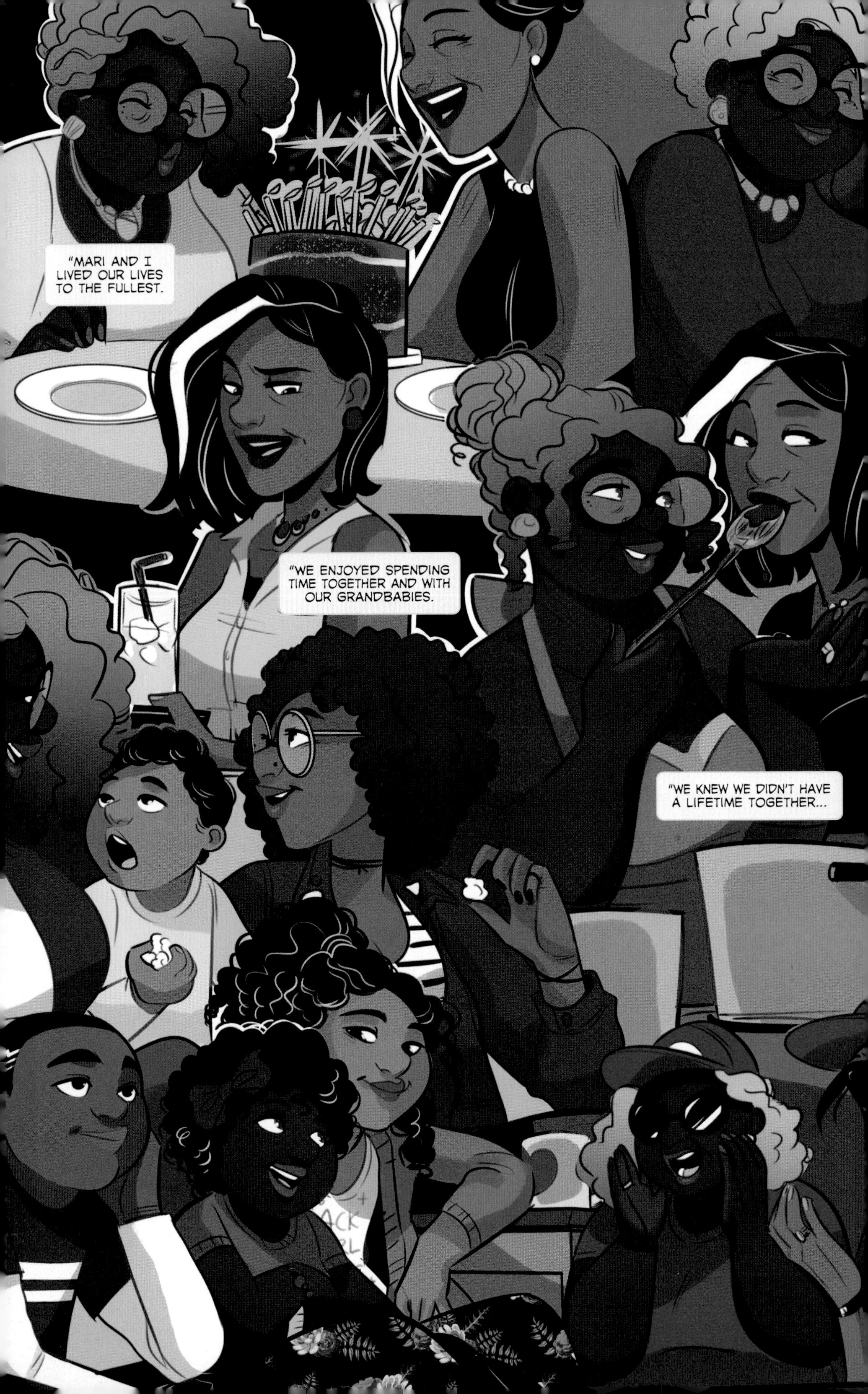
"MARI AND I LIVED OUR LIVES TO THE FULLEST.
"WE ENJOYED SPENDING TIME TOGETHER AND WITH OUR GRANDBABIES.
"WE KNEW WE DIDN'T HAVE A LIFETIME TOGETHER...

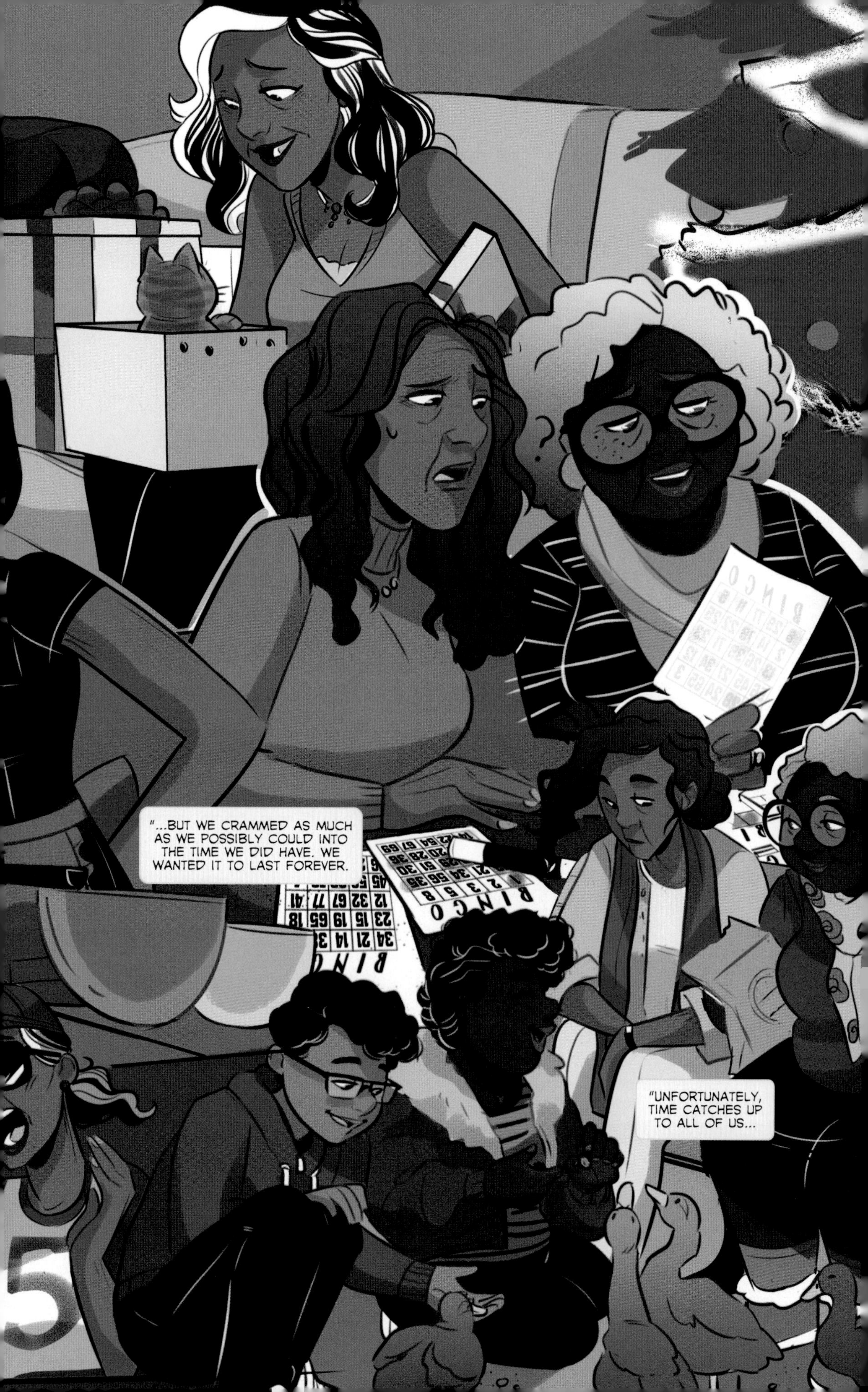
"...BUT WE CRAMMED AS MUCH AS WE POSSIBLY COULD INTO THE TIME WE DID HAVE. WE WANTED IT TO LAST FOREVER.
BINGO
"UNFORTUNATELY, TIME CATCHES UP TO ALL OF US...

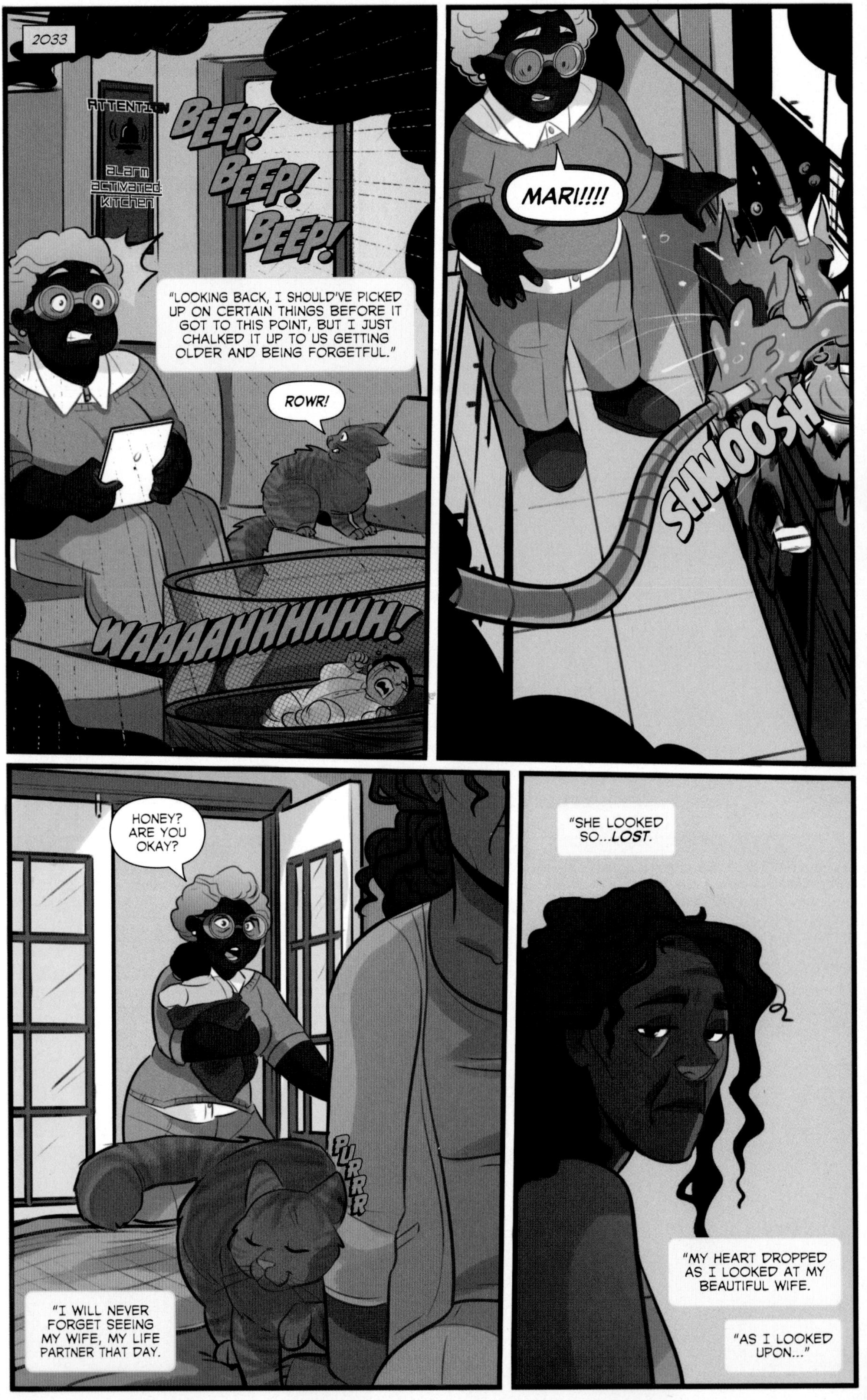
2033
alarm activated: kitchen
BEEP! BEEP! BEEP!
"LOOKING BACK, I SHOULD'VE PICKED UP ON CERTAIN THINGS BEFORE IT GOT TO THIS POINT, BUT I JUST CHALKED IT UP TO US GETTING OLDER AND BEING FORGETFUL."
ROWR!
WAAAAHHHHHH!
MARI!!!!
SHWOOSH
HONEY? ARE YOU OKAY?
PURRR
"I WILL NEVER FORGET SEEING MY WIFE, MY LIFE PARTNER THAT DAY.
"SHE LOOKED SO...*LOST*.
"MY HEART DROPPED AS I LOOKED AT MY BEAUTIFUL WIFE.
"AS I LOOKED UPON..."

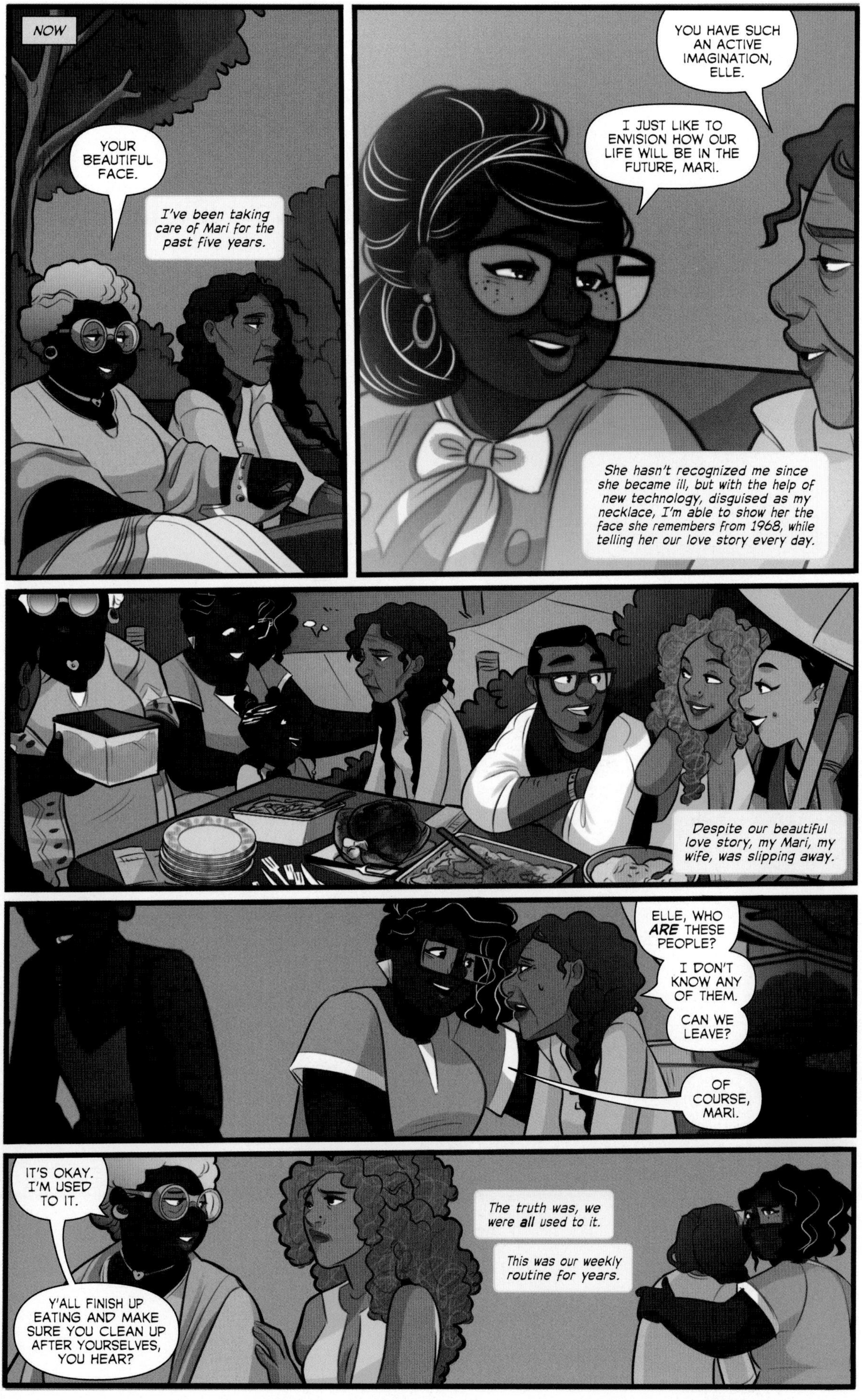
NOW
YOUR BEAUTIFUL FACE.
I've been taking care of Mari for the past five years.
YOU HAVE SUCH AN ACTIVE IMAGINATION, ELLE.
I JUST LIKE TO ENVISION HOW OUR LIFE WILL BE IN THE FUTURE, MARI.
She hasn't recognized me since she became ill, but with the help of new technology, disguised as my necklace, I'm able to show her the face she remembers from 1968, while telling her our love story every day.
Despite our beautiful love story, my Mari, my wife, was slipping away.
ELLE, WHO ***ARE*** THESE PEOPLE?
I DON'T KNOW ANY OF THEM.
CAN WE LEAVE?
OF COURSE, MARI.
IT'S OKAY. I'M USED TO IT.
Y'ALL FINISH UP EATING AND MAKE SURE YOU CLEAN UP AFTER YOURSELVES, YOU HEAR?
The truth was, we were **all** used to it.
This was our weekly routine for years.

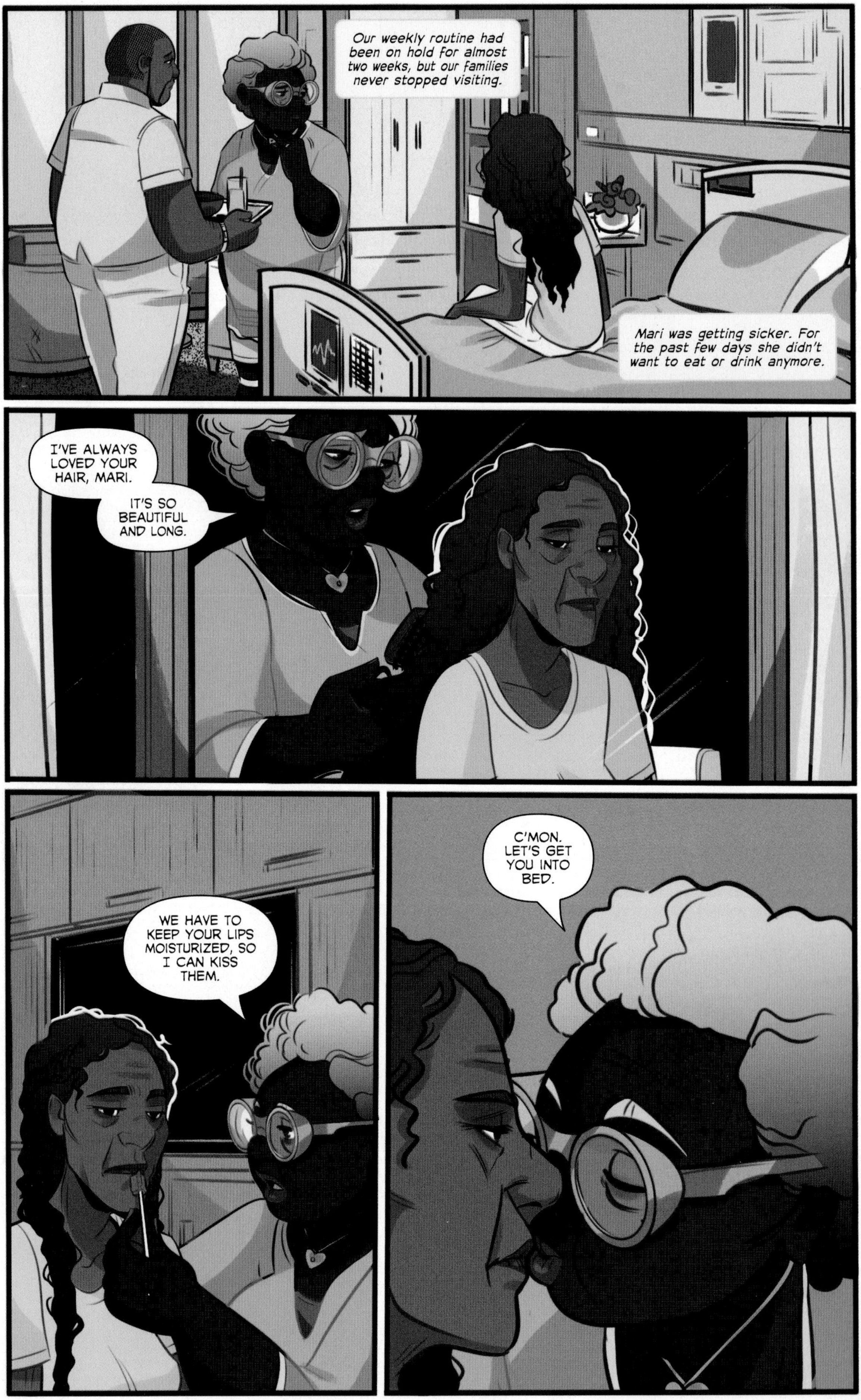
Our weekly routine had been on hold for almost two weeks, but our families never stopped visiting.
Mari was getting sicker. For the past few days she didn't want to eat or drink anymore.
I'VE ALWAYS LOVED YOUR HAIR, MARI.
IT'S SO BEAUTIFUL AND LONG.
WE HAVE TO KEEP YOUR LIPS MOISTURIZED, SO I CAN KISS THEM.
C'MON. LET'S GET YOU INTO BED.

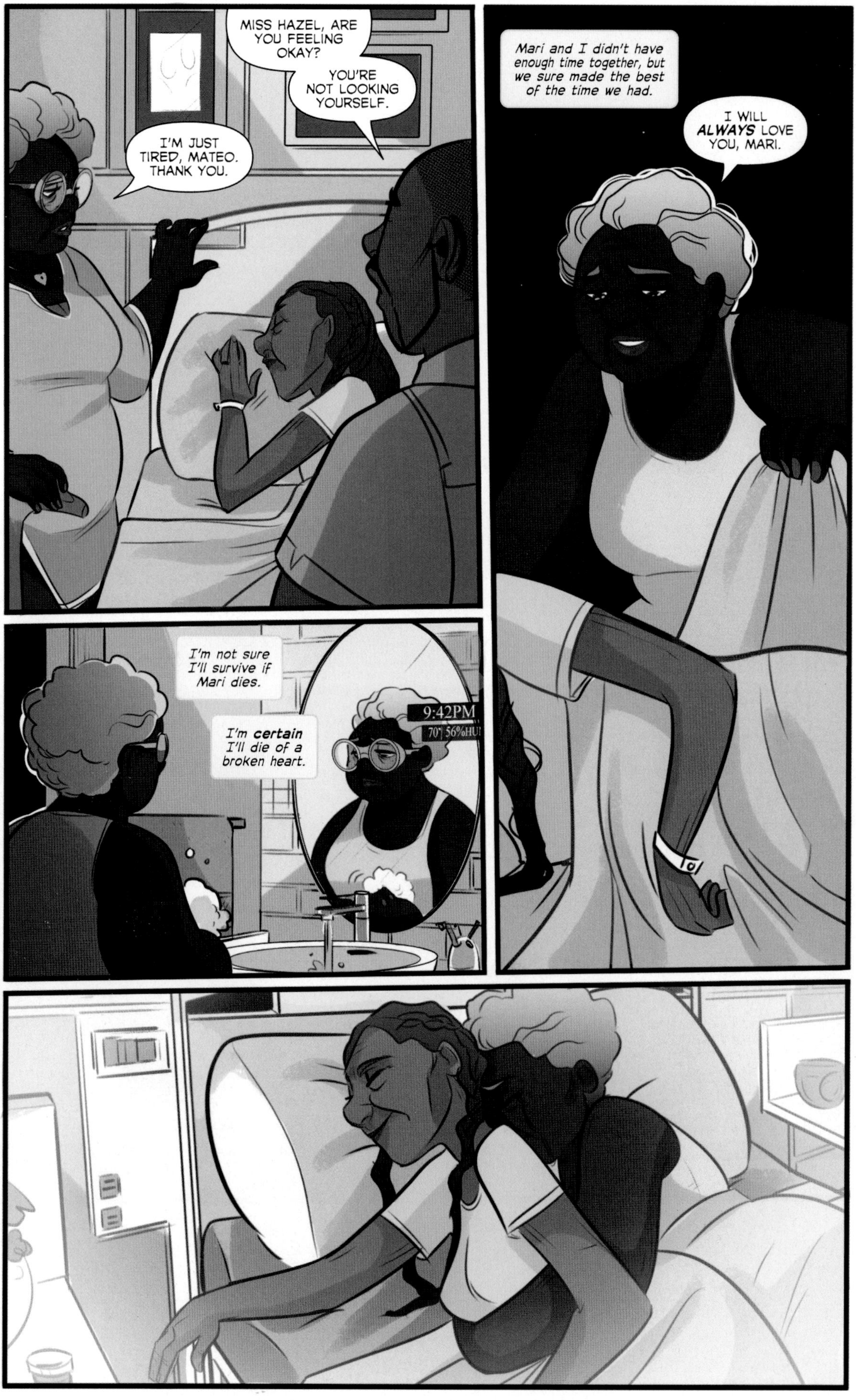
MISS HAZEL, ARE YOU FEELING OKAY?
YOU'RE NOT LOOKING YOURSELF.
I'M JUST TIRED, MATEO. THANK YOU.
Mari and I didn't have enough time together, but we sure made the best of the time we had.
I WILL **ALWAYS** LOVE YOU, MARI.
I'm not sure I'll survive if Mari dies.
I'm **certain** I'll die of a broken heart.
9:42PM

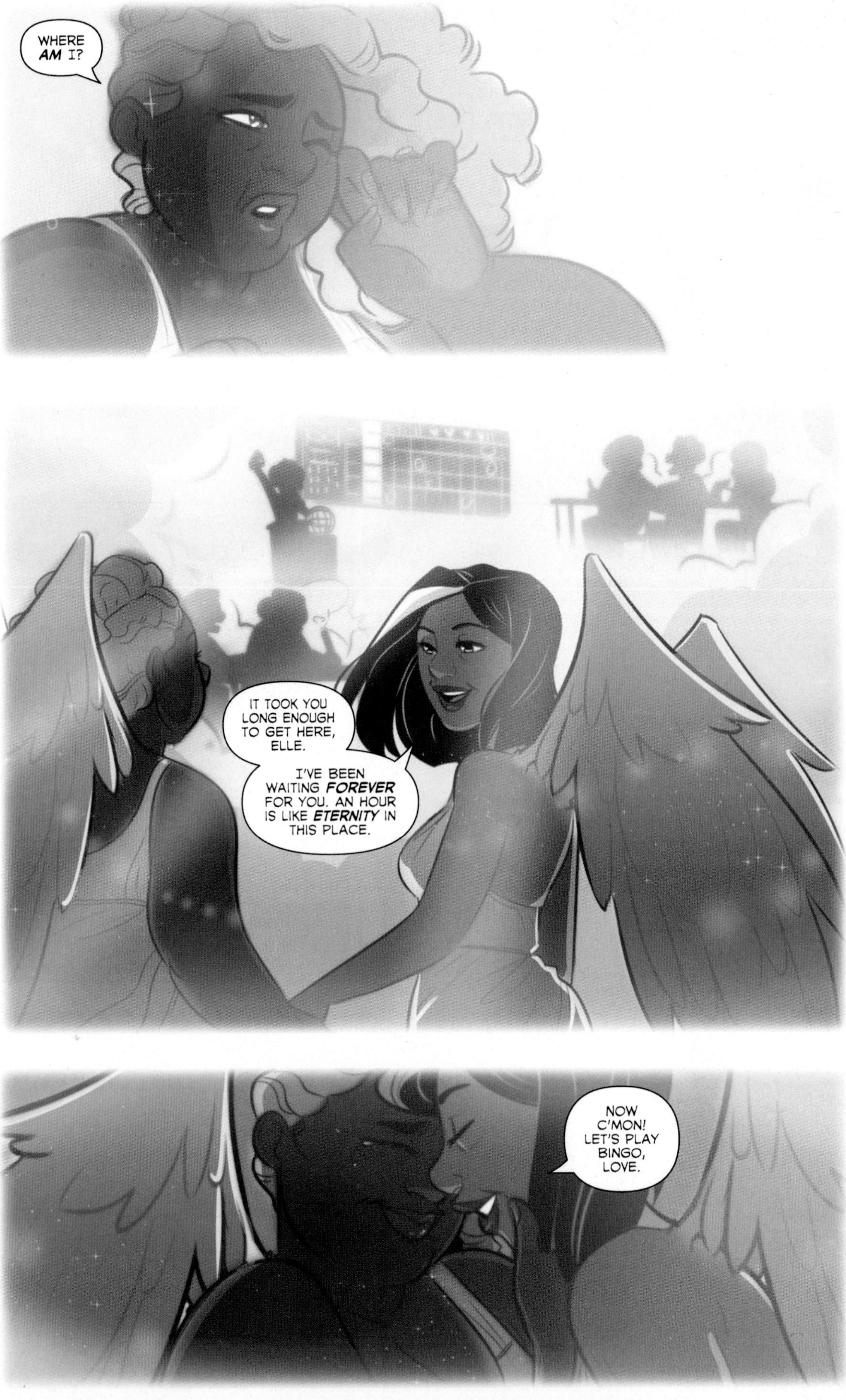
WHERE AM I?
IT TOOK YOU LONG ENOUGH TO GET HERE, ELLE.
I'VE BEEN WAITING FOREVER FOR YOU. AN HOUR IS LIKE ETERNITY IN THIS PLACE.
NOW C'MON! LET'S PLAY BINGO, LOVE.